Zainab Priya Dala is a freelance writer who has degrees in physiotherapy and psychology. Her writing has been published in a number of print publications and her short stories have received several awards. She was runner-up in the 2012 Witness True Stories of KwaZulu-Natal Competition. She has lived and worked in Dublin, Ireland, and currently lives in Durban, where she is a psychologist at a school for autistic children.

ALSO BY ZAINAB PRIYA DALA

The Architecture of Loss – a novel (2018)
What Gandhi Didn't See – Being Indian in South Africa – Essays (2018)

PRAISE FOR WHAT ABOUT MEERA

Debut Prize in the Minara Aziz Hassim Literary Award in South Africa

'Fluent narrative that sparkles. (…) The writing is crisp and sparkles with fine descriptions, and the reader will root for Meera. (…) Meera's story is an uncomfortable one, throwing up difficult questions, but Dala's telling of it is thought-provoking and beautifully done.'

—Margaret von Klemperer, *Books Live South Africa*

'Can a woman rise above her circumstances and change her fate? Though the answer is never really clear, the book crackles with life, colour and strange humour.'

—*Essay of Africa*

'Dala's novel is a haunting description of rejection. (…) That this book has come out now is ironic, a reminder that art imitates life, or perhaps that truth is stranger than fiction. (…) Her writing is a sort of equal opportunity novel of pointing out the dangers of age-old schisms and hatreds between people of different faiths, and different castes. A winner of a novel, and a brave one.'

—Jennifer Crocker, *The New Age – KZN*

WHAT ABOUT MEERA

Zainab Priya Dala

SPEAKING TIGER

SPEAKING TIGER BOOKS LLP
125A, Ground Floor, Shahpur Jat,
Near Asiad Village, New Delhi - 110 049

First published in South Africa by Umuzi, an imprint of Random House Struik Pvt Ltd., 2015

This edition first published in India by Speaking Tiger 2021

ISBN: 978-93-5447-229-9
eISBN: 978-93-5447-237-4

10 9 8 7 6 5 4 3 2 1

Cover design by publicide
Author photograph by Pranesh Maharaj
Text design by Fahiema Hallam
Set in Bembo

Printed at Shree Maitrey Printech Pvt. Ltd., Noida

For Greg

'Fiction is the lie through which we tell the truth.'

– Albert Camus

Dublin

1

What Happened at Communion

ON THE DAY THE BOY TOOK HIS FIRST COMMUNION, Meera slept with his father.

The father was drunk, playing to Irish archetypes. She was working as a caregiver at a school in the suburbs of Dublin. It was a school for autistic children. She had arrived in Dublin a month before, having taken a hasty decision to run far, far away. Still finding her feet among all the green and grey. And then came the polite invitation to a lovely little milestone, 'where our child becomes one with the flesh of our blessed Saviour'.

She smiled stupidly at the boy's mother, a Spanish vision in burnt orange and aqua, bearing a dark blue invitation card. Señora Click-Click and her posse of lisping Spaniards. Her formidable sisters, pronouncing the words 'Communion' and 'come' with their harsh, sexy 'Kh's'.

Okay, I will Khorm to his Khomm-you-neon.

They called him the click-click boy. Everyone did. It was his little clicky signature, in the big bad world. The act of repeatedly clicking his fingers next to his ears whenever he was stressed or irritated, or wanted to irritate.

Mostly he clicked to be left alone. Enough noisy clicking, and nobody tried to reach you or attempted to make you better. There were days when Meera wished she had a clicky signature, but this one was already taken. She would have to think of something else to chase people away.

She was too polite to decline to his mother's face, when she came bearing the cute little invitation cards with baby-blue and white words telling Meera that he had another name that was not the click-click boy.

She was just standing there when the invitation came. Within a group of helpful professionals. All there to treat and to serve. But never to mend completely. The children could never be mended. As Meera nodded to the beautiful Spanish mother her acceptance of the invitation, she looked across the playground and her eye caught the little click-click boy, sitting on a swing, not swinging, just staring straight ahead into the spaces in front of him. She wondered if he knew about his rite of passage, his new attempt at reaching God. Perhaps a God who did not click fingers to chase people away.

Meera skipped the morning church ceremony. The actual Communion. She didn't have anything churchy to wear. Things you wore to weddings, Communions … funerals. She only had unfashionable cheap jeans and old, worn-out boots. Some ugly shirts, all thrown together into a suitcase that smelt of incense, because it was the place she had once stored a wedding sari.

Anyway, the church ceremony for Communion was early in the morning. She couldn't get up so early. Maybe it was a Saturday morning, and maybe she was exhausted. Maybe she was too hung-over; she had been drinking heavily since she arrived in this city. Or maybe Meera had to admit she had been drinking heavily long before that. All she knew was that the mornings were always the worst. Whatever the country.

Meera trudged dutifully along behind her Australian colleague to the big, late lunch, part of a traditional Irish Communion. She looked down at her faded jeans and black button-down shirt, both old and ugly. The Australian colleague wore appropriate pearls and appropriate camel cashmere, artfully put together to show off her blonde, bouncy curls. She looked like a lady who lunched. Meera had packed away her choppy hair into a rusty-red beret.

Meera's black trench coat and faded jeans made the two of them look like an ill-matched pair, walking together from the bus stop opposite the Bank of Ireland. The Australian colleague with a thoroughly Australian name, Belinda, assured Meera that she did not look too bad. She was so polite. Polite enough to suggest that maybe they should stop off at Dunnes to get a dress or something.

Meera ignored Belinda. She didn't have the money to buy anything. Her first pay cheque had flown away in expensive overseas telephone calls and cheap wine.

But once at the Communion lunch, the fashionistas of the Spanish contingent would hear nothing of her attire. They surveyed her shaggy appearance as she wound her way into their home ground, up the garden path complete with red-and-green gnome, pansies and discarded Frisbee. They shook their perfect heads. They looked glorious in their bright colours and Mango trends. They stood on the overgrown lawn, nursing interesting drinks in plastic cups. They kissed the air beside each other's faces and warbled in beautiful tongues. Meera scanned the horizon, looking for a place to hide. There was none.

Inside the tiny house in Ballyfermot, the poorer part of town, the Irish side of the family sat, well dressed and shiny, less fashionable in the flowery pink lounge room. Stiff upper lips and hairspray, baby powder and Old Spice – the father's side of the family. Beige stockings on dumpy calves, and pale colours on pale women with pale reddish hair and pale little voices. But any voice would be pale when faced with the symphony of birds – the exotic, wild orange and red and green and purple voices of the Spanish. The mother's side of the family.

The click-click boy was nowhere to be seen. His special day meant nothing to him. He was probably hiding inside a cupboard somewhere, clicking his fingers next to his ears, waiting for everyone to leave. Meera looked around at all the people sitting on plastic chairs, lounging on pink loungers, draped over mantelpieces. It didn't look like anyone was leaving any time soon, but even before entering the house, she had planned her exit.

They had felt obligated to invite her. That much she knew. She was just standing there when they'd come to invite his schoolteacher, his psychologist, his occupational therapists, his swimming instructor, his speech therapist, his personal caregiver. She was just a stranger invited as an aside.

And so she stood among all the invited, and tried to summon up a pleasant smile. Today, it was especially difficult to smile. Maybe tomorrow …

But Meera felt the need to smile and say something as the mother approached. She immediately took in Meera's clothes. She sniffed at the air, lightly, and lifted a sculpted eyebrow. The eyebrow said, 'How dare you khorm to my only child's Khomm-you-neon dressed like a ragdoll, like a vagabond, like a beggar, while I stand before you, dressed to kill.'

But the husky lisping voice said appropriately, 'Thank you! Thank you so much for coming to Stewart's Communion, I didn't think that you would come. It is a special day for us.' She kissed the air.

Teresa. That was her name. The mother Teresa. It stayed on the tongue, an aftertaste.

Teresa spoke with a voice like a drunken woman. Like she was trying to watch her language. Like she was trying to sound Irish. She failed miserably. Her Mango dress in bright fuchsia, and her trendy sandals in gold and clear plastic made her fail miserably. Teresa was an exotic bird. She was trying too hard to sound like a pigeon on a grey column.

She had amber eyes. The same eyes as her son. His eyes were beautiful, especially when they stared into space at nothingness. Hers were slightly frightening. The under-dressed uninvited could so easily be afraid of her, shy of her, enthralled by her and slightly in love with her. Tall … watchful, in her stabbing heels, she seemed like a snake as she fixed her eyes on Meera. It was as if she knew something before something became.

'Thank you … for inviting me …' Meera mumbled as if she was the ugly girl in school, grateful to be included in the beauty queen's club. Her voice cut and broke and sounded stupid, hoarse, nervous. The South African accent, guttural, tongue-y, silly-dumb.

Meera seemed to cower before the radiance, the splendour of the Spanish mother Teresa, who noticed all the awkwardness and continued coolly, 'Yes. You are Stewie's care-worker from South Africa, yes?'

The mother Teresa emphasised the word 'worker', her mouth in a working pout. She continued in a husky timbre. 'I have seen you at Stewart's school. You must enjoy yourself, and stay till all the night. Okay? Hmmm …' And then she floated away.

Meera wanted to be Teresa right then. So beautiful, so polished, so openly tragic … everything she was not. She left Meera with a feeling of want.

Meera had no intention of staying till all the night. Someone indicated an open bottle of wine. She would have one glass. Just one. And then she would go home, on foot. No need to take a bus. Maybe a walk would shake off the feeling the Señora had left her with. She felt ice-cold, and very ugly. She felt as if she didn't want to pass a mirror and see a gaunt-faced dark girl with unkempt black hair staring back at her. She pulled herself away from the little girly group that had formed – the working girls, the girls from work, all just doing time at the late lunch, wanting to leave but politely staying. Telling themselves they had come for the boy's sake. For poor, unfortunate little Stewart, you know.

In the kitchen, surrounded by the mixed smells of saffron and soda bread, Meera went in search of a wine glass. Funny how they kept out bottles and bottles of wine, but no wine glasses. Funny how they lived in such a tiny hole-like house but wore designer shoes. All she found was one dirty glass in a dirty sink. The only wine glass around.

'You're in search of the elusive …'

Meera turned to find blue eyes taking in her faded clothes and frayed coat. This time, she didn't feel the need to apologise. The eyes understood.

The keeper of the eyes was carrying piles of dirty plates, and cloths, and many, many things in two capable arms. Golden arms, she would later recall, seeing golden arms on her too-white sheets. His head, just visible above the dirty dishes, showed long, ruffled hair the colour of wet beach sand, and silver-rimmed spectacles. The click-click boy had his father's hair.

He set the dirty dishes down on the sink and leant against the cupboard, blowing out air that fluffed his hair from his eyes and steamed up his glasses.

'Round here,' he said, leaning in conspiratorially towards Meera as if to tell secrets, 'a clean wine glass is about as rare as a badger's arse … I'm Ian by the way.'

Wink. A charmer.

Meera first smiled. A reluctant smile. And then she laughed. Out loud. And then she knew.

Later that night, after she had slept with him, after he had left to go home to the little house minus clean wine glasses, she remembered that it was that laugh that had made her do what she had done. Her laugh that had arrived from somewhere ugly.

When he mumbled the name of a pub to her as she was leaving, she knew that her laughter had brought her into a story. When he spilled his beer on her at the pub after midnight, she knew. When he walked her to her house, she knew. Some things just happen. They can't be avoided. Some things happen before they actually happen. They happen first inside you, and then they happen when you pull them outside. Inside-ly first. Then outside-ly.

As if you had a choice. You never, ever have a choice. Things happen.

The next time she saw Señora Teresa was at the click-click boy's funeral. Teresa, a mourning vision in black. A grieving mother, wailing to the north wind. With amber eyes watching Meera as a snake watches a frog. They all knew then. Everyone knew what she had done.

2

Temple Gates

ON A MORNING IN APRIL, A WEEK AND A HALF SINCE she had arrived in Dublin, Meera held a child in the throes of a massive seizure. Hard, rolling spasms, strong – too strong for a tiny body – and she found herself thinking of gates at temples in India. The tightly curled fists, the foaming mouth, and Meera thought only of how the latches of the gates at the temples were always placed at the foot of the gate. So that anyone who wanted to enter had no choice but to bow down to God. To open the locks.

The child with the seizure … Meera didn't remember the child's name when the concerned colleagues came to her, wanting to bond with the camaraderie of their common experience – life as a healer of broken children. She shrugged, and they all thought that maybe it was too much, the shock and the fear of seeing a child have a fit so soon after stepping off the plane from darkest Africa. But they sensed that the writhing body in her arms did nothing to the cold place that anyone could see deep inside of her. Unmoved.

Meera had held the child through the seizure, and when it was over she had laid the limp body across the arms of a waiting nurse and then calmly walked away, saying nothing.

Her mind remained on the bowing down at temple gates, to unlock gates, to seek out God, to ask for intervention at some point or another. All she noticed were the huddling bodies of the other children in the playground, their play so rudely interrupted by the spasms of the devil's tomfoolery, or of brain chemistry, whichever you were inclined to believe in.

It was a very serious situation, such a major seizure in school. Everyone came running from their little hidey holes to watch. The school nurse came bearing syringes and vials. The teachers stopped their lessons. The therapists stood in clumps, watching helplessly. What's happened? What's going on?

'Olive Phelan's having another Major One,' they whispered. Everyone shook their heads. They watched Meera as she held the child down and turned her on her side. The tiny child was strong. Meera's muscles ached with the effort of holding her down. The child's glazed eyes stared straight into Meera's face, but she knew the child saw nothing.

Afterwards, when she had handed her to the nurse, Meera turned to find the large group waiting to 'talk about it'. She had nothing to say. She walked away from them without saying a word.

She wouldn't join them in the dissection, in their shaking heads and *sorry poor childs*.

They began to wonder if there was perhaps something wrong with this woman from Africa. So cold and distant all the time. So silent. Meera went to the side of the building to smoke a cigarette.

Esther, the dietician, came bustling towards her.

'Oh, poor Olive, poor Olive! Third one this week. She's deteriorating, that's for certain. She may have to leave the school. Home care. Keep her comfortable till it's her time. That's what Dr Malone tells us anyway.'

Meera nodded distractedly. She had no need for words.

But Esther, for the short time Meera had known her, was aching for a conversation. 'And what about you, you poor thing? Only just arrived last week, and you had to be there to see that. Must've scared you? Well, how do you feel?'

Meera looked at her through a haze of smoke, Esther's

round face blurring slightly at the edges. Meera saw her halo of frizzy mouse-brown hair. She had nothing to say. She felt nothing at all.

Esther shrugged and walked away. The affront was too much for her. She prided herself on being the mother hen, the one everyone came to, to cry on her shoulder. She had been waiting for a tearful frenzy of 'I'm so scared, I'm so new here. This is so hard ...'

But, receiving nothing, she felt the stab.

There was something really wrong with that girl from South Africa!

For Meera the days and the nights had gone slowly by. Days of working among strange children who listened to music from a world far away, children who whooped and screeched, who flapped and hopped, who paced and ran in circles. Days followed by nights of sleep ... beautiful sleep. Sometimes dreamless. Mostly not. Mostly drunk. And she always woke up before it was light outside, and she still cowered in the mornings.

Her colleagues tried to befriend her. Words of welcome and little dainty cakes for the quiet girl from somewhere in Africa, some town called Durban, a place no one had ever heard of. Intriguing in her silence, she attracted the crowds, who thought she was exotic and found it strange that a girl from Africa could also be an Indian girl. She grew tired of explaining in disjointed descriptions a lineage of labourers who had flown the coop of a starving village in India to a life of sweat in South Africa many generations before she was born.

Are you Indian then?

No.

Are you African then?

No.

How very intriguing. How very mixed up.

And then they started to talk. The well meaning, the well dressed, the sane working professionals in their sane prosperous jobs. How can we help the poor thing?

They chose a spokesperson. The Australian housemate became the lucky intervener, telling Meera in soft tones, 'Maybe you have been under a lot of stress lately, I mean moving from your country to live here is quite a culture shock. Maybe you should speak to someone, maybe it will help. Maybe you are depressed. Maybe you should take a few days off, take a bus down to Galway with us, take in the sights.'

When Meera unpolitely told them all to get lost, including the housemate, they began to get aggressive.

How could she? How could their help not be needed?

She didn't want to be part of their little girls' club. The exotic new addition with mixed lineage and mixed signals. She did not feel the need to share life stories. She honestly didn't want tea-and-sandwiches bonding, and laughing, and sharing fashion tips and makeover ideas. Meera did not believe she needed to be improved, to be made over.

So they called her strange, and the housemate told them stories of her chain-smoking, wine-drinking, nightmare-having, calling-out-in-terror-in-the-middle-of-the-night ways. And then they felt sorry for her and came again with invitations to church, to tea, and finally to attend the Communion of one of the children at the school.

Come with us. Maybe you will enjoy it. The mother invited all of us. Come on. Come.

'No, thank you. I really don't want tea, and I couldn't be bothered with churches, but okay, if you insist, I will come to his Communion. Just because I was standing there.'

Meera's mind remained on temple gates, and smoky

prayer rooms. For months. Priests in the land of priests, in the land of priests who did things to children because they were naughty, ugly children. From a land of priests to a land of priests. The synchronicity of it all didn't escape Meera. She saw things in parallel motion, in dark tones. Like two parallel dots moving in the same direction. Like women who appear out of ovens to talk you into things. Like dots abhorrently removed, deleted. Like losing your mind, and answering newspaper adverts, and running and running to planes in the sky. Like bowing down at temples, and bowing to blue-eyed priests. Like committing adultery and becoming an outcast. Like husbands who are wrong, husbands who bruise. It's all relative, she thought. It's all relative.

3

Stew Pots

MEERA SAW HIM AGAIN. THE BOY'S FATHER. IAN Buckley. Father of clicky Stewart Buckley. He had come to drop off his son at the school. His son, whom she still thought of as the click-click boy, even though now she knew his name was Stewart. Little Stewart. Little Stewie. Little little Stew.

Meera was pushing a wheelchair filled with a child, knotted and twisted into interesting shapes, and Ian came striding purposefully across the parking lot towards her. She saw his blue raincoat with beads of silver scattered around, and she felt like licking the water off the surface. With his son safely stowed in a teacher's open arms, the father walked like a warrior to his lover.

'They will see,' Meera said, and surprised herself with the fact that she was bothered about being found out. It was not that she was afraid, it was just that she was not afraid enough. And she didn't want to have to hand out explanations. She felt she was a lousy liar. And yet, sometimes she was good at it. A professional liar.

The father didn't really care who saw him. He came with a purpose in mind. He smiled simply because he was happy. All he wanted to say was, 'After school … I will pick up Stewie. Then we'll go on into the city. The Wagon needs a tune-up, so my mate's coming to check her out.'

He worked as a tour-bus driver for one of the largest tourist circus performances in Dublin, the Emerald Wagon Tours. He took happy smiling tourists around Dublin City, Belfast and Galway, showing them the sights, entertaining them with a clichéd Irish brogue and witty descriptions as he drove. The craic …

He was never really good at his job. He hated the play he performed, the typical Irishman with the gift of the gab, flirting naughtily with Dutch spinsters and talking in rhyme to French schoolgirls. It was just a job. A way to make ends meet. He wanted to be an actor. That was his dream. He was handsome in a rumpled-Irishman sort of way, with messy hair that curled over his ears and his collar, and intense eyes, which hinted at a poet underneath his skin, and a smoky voice that chose its words with calculated nonchalance. The spinsters swooned. The schoolgirls batted their too-long eyelashes. Typical rascal Irishman. Naughty. Meera was certain most of them were secretly in love with him.

Today, as he laid out his obvious proposition to her in the schoolyard, she looked everywhere but at his eyes. She knew what he was saying. He was saying that it didn't end there. He was saying that he had not walked out of her house at dawn.

A nod, and an agreement between lovers. An agreement to cart a child along in the back seat of a green ugly bus called the Emerald Wagon. A child with watchful amber eyes, but no voice. Only a strange rhythm of clicks that would never tell about the sounds and the sighs inside the Emerald Wagon garage as he sat in the stationary bus, with a video game in his stiff hands.

How sick!

You mean they did it while the child was there? Right in front of him?

How sick, man? How bloody sick!

After-school activity. Time to go home now, little Stewie. The amber eyes looked into nothingness. And then when the father dropped her off at the bus station, and she adjusted her clothes and fiddled with her hair, the amber eyes saw her face. And they looked and they looked.

'I'm doing a run tomorrow. German tour group … up to Belfast. Overnight stay—'

'No.'

'All right then. I'm back on Thursday. We get a day off after overnights. Thursday, then?'

'Okay.'

In her mad dreams that night, a boy chased her into corridors. A boy with amber eyes. And clicks for words.

The video game became a currency. Meera bartered and negotiated with its battery-operated core. Gimme Gimme Gimme … The boy was so easily obsessed. It was in his nature, his make-up, to become so easily obsessed, so easily bought off with a stupid handheld video game of a jumping hedgehog that died with a wheezing sound when his three lifelines were used up.

Lucky, lucky hedgehog … you could resurrect him with a flick of your thumb. He never really ever died. Until the day the batteries ran out.

It became easier and easier to carry on. The father's lack of conscience became her lack of conscience. Or maybe it was the other way around. After school became a pleasant little routine. A Thursday routine. A fast run around the block away from the gates of the school, and a green bus filled with laughing leprechauns waiting slyly behind a hedge. A boy in the front seat, with arms open wide. Where is my handout? Where is the game I must play? And make sure the batteries are charged.

If anyone saw, or anyone suspected then, she would never know. The round-table girly club kept a wide berth. Didn't want to pollute themselves with such sick business. And anyway, she'll get what's coming to her. Soon.

They never really talked – she and the boy's father. Where on earth was the time? There were important things to do. What was the point of talking?

But, at times, she suspected that they just had too much to say. The unsaid sat bristling away in a corner, much like the corner in which they had placed the click-click boy. Their words walked towards each other, and then shyly walked away. And inside the ugly oil-stained garage that housed three or four green leprechaun buses, ripe with the smells that only buses can give off, the smells of machinery, and of human machinery – the multicultural smells of a million tourists who had come in search of rainbows and pots of gold, of blarney and lilting accents – there came another sound, to compete with and drown out all the others.

The halting Italian, the grunty German, the twangy American, the guttural Japanese (click click) … none could compete with the dissonance of millions and millions of conversations that had never happened. The boy's father would run his fingers through his beach-sand hair, and then through hers, and in the corner of his eyes she would see deep, deep lines. Lines of sorrow, lines of no tomorrow.

Should she ask? Should she talk? Should she?

'Where did you meet … her?' She finally ventured out of her hidey-hole, sitting on a seat at the back of the green bus, on an afternoon when he and she did not really feel like being lovers, just talkers.

He was seated in the driver's seat, and she imagined how she would look to him as he cast his eyes upwards to stare into the large convex mirror that allowed him to see all the happy faces of the passengers he had to perform for. She saw what he was seeing. His dark lover in the back seat of his place of work, and his unspeaking, unspeakable child a few seats in front of her. It was a terrible afternoon after all.

He wanted to walk up to her, to kiss her, or to slap her … or both. She seemed to inspire that dichotomy in people. He hated her face in the round convex mirror, and he loved her face in the round convex mirror, and he hated his job where he had to play the Irish fool filled to the brim with blarney tales and witty retorts and interesting facts. He had had enough of everything. And she stared into his eyes as they appeared to her in the round convex mirror, her own eyes glittering – she had had enough of everything too. The unsaid began to clap its hands. Finally! Finally, there is some damn conversation in this damn, crazy place.

'I met … Stew's mother here … in the Emerald Wagon. She had come from Spain to learn English; came on an overnight tour … to Belfast.'

He didn't seem embarrassed to talk about his seduction of the sexy señorita all the way from Gran Canaria, in her sexy sandalled feet and her tiny little skirts. He was bought … sold … delivered, for she had fixed her eyes upon the back of his head, and in the convex mirror he had found those amber eyes saying, like a snake to a frog, 'I have seen you. Now, you are mine.'

And in Belfast he had tried to duck and to dive, to avoid the snake eyes, to run away from the inevitable. But some things just happen. You have no choice. He fell in love.

Then there was a baby on the way. A baby boy wrapped up inside her, round enough to show himself, and Ian had taken her, his bride, to his mother's small house in Cork, and told his mother in his accent that had suddenly changed to a southern turn of phrase, 'Look after her, Mam. Till the baby comes. I have to drive the bus. Look after her, Mam.'

His mother had hated the pregnant Spanish stranger the moment she had set eyes on her – this tall, bubbling woman who had stolen her son.

For the mam had still nursed ideas of her son, like all Irish mams do, like all mams do … my son, my boy, my good boy… maybe he will marry a good Irish girl one day and settle down. Maybe he will decide to become a blessed man of the cloth. But Mam had stood at the sink, wringing out grey cloths, and swallowed her dreams like strong Irish tea, and had taken the beautiful canary into her cage. She had crocheted thick blue blankets, for she was convinced that her son would only have a son, and fed the girl well on special, special Irish stews. And when little Stew came sliding out into the world, the mam had fallen head over heels in love, and said as she crossed herself three times or more, he is back … thank you, Father … my son is back.

But the canary was tenacious, and her English had improved, so she packed her little babe in a thick crocheted blanket and left Mam in the middle of the night, to arrive at the doorstep of the Emerald Wagon offices in Grafton Street, Dublin, at exactly seven the next morning. Among Japanese photographers and Russian ballerinas sat a flame-haired new mama, casting about here and there for her prey. Her eyes found him, loading bags onto racks, and with those eyes she told him, I have your son. Now, I have you.

And he had loved her. Deeply. And he had created a brown-and-grey home for her then, a place to bring up children, but it was in the poorer part of town. Ballyfermot. A suburb far away from the city, a project with row upon row of council homes, semi-detached. She felt detached from all around her. This place. This is what her life had come down to.

And nobody had told her, the Grand Canary, that it was going to be like this. Marriage, baby, and the English-speaking world. There was no colour, there was no dance, there was very little music, and there was never any fiesta. She hated the days and the days, and she detested the green bus as it drove away, and the brown bricks of her castle cage, and the grey skies over the poorer part of town. The barbed wire, the graffiti, the hunchbacked old ladies in their brown serge coats, the teenage mothers in their pink-velvet tracksuits picking their nails, blowing bubblegum bubbles. She hated it!

Where was her prince, her sandy-haired Brad Pitt, her amazing Irish knight who would save her, and love her, and take her out to nice restaurants? In his place all she found was a slope-shouldered spectacled Sparrow, with bony fingers, too tired from turning steering wheels, too poor to go out eating and dancing, too dull to burst into song, too witless to be witty … It had all gone to shit!

Now, every day there were baby screams, and dirty-dishes screams, and flapping-sheets screams and apron screams and daytime-soap-opera screams and screams and screams … so many screams that the beautiful Spanish face, once glowing and sparkly, became dull and ugly, and the flame hair burnt out into ash, and the canary flew the coop. Alone. No baby in her arms.

And what of the baby, the lucky little fellow, the little Irish devil? He lies in his own mess for half a day, and he swallows his own vomit for half a day, and the green bus finally finds him after half a day of blarney. And the sweet baby-blue is as blue as his blanket, the thick crocheted one.

Mama!

He comes back to the living, the little boy, his five-month-old lungs drained clear of their stew at the emergency rooms at St Columcille's Hospital, and he lands himself in yet another soup. The doctors and the nurses all pat the sloped shoulders and tell him how sorry they are. The baby is alive.

But he will never really be alive. His brain has been starved. Of oxygen. And he will never really recover.

She comes back too, don't you know, after a week and three days – the grandness of Canaria was just too scary – and he takes her back into his bus-driving arms, smelling her hair that is now flaming and kissing her skin that is now glowing.

She is the same again. But baby-blue is never the same, and she is sorry, so so sorry ... promises baby stew-blue the world and a half, and sings lullabies to baby in sexy Spanish, in words that her mama sang to her a long time ago on sun-drenched beaches and crowded streets. But a few broken lullabies never can bring little blue baby back from the soupy stew. She becomes strange and angry at his new, changed ways. She has had enough!

She hates baby-blue as he twists and he turns, and she hates baby-blue as he foams and he howls, and she hates baby-blue as he bites and he kicks, and she hates herself because she hates baby-blue. But most of all, who she hates is the man.

All this is because of him! Of that she is certain. If only he had kept her the way to which she was entitled, none of this would ever have happened. How could he even dream of caging her up in his grey little box, and tying her body down with washing lines, and placing bars upon the windows of her heart? What was the stupid fellow thinking anyway? He knows good and well that an exotic bird of paradise deserves to be treated like an exotic bird of paradise, and who cares if he is too tired, too run down, too poor, too unhappy, too washed up?

But he loves her. Deeply.

So she accepts what her life has become. But she casts about for ways in which to feel like a queen.

Soon everything becomes better, and she smiles and she coos, caged no more … canary bird begins to sing her special, special songs. He takes the blame. And he washes, and he mends, and he pays, and he loves, and he bargains, and he pays … enough for two.

Of course baby-blue is the lucky thing who gains the most during all this strife. He blossoms and he flourishes under all the care, and all her new love, and all her trips back and forth to faith healers in Gran Canaria – the amulets and the pendants weighing down his baby jumpers seem to be working. The cost of her guilt in a few pesetas paid into grubby, greasy peasant-healer hands.

They work. Those amulets, those badges, those strings and things. They work. But just to play it safe, she becomes the doyen of therapies – every one under the sun. Nothing is too much for her little blue-baby, no therapist, no doctor, no -ologist, -ician, -urgeon escapes her timeous appointments … and she pays them in pounds … many. The bus-driving pounds the man hands to her daily. Bargaining with his bus-driving money, bargaining with a word she has never ever used … *-uilt.*

Now, baby could sit, and he could walk, and he could eat, and he could stare. That is all he could do. He never spoke, never babbled, never said Mama, Da. The -ologists had taken their time. The -icians had declared a truce. The -urgeon had taken his pound of sterling. The -pists had emptied their chambers. This was as good as baby-blue was ever gonna get! Cerebral palsy with autistic tendencies. The diagnosis. Final.

But a mama-love is a mama-love. And a mama-uilt is -uilt, only -uilt … nothing else. Baby-blue, little Stew, he was hers and she was lavish in her love for him, too late!

But there is a good little spin-off to having a broken

baby: landed in a soupy stew, suddenly she was a star! The neighbours of the grey castles were lavish, and the strangers on buses were lavish, and the housewives at supermarkets were lavish, and the handsome young doctors were lavish too … in the attention and the sympathy for the mama love, long-suffering, child-bearing. Wear broken baby like a crown.

People loved her now. People stopped to look at her now. They paid attention to her now as she carried the broken baby around like her prize. And she thanked and she thanked the Virgin for this little affliction. Finally, she was special. And she thanked and she thanked the Virgin for the soupy stew. And she thanked and she thanked herself for not feeling too much *-uilt*.

4

The 25A

ON THE RAIN-SPLATTERED PAVEMENT, ON WESTMORE-land Street, Dublin, Meera walks slowly towards the Quays. It is afternoon … only afternoon. The day is taking its time. She is waiting for the night. She has just walked away from her lover's hurried embrace, and she can still smell him all around her, his clean smell. His hands that smell of steering wheels. Meera knows that he wants her, he will always want her body, and their affair only continues because, inside it, they both do what they do best – run away from the real.

Meera has missed the afternoon bus to Lucan, yet again, becoming all too familiar with that routine. Behind her, as she sways in a light lover's step that belies her deep malaise, a green bus with a shiny leprechaun on its side and an amber-eyed boy on its inside drives hastily away. The eyes, they watch her, both the amber and the blue … and the eyes make her hate herself. But she knows that she will be back next Thursday. She still needs to hate herself more.

She must catch another bus, the 25A, the Lucan Road Flyer, at a stop further down the Liffey River Quays.

Weaving around the corners of Temple Bar, a cheeky cat in an oversized overcoat, humming a strange little tune in her strange little head.

He used to love music.

He used to hate me.

He used to love me.

I'm afraid I'm too dull and ordinary.

Sorry about that.

Sometimes there are many warbled songs in her head, all melted together, rolling and rolling their tuneless ways around a brain that has had just about enough.

'Oh, please! Don't romanticise ... like a dot progression to abhorrent infinity,' her husband had said. The dot on the screen, abhorred. Aborted.

He loved her. He hated her.

He showed it too.

Onto the bus filled with pensioners and schoolchildren, students and lovers. Because the sane and the employed, the happily married, don't take bright daylight buses in the middle of the work afternoon. They are too busy being sane and employed.

Meera sits down.

She overhears a conversation on the afternoon bus, the slow and steady bus that betrays its flightful name. Her ears slowly rotate towards it – it sounds like a good conversation. The lilting accent of the young man sitting sprawled a few seats in front of her, a cellphone stuck to his non-rotating ears. Perhaps, then, she should say she hears half a conversation on the afternoon bus. It is the interesting half.

He says he fell asleep last night on the Nitelink bus, the non-flyer ... from the Quays back home to Maynooth, from the harlot back home to the wife, from the mad city back home to the leafy suburbs.

He says he was on his way home from a gig.

He says two pints inside you and an all-night cover gig can knock the shite outta any man, even an Irishman.

He says he fell asleep on the back seat of the non-flyer, like me own bed, he says, that back seat after three pints and a gig.

He says the non-flyer became the flyer last night, and the rapid shove of the driver's foot woke him up, brought him back to the fluorescent-light reality of four pints and a gig. Where am I, where am I? Oh, only here. Okay, well I've been here before.

He says they kicked him off the night bus at its last nightly stop, nowhere near the leafy home from city to wife.

Into a taxi, lying on her back seat, from Leixlip to Maynooth – a half hour away.

Woken up again by another rapid shove, and no money to pay for his long taxi ride.

He says I am home. I am home now. I am. No money to pay, but the light goes on in an upstairs bedroom. She appears at the doorway, pink flannel nightgown, peering into the darkness with a face that never slept.

She pays his way home, and she holds his tired body, and she ignores his drunkenness, and she loves him, she loves him, she takes him home.

In a lovely house in Maynooth, the light stays on for a while in an upstairs bedroom – a golden light, a light to call you home. A light competing with the watery August dawn, coming in like a naughty cat to steal insomnia away.

He says he left his guitar… he says he doesn't know where, maybe on the night bus, maybe on the floor.

Don't worry, baby. It's okay, baby. I'll help you, baby. You'll find your guitar, baby. There's always tomorrow, baby.

The light goes out in the upstairs bedroom in a lovely house, no longer competing with the dawn.

Two sleep.

He will find his guitar.

Tomorrow.

5

Nepalese

MEERA SHAVES HER LEGS. HALFWAY. FIRST THE LEFT leg and then the right. Up to the knee in wavy lines. She uses harsh soap, feeling the nicks of a not-too-sharp blade. She wants to meet a man. She wants a dinner date. Pizza and a movie. A glass of dry sherry. She is tired of secrets and of bus machinery. She is tired of being a little hidden pleasure in a garage or at the back of a bus.

Dressed to kill, she takes the Lucan Road Flyer into the city, and stumbles from the bus stop towards the Trinity College gates. Prospects assault her. There is no shortage in this town. Short men with spiky hair watch her descent. She is aware of the intimidation of cars as they slide down Grafton Street into the Quays. She wishes one would stop, allowing her to lean into its window, looking inside for a lover. Just a dinner date.

At the Trinity College gates she feels inadequate. Academia is like a laugh in her face. The graduation gowns, the well-educated carrying books under their arms, women with laughing faces bantering about Seamus Heaney and, of course, James Joyce.

She cowers into her lack of tertiary education, her dumbness, and pretends that she banters too about sonnets in canter and the slow rhyme of psychosis. She wonders if perhaps she should begin to lie. About who she is, about what she can do. And about all that she has already done.

A blind busker stands with a thick cape around his shoulders. She doesn't know that in years to come, in the country of her birth, blind buskers will be beaten up by policemen when they try to sing Stevie Wonder songs on Cape Town streets. She tells herself that being blind is not the only handicap this singer possesses. He belts out a loud rendition of 'Bridge Over Troubled Water', and listens for the coins at his feet. Meera ignores him and walks into a kebab café.

The hanging meat of a million donors rotates in its salivating deliciousness, roasting like a cremation, the Pakistani waiters slipping and sliding with their long oiled hair towards the educated students whose worn-out copies of Joyce's *Ulysses* compete for their attention on peeling Formica. Again, she reminds herself. She wants to meet a man.

She meets a man. A handsome student. Out on the town with his tutorial group. He looks directly into her eyes, and leans into her.

'Where you from, gorgeous?' he asks, and his nerdy friends giggle like schoolboys.

'Nepal,' she lies, and she watches his interest pique.

He is brave with the afternoon of student drinking and beckons for her to come and sit on his lap. She stands inert, and then dances towards him, thinking of asking for pizza and a movie. He leaves his clever studious group and puts his arm around her waist.

'Wanna dance, Nepalese? Wanna dance?'

He takes her to a nightclub on Temple Bar. The Turk's Head. Large metal cages house dancing, prancing blonde-bobbed girls, and the ceiling is painted with a mock Michelangelo's David, one whose naked muscles are contorted like a dancer in the middle of a rave. A David who looks like the Lord Brahma. Staring high up into the ceiling she swallows a pill the boy gives her and watches a girl trapeze across the sky, her black patent boots chafing her thighs. She looks like she is having so much fun. The trance music pulses, and the strobes of an epileptic seizure begin to throb across the mezzanine level.

His name is Barry. And he loves the Church. He is a man of God, a student of Theology, he tells her, and buys her a Jameson on crushed ice. She drinks. And when she is finished, he buys her some more. Clearly, he is anticipating a repayment for his pounds. But she is prepared to pay. She wants him to be her lover. She wants him to cast her aside in the morning hangover. She wants to be one of the crowd. Young, dancing girl. Just another one.

Barry gyrates his good body. He mouths along to the beaty songs, knowing the words that have no meaning. He grabs her hips and pulls them to his, muttering the word 'Nepalese' into her ear. He seems vulnerable, in the innocent way that young boys seem vulnerable. Naughty but nice. He asks for her approval as fake fog from a smoke machine in the corner envelops the floor. He doesn't care much for platitudes. Meera clings to his aftershave smell, and shuts her eyes tight, allowing the Turk's Head to overtake her consciousness. Something, anything. To take away the whispering woman in her head.

But all she can see inside her closed eyes is a laughing Brahma in the sky. The pill she has swallowed begins its duty. The world warps and blurs at the edges.

She laughs. And spins on the dance floor. Hysterical now, with laughter, with life, with the hint of sexuality, with drugs, with alcohol, with Barry the Theologian.

The face of the painted David, a Lord Brahma seated on a swan, a four-armed god, with hands holding cups. In three of the cups he carries pure milk. And in one, milk mixed with water. The stern Brahma's swan, a once-ugly duckling, pecks wildly at his hand. The swan knows the difference between pure milk and milk mixed with water.

You don't lie to swans. Those that have been ugly ducklings.

Meera finds Barry's lips and tries to kiss them. Milk mixed with water. He kisses well. He reserves his tongue for later, and for that she is grateful. The Brahma-David in the sky breathes out the world, and the world is a trance song.

'Let's get outta here, Nepalese,' Barry says, and pinches her tummy folds, visible through the sheer top she carefully chose for seduction. To score herself a dinner date. She follows Barry numbly out onto the street. Two-thirty in the morning.

Drunk boys are vomiting at the entrance to the club. They laugh as their friends try to push them into their own vomit, they start brawls over red-haired girls. Meera wishes for drunkenness. And drunkenness comes. She walks like a ballet dancer on tiptoe following the big boy Barry as he hails a cab.

In the cab he tries to kiss her again, and she has to lean her entire torso out of the window to retch into the moving street. A sour-tasting mouth, and Barry wastes no time. He clearly isn't squeamish. He dives in for his kiss.

His house is a student digs, a decent Edwardian in Blackrock. Rich-boy digs. He opens the front door to reveal four boys, Arts and Letters students themselves, in the filthy lounge, all sharing a hookah. They stop as Barry enters, proudly showing off his prize. Nepalese.

A boy with dirty blonde dreadlocks pushes the smoking apple-scented pipe towards Meera's face, and she inhales deeply, wanting voraciously to be a girl in the night. Just a girl in the night. She wants to forget about Brahma on the swan, and about dead-eyed children, and about the past-present-future. Shut out the woman in her head.

As the lions and tigers of her memories come out of their cages, she flings her body into the waiting Barry. It is time. The recondite theologies of Barry of the Church enter her body like its sacred brotherhood, and she inhales the world full of milky water mix.

Barry is high, and he offers her his Highness, a few white powdery lines on the back of a Burt Bacharach CD case, and a freebie from the hookah. She lays her long body on his student bed. Unwashed sheets, with stains from masturbation, and a floor strewn with cracked CD cases and dirty underwear ... she falls in love. She tries to duck her head underwater. Drown, she orders. Drown. But her hair refuses to sink.

The banality of Barry becomes the aphrodisiac, commanding her sinews to contort towards his rugby sensuality. She pictures him hunched over a graffitied desk, doing addition and multiplication. Sticking out his moist tongue as he concentrates.

He assaults her buttons and, in the haze of high, each button opens itself, revealing a bone-dry core. Brown and dry. Like the twigs from a cork tree. Meera shuts her eyes, squeezes them shut, losing modesty like a race.

'Relax, Nepalese. Just relax,' Barry growls, and she watches from a distance as he removes his clothes. An incongruous body emerges, one that shows hips that are slightly feminine, and a hairy chest that is perhaps well toned.

'I'm a Kerry man myself,' he sings. 'We be hairy down in Kerry.'

Outside the bedroom, she thinks she hears a dog bark. The masculine bark of a large dog. Perhaps a German shepherd. The bark arouses her. But not enough. The guffaws of the boys with the hookah drowns out any canine conversations, and she suddenly feels her stomach turn over again and again. They are laughing at her. She knows they are laughing at her.

'Open a window. Open a window,' she pleads to the naked Barry, who lunges at her heaving chest and holds her down in the stale-smelling sheets.

Meera suddenly wants escape, immediate escape. She can't do this. Not now, not ever. Barry's showiness brings tears to her eyes, she gasps for air and, finding none, she springs up to bolt.

'Wait! You little bitch! Where do you think you're going?'

Barry blocks his doorway, his need filling the room. He now wants his due. He has not paid pounds for no return. She has drunk her way into a business deal.

Meera becomes desperate, shoving herself up against him and then realising it is a mistake, as it only serves to swell his passions even more. He grabs at her unruly hair and begins biting her neck. She writhes without rubbing against his burly frame.

She wants to scream. To the dreadlocked potheads outside the door. Scream till they save her life. Take her away from this raging battering ram.

'Let … me … out!' she screams, and Barry in his passion sees the intent in her eyes. He slowly backs off her, and stands still, guarding the door. His deadly presence burns its disappointment into the staleness of the drunk-high air.

He realises he has been defeated. The woman with the wild black hair, the flashing eyes – he will never have her now. Something inside her has flown away. And even the drugs don't work. She is gone.

'Come … Nepalese. Come …' he whispers.

'I am not from Nepal,' she tells him, and the lie makes him fallow.

'I am not Nepalese, I am Not. I am Not!' she screams like a banshee. The potheads next door fall silent. And Barry realises he has been had. He diminishes in size. From a wild Lothario to a flaccid student in one sentence.

'Well, where you from then?' he snarls.

'South Africa,' Meera answers, and then adds, 'Does it really matter?'

He shakes his head, and moves away from the door. Suddenly she feels sorry for him, and reaches out a hand to touch him.

'Liar!'

Eros vanishes as Psyche tries to perceive him.

She loses him as his light vanishes. She is a woman who is trying too hard to shed light on an angry lover, only to find a man. A boy, actually. A boy who didn't bargain for such complications..

'Go home! Get out!' He recoils from her outstretched paw and pushes her out of the room.

She stands facing the boys with the marijuana-stuffed hookah, and shrugs at their question-marked eyebrows. She holds her bra in her hands, a crumpled-up black lacy thing. The dreadlocked one offers her a smoke. She inhales deeply, one last hit, and Barry opens the door, standing naked, with a lit cigarette in one hand. He regards her. She inhales again, and then lifts her hand in a wave.

Goodbye, schoolboy.

'You need Jesus in your life,' Barry says, and then shuts his bedroom door. She hears the loud sounds of the Velvet Underground resonate into his disappointment.

Meera feels the need to hum a tune, as she leaves the house filled with boys who are high and laughing at the hilarity of all that has happened. It is, she sings, such a purrrr-fect day …

'Oh, do shut up, dollface,' a woman's voice tells her, and the barking German shepherd joins her serenade.

She slinks back, towards her world. Waiting for Thursday.

Durban

6

What Happened in Tongaat

TONGAAT WAS A DRY, DUSTY TOWN WITH ONE MAIN street that bisected the village into two unequal halves. The half where the rich lived above their expensive jewellery shops, haberdasheries and clothing boutiques; and the half where the poor survived with their cheap Morning Market, selling vegetables they had grown on farms, and poorly made baby clothes.

Surrounding the buildings, none of them over one storey in height, were fields and fields of sugar cane, and flourishes of bougainvillea. Tongaat was famous for its sugar. The oldest sugar barons from the British Empire and the Dutch East India Company had settled there, in grand manor houses that stood hawkishly looking over the town like distant relatives. Manor gardens on large estates with large bay windows that looked out onto the spreading sugary invitation and where men in too-tight khaki shorts with whiskies in their hands kept beady eyes on their Indian labourers, who were housed in barracks and occasionally thanked the Sugarman for the roof over their heads.

When Indians were freed from their indenture, after Mahatma Gandhi had starved and fought like a nappy-wearing bulldog for their freedom, the Indians remained in their barracks, grateful still for the roof over their heads. They kowtowed, still, to the Barons and their Baroness wives, and their children who had fully grown horses for pets, and happy golden retrievers.

They called the barracks the 'Newspaper Barracks'. No

one knows why. And among those living in this chattel, gossip spread faster than a fire that arose to burn the cane.

Into the town of Tongaat, on a sugar-cane farm called Emona, Meera Rekha Narain was born. She was born on the night her grandfather Returned. He had gone missing for three whole months, and her grandmother had sat on the floor like a mourning widow, with one of her only two saris drawn firmly over her head, a lavender-coloured chiffon, six metres of no pattern, just metres of fabric that struggled now to cover her wide girth.

Meera's mother was the youngest of five daughters-in-law, and they all learnt early enough that there were questions you just never ask.

So when their father-in-law had mysteriously vanished, they asked no questions, they spoke nothing of it, they accepted that this was the way things were. One stormy night in August, the Old Man had stood outside on the lawn of the farmhouse they all shared. He had sniffed the wild wind that blew and that made the sugar cane boil and roll.

And without saying anything to anyone, he had taken his fishing rod, his tackle box and his reels, and walked away from the house. Days passed into weeks and then into months, and he had not come back. His sons spoke in whispers as they huddled around a bottle of cane spirit rum. Perhaps they should go out looking for the Old Man. But the eldest son stood his ground. No. He will be back. On his own.

And he did come back. In a bakkie he had borrowed. Smiling and laughing as if he had simply gone to town on an errand. Out of the back of the bakkie he offloaded hessian sack upon sack of fish. He emptied the silvery wonders in huge piles in the courtyard, and ordered a message to be sent to all neighbours and relatives.

Come! Come, take!

Meera's mother, in the early stages of her labour, had held her rolling belly and heaved and retched at the mountain of fish, and begged her husband to drive her to the hospital as soon as possible. All she remembered through her long labour, and when the tiny child was given to her, was the smell of fish. It permeated her pores. She felt that the doctors and nurses had smelt it too. She felt that the baby had smelt it as well. And when the baby opened her mouth to suckle, her mother could only think of the mouth of a fish, opening and closing, battling to breathe.

But there was something else that came with the fish in the open-top bakkie. Seated quietly on the front seat was a man.

'I found him wandering the beaches,' was all her grandfather would say, and indicated for the man to come out and be seen. Her grandfather's trophy. A fishy man indeed.

He was a short man. A man with blue eyes, but dark skin. A strange dichotomy. He dressed in a white dhoti and a glowing saffron-coloured robe with ancient Sanskrit verse in Hindi script with the lines at the top of the words.

The people gathered, gathered that perhaps those words meant ancient prayers and hymns. The farm people, knowing nothing of the meaning of words with lines at the top, bent to kiss the robe, kissing perhaps the corner where it was emblazoned 'Meenathchi's Sari and Kurta bootik. Print will wash out if the using hot water. Please to wash in cold.'

He called himself simply India Swami. He came with a brown suitcase stuffed with books, ancient Hindu texts, chants and prayers in well-worn books with no spines. And in his broken English he stood in the courtyard filled with fish and robe-kissing men and women; he told everyone of a calling he had received while he sat under a large peepal tree in his native village in India. It was a calling to come to Africa, to go to the farms and villages filled with the children of the indentured labourers and to bring the word of God to them. With perfect white teeth he had smiled at the gathering that had assembled there and began reciting words from the Vedas, the most ancient and sacred of Indian texts.

The daughters-in-law covered their heads with silky saris and scuttled about, making tea and food, and everyone sat in awe of the holy man that Dada had found and brought to them.

They considered themselves so lucky that such a holy man had chosen their farm upon which to sprinkle his holiness, and they all vowed to treat him with the reverence he deserved. The people of Emona were mostly illiterate farmers, planting sugar cane and vegetables. They did not know any sacred texts or chants, and they felt blessed that now in their midst there stood a real proper India Swami who would civilise their children and pray for their sins.

Soon, India Swami had become part of the community of Emona. He had been given a place to live, a large, windowed, airy room. He had been given his own chamber pot, his own brass plate and cup, which Meera's father had to buy after pawning his only watch. Within the courtyards of the main house, the home of Meera's extended family, he settled too quickly into convenience. He lived among them as one of their own and began a regular regime of civilising the children and teaching them about the many Gods and deities of their religion.

No one questioned India Swami. His word was the word of God, and when he suggested to the parents of all the farm children that they be sent to him on a regular basis to learn to sing loudly the bhajans and songs that gave them access to the gods, the parents had bowed before his dusty feet.

So, in the smoky prayer room of the main house, on Tuesday evenings from seven to eight, India Swami sat with lines and lines of children before him, their dirty scabby knees reaching towards the ceiling. When they did not learn immediately and recite perfectly, they were lashed with a long thin piece of bamboo that India Swami kept on the altar of the prayer room. The prayer room itself was lined from floor to ceiling with pictures and effigies of every god, avatar and deity of Hinduism, and the children were forced to stare at these sometimes frightening pictures and bow to India Swami's feet as he lashed them into submission. On a Tuesday evening the combined voices of many terrified children rang out into the night, and the mothers and fathers smiled indulgently to themselves at how spiritual and civilised their children were becoming.

Dirty farm children, they were called. Low-caste, dark and ugly children, they were called. Filthy naughty-eyed children, they were called. India Swami was relentless and ferocious, warning the children that if they spoke of what happened inside the dark prayer room, where India Swami occasionally smoked dagga while he heard the children chant, God would never forgive them and they would definitely go to Hell and not Heaven, which is where Lord Krishna lived. And because most of the children adored Lord Krishna and his playful butter-stealing habits, they kept silent, and tried to sing louder in adoration of the gods, and in submission to India Swami.

Nobody would have believed the poor children anyway. Once out of the prayer room and among the mothers and the fathers, India Swami became the perfect benign man of God. He sat ever so quietly, ate ever so little, even though the children saw him gorging on sweetmeats while he made them say their chants. He would sit among the adults in the lotus position, his white dhoti sweeping the floor, his bare feet clean and smooth. He had taken to growing a long, flowing beard, and its sprinkling of grey made him appear more ethereal and holy than anyone they had ever seen. He gave discourses to the adults as they assembled in the lounge room, and spoke in beautiful words from the best parts of the ancient Vedas, softly intoning the Sanskrit words. Everyone felt so pure and spiritual in his divine presence, and he began receiving gifts from his flock. A shirt, a crisp white dhoti, an incense holder – and then later, as he grew more spiritually brave, he began asking for larger things, like money.

The people of Emona loved him deeply and began taking collections for cash that India Swami swore to them was to be used in purchasing more books, or a brand-new effigy. Or, most of the time, he would talk of his poor unfortunate flock back in Gorakhpur in India.

He told the people that he was sending their blessed money back to India to help drill boreholes for water, to help buy grain for food, to help send young children to school. The more-than-hard-earned money of farmers with only bunches of coriander to make their daily supper was donated abundantly. They denied their children school shoes, they denied their wives new saris, and they watched their wives in their torn, patched-up garments as they scuttled about preparing India Swami's Holy Supper. His coffers grew large, and his domination over the little children grew more horrific. India Swami lived on with the people of Emona for over twenty years, and in those twenty years he became a very rich man. And in those twenty years, many things happened in dagga-smoking prayer rooms.

India Swami had grown his nails long. He told the people that it was because of a vow he had taken at the sacred river

Ganges, that he would grow his nails and his hair if a child in his village was miraculously cured of a dangerous stomach plague. And it had happened. India Swami received a letter wrapped tightly in brown paper from his village. He read the letter to his flock in Emona, first in Hindi, which they barely understood, for the indentured labourers had arrived a long time ago from India and had forgotten their Hindi. They spoke in a mixed-up dialect called Bhojpuri, mingled and mixed with the landlord's English and the black man's Zulu.

They believed the 'Shudh Hindi', the pure Hindi, the India Swami read out. They all agreed. This was a true Holy Man. The child in his village in India had suddenly awoken from his fugue asking for dhal, and all praised the Almighty, and they revered the vow taken by the Holy Swami. His long, almost manicured nails could be seen as he doled out pieces of green apple to the people of Emona.

India Swami believed that green apples were the food of the gods, and on his altar lay piles and piles of shiny green apples. He prayed and chanted and blew ashes over the green apples, ashes that got stuck to your palate as you were forced to eat little brown paper parcels of them and smear them on your brow before school. And the people waited in anticipation for this holy food. Those apples found themselves in exalted places before being delicately eaten by all members of the family. Eating the flesh of a god.

Communion.

It was one green apple that had convinced the entire population of Emona that India Swami was indeed a sacred Holy Man. The apple had been prayed upon and then given to Anand, the poorest farmer in the entire region. Anand's crop of dhania never grew well, his herbs always wilted, and his carrots were almost non-existent, coming out of the clumpy earth like flaccid penises.

Anand bowed the lowest to India Swami and kissed his hand the most. When he complained to India Swami about his farming troubles and his haranguing wife and starving children whose stomachs were growing bloated from eating mealie rice mixed with oily dhal every day for weeks, India Swami would touch his forehead lightly, chew on a freshly made savoury samosa, and say softly to him, 'Sabr Sabr Sabr, my dear friend … patience patience patience …'

One particular day, Anand bowed extra low to India Swami and received a green apple in response. He bit into it hungrily. It wasn't just the holiness of the apple that had him salivating. He looked at the bite he had taken, and 'Hai Ram! Oh, Dearest God, Dearest India Swami … come, come look at this.'

His bite bore a resemblance to the elephant god Ganesha, complete with waving trunk and large ears.

Everyone came to see the bitten apple that was already shrivelling in its brownness. They looked at the likeness and loudly agreed, Anand was indeed blessed with the bite-shape of such a dear Lord.

India Swami himself agreed that Anand's troubles were soon to end and that the Lord Ganesha would remove all obstacles from his path.

The apple was placed next to Anand's prayer lamp and not touched for days, until it rotted into a brown blob that tarnished the brass of the lamp and became the hive of a myriad fruit flies. When it rotted and Anand's crop had still not revived – it had actually got worse with blackjack weeds and dandelions – India Swami was summoned to look at the rotting brown apple mess placed at the lamp. He stared angelically at the rotten fruit and waved away fruit flies, and all he could say to the desperate Anand was, 'Sabr Sabr Sabr …'

Anand looked at his bloated-tummy babies, their navels sticking out. And bowed again to India Swami's clean, white feet.

It all began with the long-nailed pinches. Naughty farm children had grown up into dirty adults. The time had passed so quickly. But dirty young women never spoke of what happened inside the dark prayer rooms. They looked at each other like cousins, like refugees after storms, and they sat squarely on the shelf.

'The girls must be married off before they are eighteen,' professed India Swami, who concluded that the girls had wandering eyes and needed to be 'put right'.

He began to pinch bottoms. The girl children would sidle into the prayer room backwards, afraid that if they turned their backs to him, he would rapidly pinch their bottoms.

'Ugly, dirty, farm gells,' he would say, and smoothly pat their bottoms before delivering a short, sharp, long-nailed pinch.

It didn't end there. India Swami would suddenly have a revelation about a particular girl. Mostly it turned out to be the oldest, closest-to-eighteen-year-old girl he could find, the one with beautiful hips and almond eyes.

'Say after me, gell, say after me … I am dirty, I am ugly, I am naughty … say say.' He pursued the poor sixteen- or seventeen-year-old girl relentlessly, summoning her often to his prayer room, and her parents, like true flock, sent their Black Sheep. The Girl.

And because it was India Swami, and because nobody would have believed her otherwise, she would repeat and repeat phrases of her dirtiness and naughtiness and ugliness. And she would quietly accept India Swami's pinches on her bottom, which brazenly had grown into open fondling up and down her legs, between her legs ... She would bite her lip and try to chant to invoke a god or goddess to make it stop, make it stop. Stop India Swami from making her touch his penis through the thinness of the dhoti. Stop India Swami from telling her that Lord Shiva had professed that young girls need to learn the Kundalini, the art of stroking, the art of almost penetration. For he would never compromise the virgin veil within her. She had a husband to go to. A husband who would make a way into the depths of her womb.

Nobody knew. But the children knew. The girls knew. They stopped talking to each other. They stopped sitting outside at noon making hairstyles and singing songs. And they never spoke of it to each other. They waited until it was their turn to be summoned into the dagga-smelling room filled to capacity with pictures, posters, effigies, and God.

The girls peeped from behind thick fringes, and swung their well-oiled plaits on Tuesdays, hoping for a miracle, hoping something would make India Swami die.

'You are naughty gell, Lord Krishna does not like dirty naughty gell. I am helping you reach Lord Krishna, I am cleansing you of your dirty ways. Farm gell.'

The boys were left alone. Left alone to be as dirty and as naughty as they wanted to be. They grew up into strapping, confident farm boys, strong to the core. With thick muscles, they wielded the hoe and the sickle, and spoke of dreams of Durban. The boys were given Choices. They stayed to farm the land of their fathers. Or they went to join the navy. Or they opened businesses. Or they studied Law. Or they went to work in the Big City. They had so many Choices.

The girls grew up knowing they were dirty. They blossomed into ugliness. They took overdoses of painkillers and blood-pressure medicines. They sat on shelves till they were almost eighteen, and after India Swami had pinched, rubbed and rutted his way into cleansing them, they were rapidly married off to the nearest decent offer that arrived.

No one knew anything. At all.

By the time Meera was eighteen years old, she was a married woman. India Swami had Cleansed her, and found for her the perfect bridegroom. Rajesh. Perhaps better known as Doctor Rajesh Maharaj. What a catch. The most eligible bachelor in Tongaat, and he was all hers.

7
Anjali

RAJESH LIVED ON CORONATION ROAD, THE MOST IM-portant and expensive street in Tongaat. You were practically royalty if you lived there, and Rajesh, with his medical degree, his father's massive mansion and his money, was indeed royalty for Meera, the ugliest, strangest of the farm girls. India Swami watched her hooded eyes as he fondled her. And he knew. This bird was tenacious. This bird would out him. With her flashing furious eyes, she had told him once as he handed her a sacred cloth to wipe her thighs, 'I will tell.'

Simply. With no emotion or fear. *I will tell.* And he grew afraid, fearful and paranoid. This proud, straight-backed girl had got to go.

India Swami had caught her reading one of his books, behind the borehole. She had stolen it from his altar, realising well into the first naked page that it was not in any way Sanskrit hymns, hidden behind a Sanskrit hymn cover.

It was time to get rid of her. He had warned her parents that their daughter was getting too wayward.

Because of the fear and potential of their eldest daughter flirting with the neighbouring farm boys, her parents had simply said yes. When Rajesh had arrived at her doorstep, looking every bit the handsome doctor with money, her parents had decided her future.

And so she married. But what she didn't know was that Rajesh had a mother who had watched all this develop from the sidelines, and had silently but violently protested. When Rajesh had told his mother of his choice, made not because of beauty, or charms, but simply because he was too drunk to think otherwise, his mother had pursed her thin lips and, saying nothing in response, had hastily retreated to her prayer room.

Rajesh Maharaj's mother Anjali was a deeply complex woman. She cried and she laughed and she fought and she moaned all in a single moment. She swore and cussed like a sailor. And she never ever forgot. Anything.

Anjali Maharaj prided herself on three important things, three things that made her world go round, made her live her life:

1. All of her children were doctors.
2. She lived on Millionaires' Row (Coronation Road).
3. Her prayers went directly to God, and they were always immediately answered.

The third one was perhaps the most significant point. Anjali Maharaj was known for her prayer room. It remained shrouded in mystery for most people. She never allowed anyone near her prayer room, and she always kept it locked, its key hidden in a secret biscuit box in the kitchen. Only she knew which biscuit box it was, and, given that she collected tin biscuit boxes, there were probably almost fifty to get through.

Anjali believed that she had been chosen by God. Her prayers were always meant to be answered and all her dreams had come true. She lived in a large mansion on Millionaires' Row. Her balcony was a wraparound. Her red velour drape swags in her semicircular lounge were the envy of all the neighbourhood, or even all of Tongaat. She had a real bathtub. All three of her children were doctors – Pranesh was a

GP, Rajesh was soon to specialise in anaesthetics, and Anusha was still in medical school.

Anjali was certain that her prayers were heard. By all the Matric boards, and by the professors and the lecturers, whose names she would find out from her children and include in her chant when she chanted at night.

She even chanted and prayed for the Indian cricket team, and she was always assured of their victory over Australia or even South Africa when she chanted Sachin Tendulkar's name a hundred and eight times while lighting three camphors at the feet of the strong Lord of sport, Lord Hanuman.

Her prayer room remained shrouded and hidden – a secret white door that no one, not even her own children, was allowed through. The smell of burnt camphor lingered there, followed by the pungent aroma of burnt cloves, for Anjali was of the belief that when you wanted your prayer to be answered, you needed to burn cloves that you had dried for days in the sun. If they popped and spluttered out of the flame and landed on you, then your prayer would be answered. The cloves almost always popped in her direction. She was lucky like that.

But luck certainly wasn't on Anjali's side the day her son decided to marry 'That Girl'.

By then Anjali had seen the effect the thin, dark-skinned girl had had on her son, and she had got scared … very scared. Rajesh was her favourite child. She didn't even bother to hide that fact. And his choice of wife was going to be her responsibility.

'Take this one,' India Swami had whispered to Anjali, 'she is ugly, she is quiet. You can rule over her. This girl will be perfect for your Rajesh. She won't say a word.'

So Anjali had believed India Swami, whose real name

was Naag Raaj, or Snake King in translation. She sucked back her pride and her distaste for the birdlike girl in a cheap, scratchy fake-silk sari, who entered her home as her dear son's bride. Anjali knew things that no one else knew.

What she knew was that soon, very soon … she would get her way. And the dark girl would be punished.

So even though she had allowed the marriage to go ahead, she knew the girl would not last.

And she did not. Last.

8

Firefly

HE SAT ON A WOODEN CHAIR IN THE GARDEN UNDERneath the hundred-year-old thorn tree. His daughter sat quietly breathing near him. The crickets began to sing love songs, the swallows that flew north for the winter now revelled in the December dusk and came home like obedient children to roost in their muddy homes. Not so far away, in the shacks, fires burnt and their wood smoke brought a fragrance to the night. The dew had not even begun to fall yet.

He looked with a side glance at the wild-haired child he had fathered. She seemed lost in the world around her. As always, she sat with one foot dangling off the stool and one tucked underneath her. His limber, tiny-boned girl. The daughter he knew nothing about, knew not how to talk to. He knew only that his heart would always betray him in her tiny presence. The little place-shape she took in the big wide world.

'The swallows came back, Papa,' she commented, breaking the silence. He breathed out loud and wondered why this child was lingering around him tonight.

'Yes, they have come home,' he replied and continued into his favourite time of day. When day gives herself to night.

'The old lady who lives in the shacks was selling roasted mealies today, Papa,' she said, speaking to him again.

'Hmmm,' he grunted, not knowing what else to say. Again, he wondered why the child was seeking out his presence with mundanities. The air around her asked her father a million uncomfortable questions. But she insisted on small talk. Any talk.

'I wonder why we don't see fireflies any more, Papa,' she said again, whimsically. And he recalled a day when she was five years old, as gangly as she was now, and he had taught her to catch fireflies at night and put them into empty pickle jars so they would glow. He remembered with vividness how seriously she'd set about it, chasing fireflies, how her high cheekbones would rise to the heavens in her smile when she trapped one. And how she would watch the trapped insect for only a moment before opening the lid and giving it permission to go home to its 'mummy and daddy'.

He felt assaulted by her quiet presence near him. He felt a bitter pill at the back of his throat.

Her bright yellow dress and traditional billowing pants irritated him, angered him, saddened him. A child. Barely a child still.

In two days' time, he would give her away to another man. Perhaps a man who could explain softly to her why we don't see fireflies any more. Perhaps a man who would explain nothing to her at all.

He hated himself. For giving her away. For wanting never to give her away.

But she had to go. It was her time. She had bought time by a year after she finished school. She had done well at school, well enough to get into a college. Inside his heart he wanted her to be a teacher. But rules are rules. And he was the beloved of the Holy Man, who told him that she must go. Young, fresh, freshly pinched and fondled, not even nineteen years old. With a sharp mind, a kind, soft heart, and a beauty that only a father could see. She must go.

She shifted her legs, dropping the folded one to dangle in the dust, and folding the dusty one beneath her warm body. A ripple of sand dunes from a desert breeze swayed through his heart. A ripple of self-hatred gripped his insides.

He did what he always did best when he was deeply emotional. He turned on her. His daughter. His child.

'Meera! Go inside! Now! What's this? Young girls with open hair sitting under trees at night just a few days before your wedding day? India Swami would be furious if he saw you. Go! Just go from here—'

'But Papa …'

Meera knew all too well what India Swami's fury would bring her. She shuddered. Her father took the shudder for a chill in the air, or an ill-omened wind that blew over her.

'Meera!' he said gruffly. 'Get from here. Go inside with the ladies and help to clean the rice, and also … tie your hair, and also, put on some shoes, and also learn to sit like a proper lady and also … Go from here. Now.'

She looked first at her dusty bare feet as she stood up. She looked hurt. She lingered still. And then, with those eyes that he loved and dreaded equally, she looked straight into his. A million questions were asked. A million secrets were told. If only. If only Papa I could tell you. If only Papa you would believe me.

But he turned his face away. Too quickly. Too sharply. And he heard her bare feet go padding away from a perfect moment he would never be given again.

He leant onto the hard back of the wooden Globe Chair and pulled out a cigarette. And a firefly flew benignly past his nose.

On the sweltering, stinking day he handed her over to

her new husband, he cried. Behind a pillar where no one could see him. He never saw the way she turned around in all her bridal itchy fake-golden finery, looking for him as the bridal Mercedes-Benz drove away. All he saw was the mistake he had made.

9

Ashes and Shit

In the pregnant heat, the fat flies feasted. A spreading swirl of sludge wound its way down a grassy embankment, threatening to slip and slide into a rainbow-coloured marquee. Grey-green-brown, the relentless slide defeated stones and boulders as it spread, naughtily whispering its secrets into the thick air – the sickly sweet gossiping of human excrement. It carried its message into hawking lungs and turning stomachs. It said hissingly, 'This wedding smells of shit.'

It was a day of angry heat. The start of a Durban December, the time of year for haters. Not a wedding season. A sweating season where noontimes found fat ladies lying on cane loungers, or lying on floors covered with the cool redness of cow dung.

Meera and the Good Doctor. It was their wedding day. A happy Sunday morning of ritual. A moist, sweaty morning of fragrant fires, followed by the spiciest of noonday lunches.

But again and again, the whispers rode in on the back of flies –

This wedding smells of shit.

The cesspit had chosen today to overflow. Perhaps overworked by all the shittings of a hive of guests, who had arrived in crowded buses from farms, cities and across the oceans. Eating their way into the pre-wedding rituals, watching and waiting like buzzards for a moment of the extraordinary. They had seen it all before.

The day before, a coy bride rubbed down with a thick

paste of turmeric, sandalwood and mustard oil, to make her skin fair, after which she is frogmarched to the place where two roads collide. She kneels on the dusty earth, her mother covers her eyes with a pattern of sari fabric, and she digs her bride hands into a hole in the ground. A hole recently dug by a cousin with a hoe, and then a hole rapidly filled with water from a brass cup.

And into the hole three things are thrown: a coin, a betel nut, a gold ring. And the blindfolded bride swishes her hands around the mud in the hole, the thick chocolate sauce, surrounded by a protective battalion of aunts and grannies all keening songs into the virgin air. Will she find the coin first, or will it be the betel nut?

The significance of all this is that if a bride finds the coin first, her husband will surround her with riches; if she finds the womb-like betel nut first, she will bear many fair children; and if she finds the elusive ring first, of course – she will be loved.

You always find the gold ring last. Or never at all. That's just the way things are.

Everyone knew, and every woman accepted: You always found the gold ring last.

And all this guesswork must be completed before the sun set and night-time was ushered in. Otherwise, there would be Bad Times Ahead.

The anticipation grew. The drumming of the dhol, an oval-shaped percussion instrument with tapered ends and a sound that echoed over hills, called out in expectancy. It grew wilder and faster in its drumming as the bride grew hotter or colder. It took on a life of its own, its faithful drummer, a crazy woman in a dark-green sari, twisting and turning and swinging her wild, untied hair, her open hair, as she banged out songs that made no sense.

Meera's knees, and their childhood scars, found their connection with the mother that is Earth. Kneeling, she listened to the moaning voices of the wall of women, who stood like soldiers to block out the evil eye, and she tried to make sense of their songs. In a dialect that was neither Hindi nor English, nor Zulu, but a twang cooked up into a mixture of all three, the women sang stories of the length of the bridegroom's turban cloth.

They swung their hair and danced to drums. Women gone wild. Before the sun set. They munched on raw chickpeas and sipped on local milky brews. In a collective swoon, they broke their bonds. Just this once. Just this crazy opportunity to let it all hang out. No men, no priests, no beady-eyed mothers-in-law. Happiness overran their cups, and allowed their madness to slip out of sari blouses, to jiggle their fatty rolls, to let their tightly wound metres of cloth fall softly to the ground.

The sun had set. Meera had fished around in the mud, with sweaty armpits that drained all the way down to the tightly knotted piece of string around her waist that kept her turmeric-coloured sari in its rightful place. Suddenly the dancing and the gyrating wild women had stopped, and silence descended on the air that smelt of late jasmine flowers.

Bougainvilleas in the bushes preened their showy colours and their million earbuds swivelled in the direction of a bride who found nothing but mud.

'But I swear I put them in there,' a high-pitched cousin pleaded with the flashing mynah eyes of the banshee women. They tightened their circle. An ill omen, bad luck. The sun had set, and the bride had found nothing in the thick soup of mud. They shook their heads, they tutted and muttered. Nothing at all.

Meera's red-nailed fingers, thick with the glove of sugar-cane-growing mud, appeared out of the hole like a claw held out for all to see. Nothing. Nothing in its muddy grasp. Not even the betel nut, an obvious sphere, a fertile little nutjob.

Meera's mother wrung her hands and looked around like a frightened toddler, waiting for the old ladies to stop munching on betel leaves and to profess their remedy with red-stained mouths. Surely, there must be a remedy for this bad luck. There existed remedies for everything. Old, fat women twisted red-stained mouths and shifted their bulk away from bad-luck brides.

They twirled their ratty grey plaits around their fingers, they spat at the hole in the ground. No remedy indeed. Let her take her chances. Maybe the gods would favour her tomorrow at her wedding. Maybe if she bowed lower into the mud, she would be saved the ill omens, the bad luck and the premonitions of disaster. We shall see.

The night of the ritual, the night before she was to be wed, had come alive with a cacophony of wild banshees, clapping their hands in glee. Shaking their hairdos. Not a typical wedding. A wedding begun with ill omens. And a wedding that would unfold with even uglier, even smellier, iller omens.

The septic tank on the farm had overflowed. And no one could do anything about it. The thick fetid sludge had done a slow waltz towards the marquee decorated with marigolds. A million marigolds. So thick, so pungent the smells of shit and marigolds, that Meera would never again smell marigolds without thinking of shit. Nor would she smell shit without thinking of marigolds.

And she would always carry the basket of marigolds and shit in her memories of the day she became someone's wife.

In a cream Mercedes-Benz, decorated with … marigolds, the Good Doctor arrived. A procession of Mercedes-Benzes, a haughty, well-dressed entourage, hooting feebly their arrival. Reluctant hooting, as if they would rather not be there after all. The bridegroom sat crunched up in the back seat, for too many people had wanted to squeeze into the bridal car. Too many people wanted importance.

He unfolded his folded knees and creaked from a frog squat and tried to leap from the car door into an agile stand. He failed. He slipped underfoot and landed flat on his arse on the hard concrete driveway, surrounded by the guests who had assembled for the ceremony to welcome him. He blinked, blinked up into the laughing sun, and adjusted the glasses that had slid off a sweaty nose, and felt around like a blind man for the red turban that had slipped off his head and landed in a pile of rotting banana peels.

His not-too-long turban fabric unwound itself, and his anxious uncles grabbed at the fabric from all directions. Hands and hands and hands pulling his ungainly body back into a standing position, redoing the red turban into a semblance of decency, dusting his white suit, blackened already by the dust and the dirt.

He feigned nonchalance and puffed out his chest, standing like a stuffed pigeon as the women from the bride's family turned brass platters filled with flowers and lit lamps around his pointy head. Welcome, our Prince. We give you this warm hello. Take our daughter away.

They blessed him with their songs. They blessed him with their camphor-smelling adorations. They prayed for his long life and virility. But the sludge from the septic tank decided to gatecrash the ritual, and into the middle of all the blessings a thick stain of sewage leaked menacingly, looking for a hole in which to drown.

The gaudily dressed women interrupted their throaty welcoming songs and began a hopping dance, lifting brightly coloured silk saris and revealing thick unshaven calves. Bedroom slippers gave up their ghosts, hastily worn underneath the all-forgiving saris, to prevent bunions, and anyway no one could see down there. The newly arrived importance of the bridegroom's party came undone when bisected by a line of sewage. Important rich people who lived on Millionaires' Row and who drove only Mercedes-Benzes ducked and dived away from its path. Meera's father stood drowning in a too-large navy-blue suit and gave up attempts at apologising to the wedding guests. He leant against a marquee pole with a nauseous stomach, watching people jump and fly all over the place.

The welcoming ritual forgotten, the bridegroom and his special rich family placed crumpled hankies near their mouths and entered the wedding marquee. Again to be assaulted by a thick web of smells, of the sweat of humanity in a boiling December, of cheap aftershave and Brylcreem, of babies who had vomited, of smelly socks, of bad breath, of mothball-scented old saris that were only taken out of wooden chests once every five years, of disgust and hunger and keen gossiping – all rolled into a fat, thick orb that sat in the wedding marquee like a planet.

The bridegroom shifted from foot to foot and waited in the thick of things for the loud music of the Indian horn, the wedding instrument, the shenai, to begin its high-pitched announcement of his handsome arrival.

He thrived on the attention of many envious eyes, and perhaps in the two whiskies he had hastily drunk before he got there, and walked like a Moghul prince down the makeshift aisle, with his brother on his left hand and his sister on his right. They held him upright. They knew their brother well.

Once safely stowed upon a rickety stage, surrounded by

banana leaves poached from neighbouring farms, the bridegroom soon forgot how he'd fallen on his arse; he felt important and special as the eyes of all the people looked appreciatively in his direction. So handsome. So tall. So fair. Doctor.

His mother, Anjali, lurked in circles. In the white sari of the widow, she made her circuitous movements around the bridal altar, looking beady-eyed at the drooping banana leaves, the sacred fire, the rice and the sweets and the bright Christmas tinsel that dressed the altar into nuptial welcome.

She sniffed the air. She smelt the shit. She smelt the low-caste farm people that were binding their unwashed bodies to her son, and she fainted away into a white bony heap.

Women of all shapes and sizes surrounded her supine form, raising her legs immodestly till her fuzzy hairy legs were on show for all to see. Smelling salts, perfumed hankies, water in greasy glasses – but her doctor children all kept their distance. They didn't flutter at her with stethoscopes and vials, miraculously materialised out of invisible black doctor bags. They left her. In her swoon. They left her.

Revived finally by pinches, she gasped yet another shitty breath and found herself stuffed into a waiting plastic chair, where she sat with curses in her eyes, watching the marriage evolve. So many ill omens in one hot, humid wedding. So many.

As the Good Doctor bridegroom sat on the stage and the rituals began, the rituals that cleanse the man before the bride is allowed near him, Meera sat alone in a red 1972 VW Beetle, waiting to be summoned. Nobody would have guessed that, parked at the outermost end of the wedding marquee, cushioned in the shell of the tortoise car, sat a bride who knew nothing of fainting and fallings and shit.

Hidden from all eyes, away from the evil eye, she shifted uncomfortably in her seat, the scratchy tinsel and garish gold ornaments tormenting her skin, already prickling in the boiling heat. A nine-year-old girl, a gangly little dreamer with an old woman's bun, sat on the ground near the car. The bride needed a guardian. And the guardian would be a waiflike prospect for men to keep an eye on.

In a pink starchy dress, the girl picked at her teeth, dug in her nose and drew circles in the sand, bored and ready to take on the spotlight. It seemed they were well forgotten – the little girl, the little bride, in a little car that was not a Mercedes-Benz. They must wait their turn. To be called into the not-so-fragrant marquee.

Across the lawns, avoiding the sludge, a figure in shiny black came maniacally striding. Pushing its way through shocked men who stood smoking cheap cigarettes, and tut-tutting women snaking their hairdos in all directions, the black soldier charged with a purpose and a jutting chin.

'Look at that!' they said. 'How could she? Come here to our sacred (shit-smelling) ground. How dare she?'

But the girl in black had shoved aside men, kicked little dirty-nosed children out of her path, and fixed her beady black eyes on the red VW Beetle. She arrived at its door, and shook her black-scarved head at its core.

'Ya Allah! Meera. You look like a Christmas tree.'

'Ashes! What are you doing here? You are not allowed.'

'Meera, you stupid. I am allowed anywhere and everywhere. What is this nonsense? Do you even love this ugly doctor?'

'Excuse me,' squealed the nine-year-old pink-crinolined girl. 'Get out before I tell.'

'Ha! Go tell. Go tell all the old goats that Aisha Vawda is

here, wearing her black bin bag, here to see her friend not get married. Stupid churail witch child. Go tell.'

Meera stared up into the fair round face wrapped firmly in a black headscarf, and wanted deeply to dive out of the car, to shed her scratchy trousseau and fly like a happy swallow in the rose-scented folds of black, black fabric. With genuine fear in her heavily made-up eyes, she gasped, 'Ashes, you have to leave. You know what India Swami says about Muslims. You can't come near our prayers and our weddings.'

'Shut up you Meera, you. I'm nowhere near that praying place and all that fire and all that. And I don't care about that long-haired donkey, that pervert. I'm here talking to you. What you getting married for? What a waste of time.'

'I … have to, Ashes. I have to. And anyway, you Vawdas are none the better. You all marry your cousins when you're not even sixteen.'

'Not me, Meera. I told Papa. I told Dada, I even told that stupid Zuleikha Aapa. I'm never getting married. Ever. What? Must I live my life waiting on a disgusting filthy man, what? And it's too disgusting anyway when they want to … put their things inside you and all. Never. Never. Just run from here, Meera, don't marry that doctor. Come!'

'Leave it, Ashes. Leave it now. You better go away before India Swami sees you.'

'Stupid girl, huh? Stupid girl. Meera, you remember in school we read this Afrikaans book about these four sisters? All studying, all playing tennis on the lawns, eating apricot jam sandwiches. Nobody forced them to get married. See, Meera, white girls. They don't take shit!'

'That was just a book, Ashes. And anyway, we're not white girls. We're Indian girls. White girls are too sharp.'

Suddenly Aisha's head jerked backwards and her throat

made a muffled gag. Behind her stood old Aunty Sita, dressed in wild purple and brassy red, with a garish painted-on mouth and a trunkful of fake gold jewellery roped around her neck. She had grasped Aisha's ponytail through the soft black headscarf and yanked her strong bulky body backwards. Aisha braced her thick thighs, hidden beneath a flowing black cloak, and stared squarely into Aunty Sita's black face.

'What you want here, you … you … Muslim!' Aunty Sita spat at Aisha.

Meera tried to dive out of the back seat of the Beetle, but the shackles of cheap jewellery and an ornately embroidered sari kept her firmly rooted to the spot.

'Leave her, leave her, Sita Kaki. She's just my school friend. Came to wish me well.'

'She's a Muslim! And a meat beef eater. Polluting this pure wedding with her beef-eating mouth. Get out, you fat thing. Get from here or I'm going to slap you.'

'Slap then. Go ahead. Slap,' Aisha threatened.

Aisha bunched up her fists and took the stance of a boxer. She glared into the down-sloping eyes of the aunty bat. And just when Meera thought she was going to punch Sita in the nose, punch her as she had almost all the boys back in school, the fighter Aisha backed away.

She twisted her mouth angrily at Meera and whispered close into her heavily made-up bridal face, 'White girls don't take shit. And us … we live in shit. Can't you smell it?'

Ashes. Don't go. Ashes. You were right.

White Girls Don't Take Shit.

10

A Tiger Never Changes His Spots

THE BRIDAL CAR STOPPED ITS HOOTING AS IT NEARED Millionaires' Row. Such things were not tolerated here where the rich and richer were taking their naps, not halfway bothered to attend such a low-class wedding.

Meera entered her new bridal home and was ushered into a bedroom where the bed was not even made. She sat down and posed for a photograph with her fake-smiling husband and her depressed mother-in-law. And then they ignored her. No one even offered her juice, tea, water. They ignored her. Closed the door behind them.

Her husband disappeared, not to be seen again until late into the night, drunk and drowsy. And wanting her body.

She sat and waited for hours in the room with the door firmly closed and heard the men outside her window begin drinking expensive whisky. She heard flutters of their conversation. They had set up a makeshift bar on the veranda. She heard her father-in-law's brother Premchand hurriedly tell all the men to neaten up the table strewn with used whisky glasses and pieces of fried snacks.

'He is coming here now. He just phoned.'

Who?

Meera waited. The bustle and rustle in the house had settled into a quietness of anticipation. He is coming. He is coming.

Meera never knew when He arrived. She only knew of his arrival when the door to her room swung open and before her, with her mother-in-law, stood an astounding apparition.

A woman, the beloved wife of the famous man. A woman

with caked-on make-up stuck to her ageing face like a mask of horror. A woman whose unnaturally black hair had been teased vertically into a massive beehive reaching up to the ceiling. A woman wearing the brightest red, orange and gold sari Meera had ever seen.

Meera's mother-in-law realised only then that the bed had not been made and the room was a whirlwind of chaos. Her face fell into anger. As if a brand-new bride should be on her hands and knees picking up discarded pyjamas and used underwear thrown around in haste by her husband, getting ready for the wedding.

Meera saw the anger and embarrassment in her mother-in-law's face. It was the first time she had faced that look of anger. But not the last.

The heavily made-up beehive movie star advanced towards her. Family women peeped and snaked over each other's bodies to peek into the room.

'So this is the bride?' she said. Loudly. Proudly. Eloquently.

'Yes Bhain-ji, dear sister. This is the girl our Rajesh has married,' Anjali mumbled and tried to pick up a pair of underpants off the floor before the advancing beauty queen. Anjali looked strangely as if she was about to touch the Woman's feet in subservience.

The Woman came close to Meera. She looked at Meera's face from top to bottom. Her breath smelt of cigarettes and cloves.

The Woman's eyes were heavily lined in the darkest of dark kohl. They had long points at the ends, points that were drawn in black to reach out towards her temples. She lifted a long pointed red nail and turned Meera's face from right to left, from left to right, those koala eyes stalking her with their gaze.

'Hmmm, Anjali Bhain-ji, my sister. Your boy could have done so much better. Not even fair like the first one. Not even a pretty girl. Our Doctor could have had a Queen but now he has … this,' she said and twisted her very red-stained mouth downwards. Downwards like when you are forced to look at something distasteful. Distasteful. A dead dog on the road. Run over with innards exposed.

'I know Bhain-ji. I know,' Anjali mumbled and Meera lowered her head as both older women shook their heads at the ugliness of her. The heavy gold veil that had been pinned onto her head with sharp black bobby pins dug into her scalp. The fake gold jewellery itched and reddened her skin. An angry rash began.

Quickly, to distract the woman in her fine silk sari and white-powdered face, Anjali ushered her out. Away from the ugly bride. Towards a groaning tea table. Meera's stomach grumbled as the smells of fresh-fried delicacies and brewed tea drifted into the room. But she dared not ask for any food or tea. Anjali's look of hatred had silenced her completely.

'Come come Bhain-ji. Come, sister. Let us have tea, coffee. Did I show you my brand-new crystal chandelier from Vienna? Come.'

The woman arched her back and pushed out her huge breasts. The millions of gold beads on her sari tinkled. She looked again at Meera, the bewildered, embarrassed bride, and shook her head. 'What a waste!' she said and swished out of the room strewn with underwear, pyjamas and pathos.

Meera sat alone again. Too sick inside her stomach, too thirsty and hungry, too afraid to move. For hours.

The men outside her window were talking loudly. Apologising that they had to set up the alcohol table outside the house on the veranda, blaming the women and their silly superstitions of not having alcohol enter the house. One man's voice drowned out all others.

'Don't you worry, Premchand bhai. I have sorted it out,' he boomed.

He appeared to be convincing Meera's dead father-in-law's brother that something was under control. The men all but licked the floor. They carried a single-seater couch from the red velour lounge suite to the outside table where they offered the Man his seat.

The Man held court with all the men who had gathered to shake his hand, to pump his fist, to be in his tall, powerful presence. He enjoyed the attention. He loved talking about himself and his importance.

'The government loves me!'

'But bhai, are you sure?' Premchand kept asking in wavering tones. And Meera heard the glasses of whisky clink into a toast.

'Premchand bhai, let us drink to it. It is done. Pure and simple. Done!' The man spoke as if chastising a small child. 'Your dear brother Ashok Kumar was everything to me. He was my own blood, my brother, my very own. When I started with this government, when I left the one boxing ring for the other boxing ring, he supported me. He gave me money for my campaign. He gave me courage to fight like a tiger. Like a Bengal tiger.'

'But bhai, us Indians, we are not from Bengal. They call us Calcuttias, but we are from Bihar, bhai. If I am correct? Not from Bengal.' A brave voice had ventured to contradict the Man's heritage and pseudonym.

'Bihar, Calcutta … same thing, bhai. Indians. From India. That's who we are. Not Africans. Indians,' the Man chastised the speaker, appearing to sound affronted and fazed. He quickly switched the conversation. 'Us Indians needed a representation. We had to get into the bed with the white man. A man has his needs, yes? A man needs a warm, comfortable bed, yes? So we got into PW's bed. So what? As the elected head of the party, I held the reins. But Premchand bhai ... your brother, he was my horse.'

Meera heard Premchand Uncle murmur an affirmative, and she heard as they poured and drank again to the departed Ashok.

The man continued speaking. 'This country, bhai. It was no place for us Indians. If the government released him from Robben Island, we would have been finished, kalaas! He must stay there in Robben Island. If they let him out now, he's too old now to do anything. And anyway, we will double-cross that bridge when we come to it. We have our own plans here. I met with PW many times. He is a good man. Look, I often wear the hat he wears so I can identify with him. Makes us like brothers, nah? He knows he must keep me happy. Keep us Indians happy. And the referendum, bhai ... look at the results. The whole country spoke. All the whites, they spoke. Us Indians needed our own seat in the Parliament. It's the Holy Trinity, bhai. Brahma, Vishnu, Shiva. In Parliament bhai, now we have our own Creator, Protector, Destroyer.'

'Must be the Coloureds who are the destroyers, nah? They destroy everything.' Someone made a joke and the men rumbled into laughter.

'Don't laugh, brothers. Don't laugh. Us Indians, we are the Creators. We build homes, we build schools, we create from nothing, from soil. And the white man, brothers ... he is our Protector. And he will protect us from these wild people and their shouting, screaming, marching. As for Destroyer, arre, brothers ... must have one naughty child in the family, nah?'

The men roared into laughter. Exaggerated laughter. Patting the big Man on his broad back for his witticism.

He drank deeply from his neat whisky and called forward a teenage boy lurking nearby. Rajesh's cousin Neeraj lurched into importance.

'Tell the ladies we want more samosa, burfee, bhajia boy. Go.'

Neeraj ran like a king's minion to the giggling ladies in the kitchen and barked orders at them, while they piled plate upon plate with rich food and snacks.

'He is happy. PW is happy with us Indians. He made me a Member of Parliament now. Do you know, brothers, I'm his new MP?' The man continued speaking again after rapidly mowing his way through an entire plate of samosas. 'Us Indians, we have our party, we can vote. We are citizens of this country now, bhai. Citizens with a vote. Tricameral … that is a fine word, isn't it? Such a beautiful word.'

He clinked his glass again. Meera drifted into and out of the conversation. She made the bed and hated the smell of sleeping bodies that lurked on the red coverlet. She listened to the chattering and the laughing ladies far away in the lounge room. She imagined a group of dazed and star-struck women sitting at the feet of the one with Cleopatra make-up and a massive beehive. Meera dared not undo the heavy veil with its stabbing pins. She dared not even kick off her uncomfortable shoes. She was frozen. Frozen in a moment in time that lasted forever.

Somewhere, somehow, her mind told her she had seen the Woman before. But at her foggiest with fatigue and anxiety, she had forgotten where. Hours passed and she sat on the bed. Her husband Rajesh could be heard at the men's makeshift bar, loudly demanding his fifth whisky. She heard the Big Man address him.

'Doctor! Doctor Rajesh … married now and all, hah? Well, advice to you, my boy, and my advice is gold so keep it. I haven't seen this wife of yours. But you tell her, she must always use make-up. You tell her she must always dress up in beautiful colours. For you. Every day, she must be your Madhubala. Your movie star. Every day. No jeans-T-shirt nonsense, you hear? She is married to our Doctor Saab now. She must be a beauty queen.'

Meera's eyes fluttered uncomfortably. She had packed only simple, cheap, unadorned saris and pale cotton salwar suits in her bag. Nothing fit for a beauty queen. And she certainly knew nothing about dark painted eye make-up that pointed sharply at the ends, about powdery faces and teased-up beehives.

The Big Man was speaking loudly once more, as if addressing a crowd of potential voters. 'Yes, we formed the Tricameral Government. Yes, we ignored the African National Congress. Why not! Brothers, why not? Us Indians must walk two-three ways in this world. In this South Africa. We want our comfortable life. We want our big-big houses. So, why must we waste our time fighting for the Black Man? If he is released from that jail, he will steal our land, he will tell his people to rape our women, chase us from here. When I met PW, I saw a man with a plan. I am so happy with his plan. But Premchand, bhai … you're looking so worried. Don't have stress on your head, bhai. I am a tiger. I won't change my spots. I have my ways. You have your liquor licence sorted out bhai. Relax, enjoy. Open your tavern with the blessing of a spotless tiger. I organised. Don't worry. I organised.'

As the evening wore on, and fatigue overcame her, Meera stopped listening to the men's chatter outside her open window. Their conversation had turned bawdy and distasteful as the liquor took its hold. Eventually, after midnight, the Man began his goodbyes. Her eyes heavy with sleep, she peeped through the lace curtain of the room she was kept in and saw the broad back and tall figure of a man in a well-cut navy-blue suit.

She didn't see his face as he turned away to leave, but she noticed an ill-fitting wig upon his head, and a jutting chin on his prominent profile. She had seen this man before. Everyone had. She knew who he was. He was important.

It would be two weeks later, in December 1988, when Meera, still a new bride, while peeling potatoes in a chaotic kitchen, would happen upon a newspaper article, a front-page headline with the broad grimacing picture of the Man who had held court outside the window on her wedding night.

She stopped filling the newspaper sheet with potato peels and began reading the article, hoping no one would come into the kitchen and catch her reading instead of peeling, chopping, cooking and cleaning.

The Man was in trouble. Deep trouble. He had been hauled before a Commission of Enquiry where a Justice had found him guilty of corruption and maladministration within his party. He had used his largesse in Parliament to hand out promotions to friends and devotees, and, as Meera read, she found he had handed out illegal liquor licences to his close friends.

She thought of Uncle Premchand, who had already set up his liquor store, haranguing the black boy he had hired for twenty rands a day to cart and stock shelves with bottles and bottles of spirit, beer and wine. He ran this liquor shop from expensive premises he had rented out in the heart of Tongaat, where he had placed a large television and video machine, with a spaghetti of dangling cords. This is where he showed Bollywood movies and sports matches till late. And other types of movies much later in the night. He drew the crowds. And his little makeshift tavern had thrived in that short time. He had spoken of buying pool tables and dartboards. A real man-cave.

Meera read the article to the end. PW had fired the Man from his post in Parliament. Just like that. Fired. Out. 'Get from here.'

Meera wondered what would become of a tiger that never changes its spots. She wondered what would become of Uncle Premchand's thriving tavern, now that it had been revealed that his liquor licence was fraudulently procured.

Chopping potatoes, carrots and tomatoes, she wondered about the man they had mentioned, the one who was rotting his intellect and body away in Robben Island. She had seen the 'Free Mandela' posters plastered across the walls of the post office and outside the vegetable markets. Somehow, even though she knew nothing of the man in jail, she wished him out of that jail. Because a jail was no place for anyone.

Meera's thoughts lingered on the heavily made-up wife of the Big Man, now fired, disgraced, all dressed up with no party to attend. She remembered seeing the woman on television once. A blonde white woman with pink lips was interviewing the painted lady, who sat on a couch like a queen holding court. The painted lady gushed and praised her husband and his wig, saying openly on public television to the white lady with pink lips, 'He's my hero. I will sleep on thorns for him. I will walk over coals for him.'

Meera had balked at the obnoxious gushing of a masked, golden, ostentatious woman over her husband. And maybe somewhere Meera wished she could say the same about her Rajesh, who continued to treat her like a drudge, like a maid whom he assaulted every night after he came home from his surgery, after his mother had hand-fed him balls of rice and curry Meera had cooked. Meera would dread the moment he entered their bedroom; almost always drunk, having visited uncle Premchand's tavern on his way home, Rajesh would insist she put on the reddest of red lipstick, then haul up her nightgown and throw himself into her.

Afterwards he would look at her lying still on the bed, desperately trying not to pull down the nightgown, because he liked to look at her that way. With red lipstick smeared across her cheek and a fuzzy yellow nightgown bunched at her waist. And nothing else. He would run his eyes over her exposed lower body and red-smudged lips, and smile to himself.

'You got no breasts, bitch. Flat-chested and ugly,' he would mutter and run a hand over her exposed hips. 'This! This is all mine! My property. Mine. To do with as I please.' If Meera moved or shuffled while he was near her, he slapped her across the face. So Meera learnt her stillness then.

In those dark days. She had learnt to lie frozen.

She never wore red lipstick again, after it was all over.

Years later, at her parents' house – after Meera had secretly answered an advert she had found in yet another potato-peel-covered newspaper asking for caregivers in Dublin, Ireland – she read that the Big Man had divorced his painted lady. Supernatural forces in their home had been cited as the cause of the messy, ugly divorce. And the word 'divorce' began to swell in Meera's mind. Surely if a Big Important Man could divorce his wife, maybe … just maybe … she could do the same. Stranded then in a no man's land, neither daughter nor wife, she yearned to be legally free of her husband. For four years she had endured the beatings from Rajesh, who showed her no tenderness. She had silently endured the harassment of Anjali, of Moti the Parrot and of the Fair One, Rajesh's sister-in-law. But Meera's mind was reeling. Cogwheels turning and turning, into a non-stop day–night machine song: 'I can too. I can too …'

11

The Unbearable Lightness of Skin

THE WEDDING NIGHT. A FUSTY NIGHT, SULTRY AND crying out for passion. The heat of the day was done. The putrid stinking wedding had finally ended, ripe with the chanting of India Swami's blessings. Confetti and broken-up marigolds had lain limply on the cheap carpet of the marquee.

Burnt biryani had been rapidly consumed. Rajesh had walked seven times around the prayer fire, tied to the stooping Meera with a shocking-pink ribbon and a safety pin. He had thrown rice and ashes into the fire, and had led her grimy feet down a row of seven pieces of grass, placed in an obedient line. Each step he had taken, she had taken next. Not understanding what they were doing, not understanding why, the language of a million Sanskrit virgins egging them on in their parade.

The bewildered couple had followed instructions and dropped whole husky coconuts into the wild fire, waiting for their union to be blessed. And when it was all over, India Swami had instructed in his passive-aggressive way: the bride must now bow down to the feet of her mother-in-law.

Meera had to perform a ritual where she was removed from the right-hand side of the bridegroom, the side where her parents stood with lines forming maps all over their faces. She was then placed on the left side of his jutting-out arm and told never to look back. At the right-hand side.

She tripped over the long fabric of her ruby-red sari and found herself falling like a mistake at the feet of the waiting, now un-fainted Anjali. And, urged on by the long-nailed pinches of India Swami on her rounded back, she forced her fingers in the general direction of her new mother-in-law's feet. Touching the twitching feet, Meera retched, and had to rapidly cover her mouth with her palm. Anjali had seen it all.

Back at the mansion on Millionaires' Row, the bride was taken out of a stuffed-up Mercedes-Benz and deposited in a bedroom in disarray, filled to the brim with pots.

Inside each pot sat sickly sweetmeats, gifts given by the women of Meera's family to the bride. The sweetmeats would rot in their pots before the rich women would even dream of touching their poverty. No one wanted them, made with farm ghee and cheap almonds and sugar that cost too much, and decorated like cheap ornaments. The fruit would rot in its trays covered with bright red, green and blue cellophane. No one wanted to touch it. Cheap fruit.

A few wilted rose petals strewn carelessly on the marriage bed announced their motive. They hinted at a night of first-time passion, as if wondering which part of the naked skin they would stick to.

The door to the bridal chamber remained sharply closed. The night was young.

Outside, the fair-skinned ones fanned their luminous pelts. They leant gracefully towards each other and whispered secrets. They listened with ears so fair you could see blue veins embroidered like lace underneath the whiteness.

The important guest had left. The bridegroom had showered, hawking farm dust from his nostrils, and changed into a soft pale-blue shirt and white pyjama pants. He spat out a black blob of dusty sputum and drank a tall glass of almond-flavoured milk in one go. Then he sat at his mother's feet, feeling her calloused hands rub his scalp in slow, circular motions. Her mother-mummy keening moans told him that he was still hers.

She circled his temples with her mummy massage and pushed her rough feet towards his clean hands. He picked up his mother's foot and placed it in his lap and caressed it in a motion that would never mirror the caresses he would reserve for his bride.

The bride sitting on the nuptial bed.

Fed well on almond milk, and fed even better on his mother's massages, Rajesh barged into the room. Then the door was rapidly shut. The Prince would take his spoils. The fair ones and their lacy ears listened for moans and groans. They waited for bloodstained sheets. They were to be disappointed.

The almond milk, famed for its aphrodisiac qualities, had somehow become soporific, and the powder-blue bridegroom ignored the girl on the bed. He lay down among rose petals and fell asleep.

After courting his snores for an hour or more, the anxious bride stretched out beside him, and, braving the scratching and the itching of fake gold threads, and the aching of a million pins that kept her heavy sari firmly pinned to her head, she feigned sleep in a stifling night filled with the sounds of crickets.

When morning arrived, the purple dawn found two beady eyes staring into hers through the velvet of dawn.

'I want it now,' Rajesh said, and made a grab for her body. Meera twisted away, hearing the people of the house awaken, feeling revulsion and shy fear overcome her. She noticed that Rajesh's nails were painted, and that they looked feminine and naughty as they shoved dead roses aside and began to rip at fake silky fabric.

'No, not now. Not now. Everyone is awake. Not now,'

Meera feebly protested, batting his tentacles away from her body.

He grabbed her chin and swung her sleepy face towards his and growled through clenched teeth. 'I said, I said … I … want … it … Now.'

The scuffle began, a useless scuffle, for he was strong and relentless in his morning glory, and he held her torso down with force. Not bothering to remove clothing, he pulled down the elastic of his pyjama pants and ripped and forced his way into an entrance.

The fair ones, who had fanned themselves to sleep on moist verandas, did not hear the rutting, grunting noises competing with the morning birds and the boiling of the morning milky tea.

He thrust and he grunted, and was almost ready to contort into a full satiation when there came a manic knocking on the door. Rajesh swore loudly, but the knocking became banging, and when he heard his mother's voice boom loudly from the other side of the door, he went flaccid inside his too-tight bride.

'What? Ma? What you want?' he shouted brusquely, and tried to fiddle around with himself, with his painted nails, hoping to resurrect the fallow fellow in another attempt.

But his mother's crazy, frightened voice rendered him limp, and he rolled away from his bleeding bride and pulled up his white pyjama pants, not noticing the buttery-smelling blood that smeared a little over the front. He was fuming. He was seething. But, swinging open the door, he saw his mother's face and he forgot his wild needs. The bride on the bed twisted sharply away from the gaze at the door and tried desperately to cover up her exposed ankles.

Anjali knew. It had been consummated.

'What, Ma? What's wrong?'

'Your sister. Rajesh, come. Come see Anusha. Something is wrong.'

Rajesh swore under his breath and, with barely a glance at his crumpled-up bride, charged after his mother into her resplendent bedroom. The opulence of red velvet swags fringed with golden Rapunzel tassels and a low-hanging crystal chandelier invited him in, to find his sister Anusha lying face down on the king-size bed, crying loudly into the approaching morning.

'What's wrong with her? Anusha, what's wrong?' Rajesh said and grabbed his prone sister and turned her around. She covered her face with her nut-brown hands and sobbed in a rasping staccato rhythm as her brother tried to prise her hands from her face.

Moving aside a curtain of frizzy hair that had been hair-sprayed to perfection for yesterday's wedding, he found a face so ugly and smarting, he had to turn away. Covered in thick angry welts and ripe red pustules, his sister's moon face stared up at him, competing with the redness of the velvet drapes.

'What's this? What happened to your face?'

Through a mountain of sobs the sister laid her head in her brother's bloodstained pyjama lap, and told him a story of fair skin.

She had lathered a thick layer of skin-lightening cream on her face the previous night, and had woken up in the morning with a festering visage.

Anusha was a dark girl. The fairness in the family had, in a twist of fate, landed on the faces of her brothers, who didn't really need fair skin at all. Anusha's life had been peppered with attempts to lighten her skin. She had endured her mother's haranguing as she grew into a teenager, a mother who locked her in her bedroom during sunny days and placed thick dark-brown drapes on her windows, a mother who had ritualistically scrubbed her face on Sunday mornings with a concoction of turmeric and rose water, and who had made her bathe daily in a brew made of bitter syringa leaves. All to try to make her fair-skinned.

Failing, her mother took to calling her 'blackie' and had cursed her darkness out loud, but had softly prayed in her prayer room for her daughter's skin to turn fair. Anusha of the Medical School had ignored the pharmacopeia of warnings from real doctors and professors and had secretly begun buying skin-lightening creams. She had sent out to India for catalogues, where the skin-lightening industry thrived in its assault on sun-browned women. She had hidden all the thickly wrapped brown-paper parcels that arrived by registered post, carrying her bright treasures from India.

Fair & Lovely, Super White and Vicco Turmeric Light and Bright sat in chubby, twisted tubes at the very bottom of her panty drawer, and she layered them all on into a smelly burning mask every night before she fell asleep, dreaming of the sloughing off of brownness. The creams never really delivered on their promises, and her complexion had settled instead into a muddy greyness.

Passing every mirror, she would examine her face for spots of light, convincing herself that she had seen them. Her mother had given her an amulet to wear around her neck, a necklace made of holy ashes and a dried-up, shrivelled old lime, a medal that had been prayed upon and placed at the altars of the fair-skinned goddesses who reached out their six arms to soothe the black black skin.

At her brother's hot, sunny wedding, the grey-fair Anusha had found the darkest, least sun-filled spot in which to plant herself, and had waited and waited to go home and lie in the darkness of heavy brown drapes. But a fair-skinned wonder, a god in his luminescence, had found her and had sat down beside her and talked sweet talks.

Vivek Patel. The Gujarati. The gorgeous Gujarati. He was what dreams were made of. Fair of face, so handsome, so clever, so rich with his family jewels – for he came from jeweller stock, the people who had arrived into black Durban not as labourers but as rich traders with land in villages that Mahatmas were born into, and a talent for melting gold and mixing gold with cheap alloys, and then selling gold with all its impurities to the gap-toothed indentured labourers from the sugar-cane farms.

Vivek the handsome jeweller boy was the man of Anusha's fantasies, and during Rajesh and Meera's stinking wedding he'd been bored. He had wanted to pass some time. He had placed his devastatingly handsome long-legged body near the ugly Anusha and wasted some time flirting with her. He had no intention of taking anything further, knowing full well that his fair-skinned Gujarati bride awaited him in Surat. He liked playing games. He liked taunting this dark thing into hopes and dreams.

As a little boy, Vivek had loved to play with flies and ants, squashing them into the ground. But never completely until they were dead. He had enjoyed their entomological legs waving in the air, desperately asking him to squash them to death. He never did. He left them there, half alive, half dead, in limbo. He was cruel like that.

His attentions fawned upon the desperate Anusha had unleashed a torrent of mad, helpless love into the dark girl's heart, and, later that day when she had arrived back within the chocolate-brown bedroom drapes, she had examined her skin and compared it to his. She had lied to herself that she was almost his colour.

She'd lain on her bed and stared up at the light-brown stains on the ceiling and imagined a world where she was bright and fair, and Vivek would be lightly kissing her luminous face. In a love-filled trance she had dug through her panty drawer and taken out every single tube of skin-lightening cream and, ignoring their smelly expiration dates, she had created a chunky mask of the stuff, spooned and rubbed the amalgam like an impenetrable fortress onto her waiting face.

She had lain down to sleep, taking care not to rub even a tiny drop of the magic ointments off, and dreamed of the goddesses who sat on the backs of tigers, the ones who sported red lipstick and rosy cheeks. And when the morning came, and the hopeful girl had tried to open her eyes … she had found that she couldn't.

The lovely alchemic mask had betrayed her. And her face would be damaged forever. The chemicals of the amalgamation had worked their melanin-eating magic and left in their wake a face covered in craters and blisters. Howling into the dawn bathroom, the girl had attempted to scrub her face down with rough cloths and steel wool, serving only to ruin herself even more. Her Vivek-dreams flew like black bats to cling with strong claws to the chocolate drapes.

In agony, Anusha had run to her tormentor, her mother, who had recoiled from the ugliness and pushed the girl face down onto her bed, trying unintentionally to snuff her out. Better off dead than this. And finally as the girl wailed loudly in pain, the mother had gone in search of her son. Her fair, favourite son.

With a finger that had recently prodded his bride, Rajesh prodded at a bright, ripe boil, and as it vomited out its toxic contents, he hated the fact that he was a doctor.

'My glasses. Bring my glasses,' he commanded, and his

mother, who refused to remove herself from the sight of this car accident, screeched into the air, 'Girl! Girl! Hey, you deaf or what? Tobokile!'

The short black maid, a casual who had just arrived from the squatter camp to earn her daily loaf, took a moment to realise she was being called. Well into her fifties, she didn't realise she was the 'girl'. She dashed her round hips into the royal bedroom, and almost immediately covered her face when she saw the monster on the bed. She stared. She couldn't help herself.

'What you staring at you stupid idiot? Go bring Rajesh Baas's glasses from his room. Get!' Anjali shouted and hit the woman on her head.

Tobokile ran with cracked bare feet down the dark orange-carpeted passage and barged into Rajesh's room, where she found the still-dressed bride curled up on her side. She mumbled awkwardly, not knowing what to make of the miserable creature, and then grabbed the glasses from the nightstand.

Thinking she was doing a good deed, Tobokile smiled a beautiful toothy smile and handed the glasses to the bride. *You give him. You take it. Maybe he will be happy if you take it. You are his new wife after all.*

Meera, not understanding at first, had stared dumbly at the maid, and then finally, slowly, she had taken her husband's glasses and crept out of the bedroom and down the orange passage. She had heard the moanings and wailings of the smarting Anusha. She approached the room where all the action was unfolding and, knocking lightly on the door, she entered. She stretched out her hand and displayed the husband's glasses like a shield.

But as her eyes grew accustomed to the bedroom, which dazzled the retinas with its red velvety magnificence, she caught sight of the oozing-faced monster on the bed. Not able to help herself, she gasped out loud and almost fell backwards onto her raging mother-in-law, who stood like a guard at the door.

Anjali's rage bulged into a hate-filled hot-air balloon, taking over the room in its seething engorgement. How dare this ugly thing, this bride who had been forced upon her family, stand and stare at her daughter's horror?

She grabbed the bride by her shoulders and slapped her across her smeared face, where the clotted make-up from her wedding day lay in clumps across her eyelids, down her cheeks, up her thin neck.

'Get out from here, you ugly bad-luck bitch! See what you have done! Brought bad luck into my family right from the start. This is all your fault.'

She shoved the dazed Meera backwards, and as Meera reached out to steady herself, her husband's glasses fell on the floor, to be trampled with a crunch under her sandalled feet. She bent over and tried to pick up the broken pieces, but a yanking of her neck drove her up against the wall.

Rajesh, the Good Doctor, whose irritation was growing after his tumescent ruttings had been interrupted, and whose bad mood had grown with the train wreck that was his sister's face, grabbed his bride by the neck and pushed her up against the wall.

'You stupid bitch,' he seethed, 'you bloody stupid bitch. Look what you have done. Wait for me in the room.'

Meera had stared into his glasses-less myopic eyes. And she had fallen deeply. In hate. And fear. And after she had received her virginal blows, slappings, punching, she had crept and crawled into the bathroom to wash the blood off her face, listening to the howls of Anusha as her brother applied steroid cream to her volcanic face.

It was only morning. Still time yet.

It is a ritual practice that the bride is returned to her family on the morning after her wedding night. She is Sent Back. To be examined, to be questioned, and then to be packed off again. Meera approached this ritual with glee. She pictured the dry courtyard of her parents' home, she tasted the food in the pots. She lied to herself that she was being returned forever. They had starved her at Rajesh's home. Unintentionally, of course, because no one could think of food after the bubbling pustules of Anusha's face had burst.

Meera didn't know where the iron was, and was too afraid to ask, so she had changed into a crumpled brown sari. She felt self-conscious, as if her parents would smell the husband smell on her. She had been too frozen and afraid to use the shower.

In a rumpled unironed sari, she sat at the foot of the rose-petal bed, listening to the moans and howls of the faceless Anusha. She fastened the black and gold beads around her neck, the mangalsutra, the chain that would chain her to Rajesh forever. Seven lifetimes, the priest had said. A life sentence lasted one lifetime. A marriage lasted seven.

She applied cakelike make-up to obvious wounds and hoped no one would see them at home. She dutifully applied a big red dot and bright garish sindoor into her middle path, and waited alone while Anusha was driven to the hospital.

As noon approached, the sound of a 1972 red VW Beetle hooter at the paisley gate drowned out the rumblings of her stomach. Her father had arrived. To ritualistically take her back. Home. For a day.

Her father, accompanied by two old aunts, stood hat in hand at the doorway, smiling the smile that Meera hated.

That smile that he reserved for rich men. The poor-boy smile, shaking his head back and forth, front and back at the doorway, asking for his child back. Just for a day.

Drive off. Drive really fast.

The sight of the old farmhouse sitting on a green hill brought fresh tears to Meera's eyes. It had been only a day, yet it had been a lifetime. A long, frightening lifetime.

Approaching the dusty driveway, Meera saw a welcoming brigade, a waiting wall of relatives. But as she neared the house she soon realised that the straggly group of uncles and aunts was not there to welcome her after all.

A man was being sjambokked in the driveway. Her uncles took turns swinging the long snaky whip upwards into the skies, and then, as if casting a fishing rod, bringing it lashing down on a contorted black body jumping on the ground.

Caiphus 'Smiley Montezuma' Zuma – the gardener. Being beaten senseless on the day Meera arrived home from a loss of virginity and a loss of sanity.

'Smiley! Papa, why are they whipping Smiley?' Meera screamed, and even before the red VW Beetle had stopped, she had dived from the car and run into the mob.

'Meera, you get back. Get out of there. This is our business. Out!' her eldest uncle growled at her as she ran into the circle and stayed the swing of lashes.

'But Smiley ... what's happening?' Meera cried, and forgot her new bridal status, and bent, tripping over her unironed sari, to try to reach the bleeding body. Caiphus Smiley could not smile, but a lash from a sjambok had split his cheek, and the sideways smile appeared through bloody flesh, revealing an ape-like grin of perfect teeth. His wheezing breath came rattling upwards from a beaten ribcage, and his body buckled over into submission. He was close to death.

'Meera, get out of here!' Her second-eldest uncle grabbed her by the arm and shoved her into the waiting arms of her distraught mother. This was no place for a bride.

A place of beatings. Yet a bride had begun her marriage with her own fair share. Meera's mother grabbed and shoved her into the open doorway, where Meera leant panting against the frame. The lashing of Smiley began again, and Meera was certain she heard a death rattle. Or perhaps it was her own rattling breath.

'What happened?' she finally asked her mother, but her mother turned away, shame in her eyes.

'Sies! They found Smiley in the sugar-cane fields making love to a man. Bloody moffie!' her cousin Neetu whispered to her. Meera heard the men grunting as they beat down again and again on the body she was sure was a dead one, and she ran madly down the passages and courtyards before she came to her bedroom and threw herself onto its yellow-and-pink bedspread.

Gasping for breath, she pictured the beautiful Smiley as he planted fat green pumpkins and whispered to the dandelion weeds in apology for having to take them out. She pictured his radiant smile as he pulled carrots from the ground and presented them to the clapping children like Christmas presents. And she saw his black, strong body lying in a bloody mess on the ground. This was all too much. Too much.

She began ripping at her sari, tearing the six metres of brown fabric off her body, ripping it to shreds, flinging gold jewellery in heaps, and finally, as she collapsed onto the floor with wild open hair and dressed only in her beige slip, she allowed the oily tears to fall.

Her crying was almost a breathless, racking prayer.

'Oh! So nice … so sssso nice … gelll …'

India Swami.

He had crept into the girl's bedroom, and, seeing the lovely brown body clad only in a slip kneeling at the foot of the bed, smiled sluttishly to himself. Meera looked up and, through a curtain of tangled hair and hot tears, she saw his long-nailed claw reaching out to touch her skin.

She roared. She screeched and she screamed like a wild animal. But no one came running. Everyone was watching Smiley die in the driveway.

'Don't … Touch … Me!' Meera howled at India Swami, who withdrew his claw into his pants pocket. As she saw the fingers moving rhythmically there, Meera retched.

India Swami softened his gaze into a glazed passion-filled wonder. He stood over the half-naked girl kneeling at his feet, bent low to the ground and whispered, like a hissing Kaa, into the distraught girl's exposed ear: 'How was it gelll? Tell me … Did you enjoy it, dirty gelll? Did you lift your hips? Your hipppps? Did you?'

'Get out!' Meera yelled, and threw a shoe at India Swami's head.

He ducked and continued fiddling with his pocket, as he laughed and moaned and sidled out of the room, imagining lifted-up hips and beige slips. And somewhere in between his moans and grunts she heard him mutter Sanskrit hymns. All mixed up into a bundle of wrong.

A song began in Meera's head. A soft little lullaby. A song that started off as a hum, and then collected beautiful words along its way. Words that said,

White
Girls
Don't
Take
Shit …

Meera sang her song the following morning when a cream-coloured Mercedes-Benz and a half-blind doctor with no spare pair of spectacles came to take her. Home.

12

Pietà

RAJESH WAS A HATER. HE HATED PROFESSIONALLY. Inside his belly swarmed angry beasts that spewed venom. Towards women. From a distance he felt the poison of hatred exude from his mother's pores, from the sour-sweet smell of her armpits and from the undyed roots of her thin hair as it lay flat and lifeless against her scalp. She had taught him how to hate. How to love. And how to hate because of love.

Rajesh craved his mother. And his mother craved him. But they circled each other, staring at floors and walls, never once reaching the place where this fountain of unrequited love could flow and flow.

It was a strange kind of craving. Poison lurked between mother and son. Poison and love. Dark-purple love that didn't know its place in the large mansion with polished marble tiles and gold taps.

Launching into puberty like a heat-seeking missile, Rajesh had detested his simple, dumb brother who saw life as simply as the cartoons on television saw life. He barely noticed the existence nor the angst of a dark-brown sister as she spent hours examining her complexion in gilded hall mirrors. He only saw Anjali. Younger then, with a semblance of attractiveness still lurking behind the widow's white veils, she called him into her dreams at night. And he came. He came.

'My mother, mummy mine,' he ached to whisper to her as she rushed past him, away from him, when she saw that look in his eyes, 'Mother, hug me. Smooth my brow. Notice me.'

But instead he said nothing. And nothing soon became something that lurked inside his heart. A something that would hate all women.

Anjali was astounding. She glowed before him as she swiftly churned out profits from his late father's thriving business. Every evening after she had fed the children, washed up and scrubbed her kitchen to a sparkle, he would find her sitting hunched over at the dining-room table, poring over sheaves of paper. Her lack of education troubled her. She strove and struggled every minute of her life to grasp every aspect of the business. So even though she did not know balance sheets and stock charts, she would sit at the ornate mahogany table, and her toes would tickle the ball-and-claw feet while she mouthed figures out loud. Reading as a six-year-old does, with a pointed finger running across the page and a tongue sticking out, Anjali taught herself a system of business that only she understood.

The transactions of purchase and sale became a foreign language to her employees, as she filled notebook after notebook with her strange debit-credit system. Clients and merchandisers of cotton, silk, linen and rayon were reduced to caricatures in her notebook. Suppliers were described by the quirks she saw in them, and not by name, so that Mr Lockhat, who supplied the fine linens for sheeting, was noted down in her book simply as 'Mr L (hooked nose, green fence – 20 bales, still to pay. Don't talk to Mrs)' Roughly translated, this described to Anjali his appearance for identification, his address for dispatch, and his particular quirk that kept him true to her as a supplier. 'Don't talk to wife' was Anjali's way of saying that that was how Mr Lockhat preferred to do business, ensuring a wife who was hidden safely behind her black veils as she stood in corners and watched her husband bargain and deal with the daring woman in white. It was also Anjali's own way of preserving her widow's chastity, for Mr Lockhat had locked on to her and, even though she was a widow in an ugly white chiffon sari, unadorned and unmade-up, the sari still clung to her young hips, and her face was still interestingly pretty.

Anjali could have had lovers. Remarriage would have been totally frowned upon, but she could have taken men into her bed after her husband Ashok killed himself. There was no shortage of men who would convey their intent by their seductive eyes. But something in Anjali made her detest all men, all glances. A surreal, strange love arose in her for the dead Ashok, whom she had never loved as a living man but clung to as a dead one. There were nights in summer when her still-young body craved the length and strength of a man lying beside her on the bed with its gold seashell headboard. But Anjali banished all desires as she banished lazy employees. And when the sultry heat washed over her skin, she would grab a black notebook and begin reciting figures and transactions, whispering them into the jasmine-scented air and falling in love with the sound they made as the debits and credits balanced.

But she was blind. Blind completely to the three children growing up before her. She fed them well, she clothed them beautifully, but she avoided their advances. With vacant eyes she would take one of the trophies or book awards they regularly brought home, and, delivering no congratulatory hug, hold it for a second and then shove it back to its proud recipient as if it burnt her hands. Her children grew used to their inattentive mother, her inability to hug them without stiffening her back into an ironing board. But they all desired her in different ways.

Rajesh dived into puberty like a rough-and-ready seal, allowing the admiring glances of young girls to wash off his broad back. He was handsome, the fairest of Anjali's children, the one furthest in resemblance from Ashok. She watched him grow an Adam's apple, his voice deepen, his body take on a lean but hungry musculature. His intelligence brought him awards and fame. It brought him the first place in the country in the Matric final examinations. But it never brought him the one thing every cell in him craved: Anjali.

It was only one night, late and heavy, in the year he had won the first place in the land, that his mother decided to show Rajesh her love. In the most disturbing of ways. He had awoken at midnight to find that she had crawled into bed next to him. He pretended he was asleep, not wanting his awareness to chase her away.

Anjali had spent most of her day bargaining for silk and cotton bales with Mr Lockhat. His advances towards her had begun to reach aggressive proportions. Strangely, Anjali felt her body responding more to his aggressive grabs than she ever did to his whispered innuendo. His burka-clad wife had gone home to her mother's house in Ermelo, and Mr Lockhat had found himself with a silent house and raging thoughts. He had watched Anjali bend over to finger a length of Thai silk, and then pushed himself into her bent form. She had immediately stood up, finding herself pressed firmly up against him. Saying nothing, he had grabbed her ponytail and tilted her head backwards, leaning into a kiss. Anjali wanted that kiss. It had been too many years. Too many dry, dusty years of craving. But she had dived out of his embrace, and, saying nothing, grabbed her handbag and run out of his warehouse.

As evening approached, Anjali thought of Mr Lockhat's firm body pressed up against hers. She felt dazed with thoughts of his taut muscles. She burnt the rice, she scalded the milk, she took two baths and spent an extra hour reading her contorted balance sheets. And after tossing in her beautiful bed for hours, she softly padded towards the comfort of her favourite son.

With open hair and a soft, sheer nightgown, she had lain quietly next to the teenage boy, taking in his smell, his length, as he lay on his side. And from a place that she had never visited before came hot tears. Angry, desirous, racking sobs that she muffled with a fist stuffed into her mouth. Rajesh lay there, listening to her sobbing and instinctively knowing why. Minutes passed into a full hour. He dared not move. As Anjali's sobs reached a crescendo where she could barely breathe, he heard her muffle words into the sobs: 'I want … I want …'

And his heart lurched. For her loneliness, her sacrifice, her strength that now seemed so brittle. He reached his hand across and placed it on his mother's head. She stopped sobbing immediately. Her breaths became even and calm. And he kept his flat, warm palm on her head till she was cocooned like a baby, silent and peaceful. When he heard her sigh softly, he whispered into the air, 'Ma.'

And immediately Anjali bolted upright, and, like a sylph that had never been there, she disappeared. She ran in her bare feet back to her bedroom. When morning came, over the clatter of tea and toast, neither spoke to the other. Neither looked at the other. Again.

13

Moti the Wondrous

MOTI THE WONDROUS WAS A PRECIOUS PARROT, THE wonderful incarnation of all things good and all things great. He was Anjali's most prized possession, after her red velour swags and her crystal chandelier, of course.

Moti, an African Grey, wandered the house, the large mansion on Millionaires' Row, and surveyed all that was his kingdom. Anjali loved him as she loved her own children. He was the last thing her husband had given to her before he killed himself. A tiny baby parrot with a beak that opened and closed, demanding sustenance and love.

He was old now, and with age Moti had become impudent and cranky, fussing about the house and taking to hissing at people like the domestic helper or the gardener. Anjali loved that Moti was so feisty. She boasted often that it was she who had taught the parrot to swear. And Moti lived out his days braced for battle, swearing loudly at anything that troubled him.

Anjali refused to believe that her husband, Ashok Kumar, had killed himself. Admitting it would be a great affront to her. People would blame her, for they always blame the wife. But the evidence was obvious. He had gassed himself in the cream-coloured Mercedes-Benz that sat luxuriously in his garage, sharing a patriarch's place with three other cars. Rajesh was only four years old when it had happened, Pranesh was eight, and little Anusha was barely three.

Anjali told people that he had been sitting in the car and had had a massive heart attack. That would explain it all. But people talked. People knew of the gasoline smell that permeated the car, the house. People wondered, how could a man who clearly had everything his heart desired – wealth, riches, a beloved family, a holier-than-holy wife and a crystal chandelier – kill himself? It just didn't make sense. In her most private moments Anjali cursed Lalitha – the reason her husband Ashok had killed himself.

Days and days spent chanting and burning cloves in her prayer room had not banished the evil-eyed Lalitha from her husband's life. But Anjali held on to Lalitha like a noxious vine, knowing that it was always the case that God would answer her prayers, and Lalitha would disappear from her husband's mind forever.

It was not that Anjali loved Ashok. She didn't. He drank too much, he was too fat and flatulent, and every other morning he awoke from his snoring and beat her with his shoe. She knew also that Lalitha had not been the first, and would not be the last. What she didn't know was that Lalitha, too, was as tenacious as a poisonous vine. She had twined her way into Ashok's heart, into his life, and become part of him. When Ashok beat Anjali, he did it because he deeply loved Lalitha, and by beating his wife he was pledging allegiance to the sari-shop counter girl with the round hips and deep black eyes.

Anjali could keep many secrets. She stored secrets inside a locked biscuit box, deep inside the ventricles of her heart. The Lalithas and Mumtas and Shobhas of this world meant nothing to Anjali. The beatings and the slappings meant nothing to Anjali.

All that mattered were the crystal chandelier, the red swags, the glass-top stove and the outside gate with ornate wrought-iron words that were supposed to say 'Welcome' in Hindi, but failed miserably: they looked like an upside-down paisley pattern made by a dyslexic spider. On the day she found Ashok slumped over in the Mercedes-Benz, the motor still running, she had quietly turned the ignition off, removed the garden hose from the exhaust pipe, and set to the task of cleaning.

'Chalo. Go!' she whispered to the slumped body.

She scrubbed. She wiped. She went on hands and knees and made everything glittery and sparkly. After all, there would definitely be so many people coming to her house for Ashok's funeral. She warned the children to bathe and dress their best. The confused children were hit with a loud clap on the ear if they tried to go near the garage where the gasoline smell attracted them. And after she had scrubbed the entire house clean, she had bathed herself in her magnificent seashell-shaped bathtub and then set about the business of calling everyone to tell them: Ashok had died.

'A massive heart attack? So young?' people questioned, but Anjali had been strong and steely, not answering too many questions, holding her beloved children close as the incense-filled funeral took place, and grieving as a good widow should grieve. With vacant eyes, from which she wiped vengeful tears, she scanned the swelling crowd (for Ashok had been a popular businessman in Tongaat), for the face of Lalitha, the sari-shop counter girl. But Lalitha had not braved the crowds to come to Ashok's funeral.

He was of course useless to her now, but Lalitha recalled how she had harassed and lied to him about the baby in her belly. Well, there was no baby, Lalitha was just trying her hand with him, making him choose to leave that bat out of Hell. Lalitha had sworn and cried and pleaded and finally she had threatened to tell everyone, including Ashok's family, about the baby that was growing in her belly.

Ashok was a weak man. Weak in his affections for beautiful but conniving shop girls. He ran his sari and Indian-clothing store and fabric warehousing business with absolute efficiency, but his resolve broke every time he saw a flirty girl swan past him in a neat little dress that showed off her hips and buttocks. Lalitha had known that this was indeed the boss's weakness, and had stalked her prey like a lioness in a pretty dress, and now … it had all come down to nothing. She didn't bother with Ashok's funeral, and didn't question like everyone else how a perfectly healthy man in his late thirties could slump over the gasoline-smelling seat of his car from a massive heart attack.

But Anjali waited. The funeral and all the Memorial Day ceremonies had been done, and she hugged each of her children and told them that they need not worry, for now she was in charge.

She ran away, first to her mother's house on a pea farm in Camperdown, where she sat under trees, ignored her children, rocked back and forth, and thought and thought. Finally, after a week of complete silence, she grabbed her eldest son's hand, told her mother to keep the other two, and returned to the mansion where the velvet drapes and Persian rugs awaited her. She ignored the screaming and crying of her youngest babies, and walked away from them for a year, leaving them in their grandmother's senile care.

Back in Tongaat, she took over Ashok's clothing factory, and with a Standard Six education and a penchant for swearing, ran the business even more efficiently than Ashok himself had. Nothing and no one got past her beaky stare. Lalitha was fired immediately. Anjali hadn't done the deed herself. She had instructed the runner boy, Indran, the one who carried notes and files, to tell the hooded Lalitha that her days were up. Lalitha twisted her lips into irreverence; it was no surprise to her. And anyway, she had found another benefactor, a weak, bearded Muslim general dealer who had already taken her into his bed.

After a year of good profits from the textile factory and the sari shop and many other little businesses she had set up, Anjali returned to Camperdown to her dead mother's house. There was no one to care for the young Rajesh and Anusha now. She grabbed their little hands and took them back to Tongaat, where she tried but failed to love them and hoped they would forget her abandonment. Children forget. But inside their recesses they never forget. They got over it, and bloomed and blossomed into matriculants who topped the country in their marks; they appeared in newspapers holding trophies and certificates for spelling bees. She sat back indulgently as they entered medical school and rapidly flew through the difficult courses, for she had invoked all of God's blessings in chanting the names of their professors in her prayer room.

So many years had passed since Ashok had died. Anjali, stooped over and shrewd, forgot his face. But she clung to his memory, his money-making memory, by indulging and spoiling Moti the Parrot.

It was Moti the Parrot who harassed Meera the most when she married into Rajesh's family. Moti the Parrot had been trained well. Into the late nights of sleeplessness, before her son married Meera, Anjali had confessed her fears and hatred to Moti as he sat on the pillow next to hers, occasionally dropping a tiny blob of bird shit which Anjali wiped away with soft tissues. Moti listened. He remembered the swear words his mistress had whispered in their late-night trysts. Clever parrot. He was loyal to his Anjali.

Meera remembered taking the seven steps around the sacred fire during her wedding, and one of the steps was a vow to be kind to all animals. Meera knew she couldn't keep that vow with Moti the Parrot. She occasionally kicked him with her soft bedroom-slippered foot. She denied him his sunflower seeds every morning, as feeding him had become her job while Anjali and Meera's Fair sister-in-law lay languishing in bed till ten.

Moti became everything that was wrong and terrible about her marriage. On the day of her wedding, when she had entered Rajesh's house for the first time as his bride, Moti had pecked at her ankles and torn holes in the bottom of her silk sari.

The parrot took to swearing at Meera whenever he saw her, using the foulest of language and in the loudest of tones. Moti loved Pranesh's wife – Meera's elder sister-in-law – and would lovingly croon when she was around, 'The Fair One, The Fair One …'

And she was fair, very fair. Her skin was luminous in its fairness. People came from far and wide to see her fair skin. Even parrots and dogs and children noticed. The Fair One. She wore her fairness like a crown, walking through the mansion on Millionaires' Row like a princess, swinging her long plait, and batting her eyelashes at people, dogs and parrots.

As the Fair One was called the Fair One, Meera became the dark one. She knew deep inside her that Moti was not just a law unto himself, he had been taught his rantings and ravings. So she forgave Moti. She stopped kicking him. She added little sweet pieces of chopped apple to his sunflower seeds. She stared at him while he sat on his perch, a sizeable tree branch decorated with all manner of trinkets and birdie toys, and she knew he stared back. And swore at her. She felt that Moti could see the dark-red bruises on her face. She felt he could hear the sounds of the punches and the slaps. But Moti still swore at her and pecked at her ankles.

It was only rational that Meera would take on all the household chores. Why pay for a domestic maid when there were two daughters-in-law in the house? But one daughter-in-law complained of fair-skinned ailments and took to dusting only the mahogany mantelpiece filled to the brim with graduation photographs and fake plastic roses. The Fair One would sneeze the way princesses sneeze, and complain that dust made her sensitive skin itchy. And because Anjali wanted to preserve the fairness of her skin, the Fair One was neatly absolved from all major household chores. Which left Meera. Daughters-in-law must work. Only dark ones. After all, the people came from far and wide to see the luminous skin of the Fair One; how could they put that skin at risk?

Meera began a life of cleaning. Robotic. Harassed by a parrot who swore at her when she tried to clean his perch. Her mother-in-law spoke of collapsing vertebrae, hot flushes, arthritic fingers and migraines. The Fair One took to her bed with a fair hand thrown over her almond eyes. A baby formed its perhaps fair self in her belly, and her dizziness and nausea rendered her incapable of movement. Meera carried soups and toast with thick butter to her in her bed. Meera cleaned. And she cooked. And she only ate after the men had eaten. The dregs of the curry left in the pot.

Days and days of it. Anjali clapped her hands in glee. India Swami had been right. This ugly dark girl would meekly do all the work set out for her. She was so desperate to be married into such a family. The house sparkled. The house shone. Meera's face became accustomed to purple bruises. She knew before he did when Rajesh would deliver punches and slaps. All was well with the world.

Until it was not. Until the morning Meera woke up, received her day's share of purple bruises, and then vomited in the oh-so-clean bathroom. Moti, who was doing his morning rounds waddling throughout the house, dropping shit in every corner, saw Meera come out of the bathroom with a pale, clammy face, and it was Moti who finally said, 'Bitch. Ugly.'

And it was Moti's words that set a path in motion. Bitch Ugly.

Enough!

Bitch Ugly cracked. Like an eggshell.

14

Purple and Oak Boxes

ONE MORNING HE SAID TO HER, 'MY MOTHER AND FATHER fought.' And because it was early days, she held him through the memory of fights.

And then every other morning he said to her, 'My mother and father fought.'

So, they fought – so they fought! So they fought.

And she thought, 'So what if they fought? So, he hit her. So what? So he broke furniture, punched walls, tore curtains, slapped her, slapped you, till you peed in your four-year-old hand-me-down pants. So what? So he killed himself? So what?

'So, she ran away. So she ran away, clutching you and your sister with her rough washing-stone hands, her winter hands, into the road and to the pea farm. So what? So she came back to the mansion in the sky, and gave you everything in the world but her love and attention. So what?

'So, you were just a spotless four-year-old boy with a spotless runny nose and drops of sweat on your upper lip and hands that clasped at her winter hands.

'So what?

'So, you never were a little boy, and you never knew what was normal, and you only are the way you are because you never learnt how to be without the stiff, sweaty upper lip, and your hands have never learnt of summer, and you are there, little baby boy, holding on to his light-brown pants, saying daddydaddydaddymine …

'So he slapped you babybabybabyboy who never had a

daddydaddydaddymine, until the day he died and someone asks the four-year-old you, "Who's in the box?" And you say, quickly, spotlessly, "Daddy … mine."

'So what?

'So mother keeps coming back to you, bearing in her winter hands two birthday cakes on a morning in March when actually your birthday is in February, with her tap-ping-tapping mummy steps on the road and the pea farm. Why two cakes, mummymummymummymine?

'Because, my son, my spotless thing who peed in his pants and saw into oak coffins, because son, my son, my baby mine, because I bring one for next year too, because son, my son, I won't be tap-tapping along minding my peas and queues for a long long time to come. Maybe a whole year without me. I have a business to run. No time for children.

'So you cried.

'So what?

'So, you ate cake that day, and you learnt how to hurt someone that day when you saw rainbows in the sky of the pea farm where it had not rained for manymany months and you learnt that her eyes filled with tears that day when you cried with your spotless four-year-old, five-year-old, thirty-three-year-old mouth to mummymummymummy. And she twisted away, and your eyes saw the future and the past, and you knew that you had learnt that day how to hurt how to hurt how to hurt, how to love …'

'Love me,' Meera had said, 'and then I'll love it all away. The spots and the peas and the expensive oak boxes and the goodbye daddys and the absent suicide notes. Love me and then it will all go away with the freshness and newness and the glory of my affection.'

It's early days. Early days.

She is his woman. His woman screams, when the days

become later, and she is no longer fresh, no longer new, not sparkly and glittery, has become common, and asks for love back from him.

But her screams are all inside-ly because she is afraid to bring them outside-ly because he stands at the doorway, and he laughs in her face when she tells him, 'So what if they fought? Love me instead. I'll help you forget.'

But the demons are still here.

As they creep and crawl into yet another today, and his flesh crawls as she creeps into their bed, he hides his head, and remembers decadent things, and she knows how he hates the morning smell of her.

'Is it morning now?' she asks.

'It is morning now,' he says.

'But it is not even bright yet,' she says.

'It is still morning,' he says and he remembers that this morning she is not glorious, not new, not fresh, not shimmery, glimmery …

She can see the shadow of last night with its black purple, dark purple, bruise purple, and she can see the shadow and the sleep crystals at the corners of half-open eyes.

There is so much fear here.

In this room, there is so much fear.

The morning creeps and the morning crawls and then it is today, and her hair and his hair flying across the pillowcases weave a lovely basket, waiting to be filled with good things, like rice and sweets and sunlight.

But the hair lying flying across the case covers purple purple, red purple, her purple, and she knows that he will awaken and then he will turn the blade (the shoulder blade, you know), and when the crystals clear from the corners of his eyes, he will look at the purple, and he will yawn loudly, and say to her, 'My mother and father fought.'

He is waking up. Ready to start his morning rituals of silence. His bargaining will begin. Bargaining with God, bargaining for moments with less hurt, less pain, less whispering, less silence, less rage, less memory, less nonsense ... fresh, new, glittery, sparkly.

You did not do your job, hateful, spiteful, lying, ugly, filthy woman ... You did not do what I brought you here to do.

Bitch!

She doesn't hear his silence, she listens only to his breathing. Inhalation, exhalation, breathe in the world, wake up, wake up, my beloved god, wake up, my deity wake up, my idol wake up ... No, don't wake up. Stay asleep. She hides her face. From blows.

But he breathes a deep waking-up breath and arches towards the morning, and he casts a glance at the basket and the happy purple, and then covers his eyes with a palm full of lines.

Not seeing, not looking at the bared breast, nor the morning red-lipstick pout, nor the colours of the rainbow that form on top of skin, inside skin, within and beneath flesh, inside-ly more and outside-ly less.

Once she was a goddess. A vision in red and maybe some gold. A bride who was supposed to make ugly things disappear like magic.

But she has lost her sparkle.

And he must look ahead. He must not taste bad things, like bitter tastes, and salty tastes, and morning tastes.

You leave a bad taste in my mouth. You have lost your sparkle.

And she longs to kiss the morning mouth of him, with its combination of tastes, the spoilt-milk tastes, the musty tastes ... maybe this kiss will call him back home.

'Put that tongue back in,' he says.

'That tongue can do no good for me,' he says.

'That tongue is forked,' he says.

'You have not done your job,' he says.

The demons are still here.

Bitch!

'Can you love me?' he had asked, in starry-eyed desperation. 'Tell me you can. Tell me. You can.'

She attempts to quell his questions with a feeble squeeze. A possibility of a hug. She barely knows this man, this idol. He is nothing to her. She has followed him around fragrant wedding fires; she has burnt with him on the rituals of pyres. But he is a stranger to her. A stranger tied around her neck.

She used to be a goddess.

She is supposed to be his goddess.

In the morning, she wants to say to the man who is curled up like a fish on his side, cold and clammy after battling oak boxes and pea farms, 'I can love you. I can love you in many ways. I can take some of it away. But I can't take all of it away. If you let me I can. I will. Tell me I can. Tell me. I can.'

But he doesn't hear any words. He doesn't speak and she doesn't speak. The moments for speaking are over. The time has come for flinging, and slinging. Of arrows.

In the brightness of morning the happy purple shines. In the brightness of morning, with the slamming of car doors, with the barking of dogs, with the boiling of the kettle, she cannot, cannot speak. She has lost her sparkle.

The demons are still here.

He lights a cigarette.

Cover it up ... cover it up ... the happy blue red purple ... cover cover cover ...

It up.

He blows half-circle smoke circles.

Circlescirclescirclescirclescircles …

Get out of my home.

Do you want me to spit on you?

Get out!

'Take me back. Take me back. Beloved, I am sorry. I will make it better. Please take me back!'

'You have lost your sparkle. You are nothing.'

He takes a bridal pot, a gift from a beloved aunt. He throws the pot at her head. She ducks in time, and he flops around like a beached whale. Rage.

He throws another one. And the pot made of stone and bone tells her, 'Watch this man. He will throw stones at you. He will pick the bones of you. Watch this man.'

15

Iqbal the Muslim

IQBAL THE MUSLIM LAY DOWN TO SLEEP.
On a night of a new moon he began counting sheep.
The bleating of lambs that tomorrow he would slaughter.
Iqbal the Muslim in love with a favourite daughter.
In his rumpled bed, Iqbal tossed and turned.
His love for a good girl heaved and it burned.
Iqbal the Muslim lay down to sleep.

He was deeply in love with Rooksana Vawda, the elder sister of strong-calved Aisha Vawda. The Aisha whom everyone called Ashes, because when she hit a boy in the schoolyard, she always shouted into his ashamed face, 'Ashes to ashes, dust to dust.'

She had pummelled her way through primary school. Beating up stunted-growth Selvan and Kevin-who-knitted-foot-blankets. Aisha and her invisible friend, the sticklike girl from the neighbouring farm, that poor unfortunate Meera Narain. They clung to each other like the number ten.

Aisha beat and slapped, Meera chewed gum and stared into space. Boys kept a wide berth. They called them lesbians and guffawed as they picked at their teenage-boy zits. They balked as the two shared ice-cream cones unwrapped from brown paper wrappers and spent their pocket money on sherbet that whizzed and popped in your moist mouth. They called Aisha Vawda the Black Pig. Although she was as pink as a ham, not black at all. It was just a name. A misnomer.

Rooksana Vawda was a beauty to behold. Although covered by a headscarf and flapping around in loose clothes that should never show her curves, she had a beauty that extended beyond shapeliness and open hair. She made you fall in love with her by her eyelashes, those long black brooms that swept the chambers of your heart.

Iqbal knew about love. He had seen mature love settle like a shawl over the shoulders of his old parents who had defied all tradition by being arranged spouses who had fallen for each other. They spoke freely of their earliest years, where they were promised to each other before either had even turned twelve, and how at sixteen they had sat at opposite ends of a courtyard, facing a bearded priest, and repeated three times the agreement of marriage.

– Do you agree to marry this boy?
– Jee, Qubool hai … yes, I agree.
– Do you agree to marry this boy?
– Jee, Qubool hai … yes, I agree.
– Do you agree to marry this boy?
– Jee, Qubool hai … yes, I agree.

Their old families had thrown scented rose water at them, hot mutton biryani had been eaten, and, easing into the world of matrimony, Hajra and Ali Bux slid. They had immediately loved each other. They had taken to this love with natural ease, and the products of this love had taken naturally to love as well.

Iqbal's elder brother Haroon had fallen in love with Nisha, the Hindu girl from a farm across the sugar-cane fields. Nisha belonged to a family whom everyone whispered were low-caste Hindus. They were rumoured to come from the shoemaker caste in India, the barbers and the ones who cleaned rich people's toenails. It was never openly said but the people knew that this family of mainly girls with their long dangly earrings and their fat nose rings and their love of clashing bright colours were secret pig eaters. An abomination for Hindus and Muslims alike.

And an even greater abomination when the eldest of the girls, Nisha, had rapidly and comfortably thrown her religion aside and sworn allegiance to Allah, and to the Prophet Muhammad, and soon Nisha became Aneesa who had married Haroon and sat happily in her new beef-eating home, doling out her laughter and sweets to relatives and friends. Nisha had once sat next to Meera, singing loud Hindi religious songs and spurning as best she could the advances of India Swami. And Nisha had been the bravest of them all. When the time came for India Swami to find her a bridegroom, she had defied everyone and secretly run off to the mosque at dusk and married Haroon, who protected her like a jewel. Meera envied Nisha – she had escaped.

She had smiled her dimpled smile through two jolly babies, and had taken to wearing a black cloak like a real Muslim. She had fasted at Ramadan, not touching food or water from sunrise to sunset, and had learnt how to kneel and bow on her prayer mat like a professional, an act she performed often. Even Haroon, who sometimes had faltered in his five-times-a-day prayer, Aneesa, who was once Nisha, would prod out of bed at dawn, sharply admonishing him for forgetting to do his early-morning prayers.

It was one morning after the call to prayer had resonated from the loudspeakers of the local mosque, calling the faithful to come and kneel on carpeted floors and beseech the one true God, that the ugliness had happened.

Eid morning. The Other Eid. The one where you slaughtered lambs and goats and ate their fresh fried livers with salt and lemon juice, before the corpse had even stopped pulsing.

Haroon had been poked and prodded out of his warm

bed, where he had prised himself off the toddlers that now clung to his sleeping body and separated him from the warm soft folds of his Aneesa. In the cold bathroom he had performed the ritual of washing his hands, face and feet with hot running water.

In the misty bathroom mirror, as he stared at his unshaven face, Haroon felt helpless. The deep, sonorous love poems echoed through the house – the poetry that walked a thousand sweet miles inside his younger brother's head. Haroon, who knew love so well, could smell love being boiled in the pots of a young man's heart.

Life was not poetry, Haroon knew. Life was divides, and hierarchy, and places where certain people did not belong. The girl came from rich, snobbish stock – the ones who felt above everyone else for the language that they spoke in their clean lounge rooms. Rooksana Vawda, a privileged Surtee girl, whose family hailed from a money-filled village called Khator in Gujarat. They looked down their prominent noses at the Urdu-speaking Bux family.

'Aapro waalo nee malle …' they told each other. 'Not one of our own people. Hedroo che.'

A derogatory name for the lower class: Hedroo. A shortening and parody of the word Hyderbadi, because most of the Muslims who came to South Africa that were not of the Gujarati-speaking trader class had come from Hyderabad, India. Iqbal was a Hedroo. To the rich Gujarati-speaking family with the ever-producing sugar-cane farm, who indulged the handsome Iqbal when he took them presents his hands fashioned out of pieces of newspaper – poor Iqbal was a Hedroo.

They displayed his fans and birds and many-petalled roses in all their creative wonder on their mantelpiece, and told relatives who visited from far-off Durban, 'Oh *that*? Yes, the Hedroo boy whose father is the foreman at the next-door farm. He made it. Talented boy, that Hedroo boy.'

But Iqbal, with a head filled with love poems, didn't see the divide. He only saw Rooksana's benign, beautiful face, and knew with all certainty that she would be his. She appeared to him like an angel, like the ones they promise you will be your companions in Jannat, in Heaven. It was all in her eyes. They drew love out of you as they swept across your face. Rooksana knew the Hedroo origami neophyte was in love with her.

But she was ambivalent. She knew she would eventually marry a very wealthy businessman from Durban. Maybe a mansion in Musgrave. Maybe a home in Dubai. But she loved looking at Iqbal. And she accepted his flirting, knowing nothing would come of it.

'Eid Mubarak, Bhaiya,' Iqbal had whispered into Haroon's fresh smell, drowned in the scents of ittar. Ittar, a strong concentrated perfume brought from the holy lands of Mecca, with a fragrant name like Khalifa, in a tiny golden bottle that sat on a shelf. A shelf that carried a green satin-wrapped Quran and a myriad of holy books written by well-meaning maulanas and clerics from Pakistan and Saudi Arabia.

'Eid Mubarak, Small Boy,' Haroon had replied, and hugged his tall handsome brother three times, twice on the right and once on the left, before planting a happy brother's kiss on his freshly shaven cheek. Haroon knew that Iqbal was in love with the elusive Vawda girl. He knew this love spelt danger, but he didn't have the heart to damage the poet brother who sat up till late in the nights quoting love sonnets from the eternal provocateur, Rumi.

The local mosque sat in the valley, its tall minarets reaching up to the sky. It was a pure white building surrounded by yellow-green *Duranta* bushes that glowed in the afternoon sun. It had been built by the old man Solly Vawda, Rooksana and Aisha's grandfather, the rich one, who owned the largest farm in Emona, the farm that grew the most sugar cane. The old man had lived out his days praying his obligatory five-times-a-day prayers in the quiet of his own bedroom, only venturing out of the farm to pray in the mosque in the village of Tongaat on Fridays. A twenty-minute drive away.

But Solly believed purely in the Sunnat, the teachings and behaviours of the Prophet. And these teachings told you it is most blessed to walk to the mosque. To walk towards it on one path, and to return from it on another. Solly Vawda vowed then to build his own mosque, within walking distance of his house. A house of prayer, for all to come to.

And one day he had decided: It was time to form a congregation. A long, happy line of white-clad pilgrims walking with glowing faces to their local mosque. It had to be done. His pilgrimage to Mecca for Hajj had teased his senses with the beauty of Arabian architecture, and he had returned from his pilgrimage with rough drawings in an old worn notebook of the shrines and the mosques that he had seen.

The building of a mosque in the farming community of Emona drew everyone's attention. A majestic building with Arabian calligraphy adorning its white walls and perfectly rounded domes made of green ceramic tiles, the Emona mosque had even surpassed the one in the town in all its beauty.

And with the mosque had come a madrasah, an orphanage, a soup kitchen and a secluded ladies' section. The gardens of the mosque grew resplendently, blooming with late roses under the happy songs of Amos, the Zimbabwean gardener, whose Christian hymns were not minded at all. The mosque and all its activities brought beauty and liveliness to the dusty farms, and the five-times-a-day call to prayer that rang out in the valley punctuated everyone's lives.

As Haroon and the dreamy Iqbal walked to the mosque in fresh sandalled feet on Eid morning, they watched the sun rise on the glowing minaret, and suddenly all was right with the world. But, all was not.

Gathered at the gate of the mosque, in the dewy fresh gardens, stood an anxious group of men, like men at a funeral, with heads shaking to and fro, and shoulders heavy with worry. Haroon walked faster, and Iqbal hastened to keep up.

The morning Eid prayers were about to start, but the men just stood in their places and made no move into the waiting mosque where the mufti, the priest, stooped at the door, wringing his hands.

'Fazel, Fazel!' Haroon called out to one of his friends standing in the group. 'What's wrong, brother?'

Fazel Hajee, fat and spilling out of his starched Eid kurta, looked into Haroon's eyes and shook his head. Tears seemed to appear in his eyes.

'What's wrong? Brothers, what has happened?' Haroon asked.

'A most horrible thing, Brother Haroon,' Saleem Khan, the Pathan, said. 'A disgusting, heinous act. And on Eid Day! Ya Allah ... on our most holy of days.'

'What, brother? What?'

'Brother Haroon ... this early morning, as old Solly Vawda bhai opened his front door to allow the farishtas, the angels, into his home after performing his morning washing ablutions, Ya Allah ... what did our dear old father find on his front lawn? A ... a severed pig's head! A filthy pig's head, brother.'

'What?' gasped Haroon and Iqbal in tandem, both almost

reeling backwards into the moist *Duranta* bushes, the shock of such an act bringing dark bile up into their throats.

'Ya Allah, my brothers,' Saleem spoke out loudly to the group that had refused to move forwards into the waiting arms of the mosque, 'this is indeed the greatest of insults. An item, most hated, most disgusting as that haram filthy head of a shit-eating Soowar pig … thrown onto our old father's lawn! And the shock, dear brothers, the shock of seeing that filth as he prepared himself to come for Eid prayers was so much for our dear old father that he has collapsed and now lies mute on a bed. Even Doctor Rajesh Maharaj who we had to call from town says that maybe dear old Solly bhai has had a stroke. We must act, brothers! We, our group, must Act!'

'Come inside, brothers,' the priest, Mufti Kazee, called out from the mosque door. 'Come inside now, the Eid prayers have started. We will talk later.'

And later, a large gathering of thirty men in white flowing kurtas, all smelling of the fragrant intoxicating ittar, sat cross-legged on the floor of the mosque, listening to the words of their mufti.

'Who are we, my brothers?' said the tall Pathan, Saleem Khan. 'Who are we, but the defenders of our purity, the defenders of our beloved Faith. We must all come together on this terrible, terrible morning. A morning that is supposed to be our happiest, our Eid day, defiled by an act so horrific that it has placed our father on his deathbed. We must become the soldiers of our purity. We must seek out who has done this. And we must kill. Kill, my brothers. To avenge, and to sanctify our faith. We are now warriors. We will call ourselves the Mufti's Warriors al-Haq! And we must destroy …'

The newly formed Mufti's Warriors al-Haq, or MWAH,

raised their voices and praised their purity, and with eyes that burnt for revenge set out to find out who had thrown the severed pig's head onto the Vawdas' lawn.

'It is that Chamaar family,' someone said, and Haroon's skin began to crawl.

'Yes, it has to be that Hindu family that lives down by the river. Those shoemakers, those low-caste barber people … we all know that they eat pig!'

Haroon looked around wildly at the angry crowd, thinking of his wife's family, in their over-bright clothes and dangly earrings. He grew desperate as the crowd of men all shouted their approval. Yes, it is that shoemaker pig-eating family! Let us kill.

'Wait, wait dear brothers …' Haroon said feebly, but the swelling crowd of MWAHS had already begun racing across the mosque lawns towards the poor hut where men sat mending broken shoes, and women sang early-morning songs to babies with rainbow-coloured strings tied around their naked waists to ward off colic and the evil eye.

Haroon looked in anguish at his brother Iqbal, who immediately understood what Haroon was indicating, and, as the raging men raced towards the hut, Iqbal bolted in the opposite direction towards his house, where he would run into the kitchen to find his sister-in-law frying samosas. He had to warn her.

The fuming mob of MWAHS surrounded the hut, shouting for the men to come out, and, as they rubbed the sleep from their eyes, the benign brightly clad men with gold earrings in one ear stumbled out of the hut. The sight of thirty angry Muslims with sticks, guns and scythes met their dazed eyes.

'No, brothers, no! It wasn't us. We would never do such a terrible thing!' they pleaded, but the crowd was deaf in its fury. Haroon watched his father-in-law begging at the feet of a Pathan with a rifle, and he tried helplessly to push his way forward into the throng. He felt a strong hand grab him, holding him silently in place.

'You stay here,' a menacing voice muttered into his ear. 'This is not your family. These Hindus are not your own.'

Iqbal came running wildly down towards the hut, with his sister-in-law Aneesa, who was once the Nisha of the hut household, in his wake, her black cloak flying against her body as she raced into the crowd of men. She saw her father kneeling on the ground, a rifle at his head.

'No!' she screamed, and pushed her way to her father's begging form.

'Get out of here, woman,' a man with a panga shouted, and grabbed her by the shoulders and threw her away. She landed on all fours on the dusty ground, her body immodestly showing itself to every man as the cloak rode up her buttocks. Desperately she tugged at the cloak and tried again to run towards her trembling father. She saw her brothers, all lying face down in the mud with weapons attached to their temples, and she felt the cold steel of fear grip her bowels. They were going to kill her family.

Blinking madly into the sun that had fully risen, she stared into the crowd and saw her husband standing inert within. Her eyes found his, begging him to act, but he stood unmoving. The terror and revulsion wound its twisted grip even more around her insides. Why was Haroon not doing anything?

This was her family, her own flesh and blood. And even though she had forsaken her name, had taken the testament to the One True God, Allah, and had accepted the Prophet as his messenger, these were still the people from whose brightly coloured mismatched wombs she had been born. She screamed a hoarse, wild-woman's call, and threw herself at the feet of the Pathan, Saleem.

She invoked his raucous laughter, his jokes and his voracious appetite as he devoured the tasty fried food that she had served him at many happy, friendly dinners at her house. She remembered how he had sat at her kitchen table, telling her, 'Aapa Aneesa, you make the best bean curry in all the world.'

But now, his eyes were as cold as ice as he held an angry rifle to her father's head. The happy times were forgotten. These were just Hindu people, and she was just a girl who used to be Hindu.

'Please my brother Saleem,' she whimpered, 'please don't kill them. They are innocent.'

Saleem stared at the woman begging at his feet. And he thought about the filthy pig's head on the manicured lawns at the Vawdas' house. He prepared to shoot.

A sudden loud blast rang out through the silence. It was not a gunshot.

The MWAHS looked upwards from their waiting weapons. A great cloud of black smoke shot up into the sky. Suddenly the screams of women and babies filled the air. The men forgot their weapons and ran towards the screams. Before them, at the very bottom of the valley, a wall of fire assaulted them. The shacks. Ablaze.

The fire razed through cardboard dwellings, destroying everything in its path. It burnt through sleeping babies and women who were hunched over washing tubs. It didn't stop until it had destroyed the entire world – an entire world of people. The maids and the gardeners, the labourers whose shiny black hands had cut sweet sugar cane, the old men and women whose job it was to pick out the seeds from drying coriander. All gone. Gone. So rapidly. Cardboard and Masonite homes burn fast.

Their hackling of the low-caste shoemaker family forgotten, the men of the MWAH stood watching, doing nothing amid the screams, the stoves that blew out their paraffin cores, the wild, crazy shack people running in all directions. What was happening here?

And through the thick black smoke of the shack fire, a boy with poetry in his eyes and a kurta that was once white but now streaked with black, came striding, to stand among the amazed men.

Iqbal. The Muslim.

'I did it!' he announced. 'I started the fire.'

His brother Haroon, secretly relieved that the attention had been diverted from his kneeling in-laws, grabbed Iqbal by the shoulders, and, through the smoke, he shook him. Why? Why?

Iqbal had been standing quietly near the crowd that was terrorising his sister-in-law's family. He had looked away when her cloak had ridden up her thighs as she was flung to the ground. And as he stood paralysed, a voice near his ear had said, 'You want to know who did it? Who threw the pig's head on the rich people's lawn? It was the amakwerekwere ...'

Akash, the cripple, who could never sleep, swore that he had seen the Zimbabwean gardener, Amos, with a hessian sack under his arm, a hessian sack that was big enough to be pig-headed, heading for the lawns that he had just himself cut the day before. Amos who had a pig's bone to pick with the old Vawda man who had not paid him two months of wages after three months of back-breaking work.

It was the amakwerekwere ... the foreign ones. The blacks that don't belong to us. The Zimbabwean ones.

The ones who had run away. The ones who had crept across borders. The ones who had stolen our people's jobs.

Not our own people.

Aapro waalo nee malle.

Iqbal, whose love for Rooksana had somehow become mingled into a world where he needed to avenge the clean lawns where she placed her light step, had stolen the petrol from the Hindu people's barn and set fire to Amos's Zimbabwean shack. But fire being fire – naughty and unrefined – it had not made a distinction between our people and not our people, and had sped through all the shacks before anyone had even had breakfast.

Iqbal had set the fire, and then watched the fire, and he told himself happily that now Rooksana Vawda would be his. He had performed the ritual of cleansing, had avenged the act meted out against her family's purity, and his due worth was her hand in marriage.

'You did this?' asked Muhammed Vawda, the eldest son of Solly Vawda, as he watched the fire die down into embers, revealing dead and dying beneath it.

Haroon watched in horror. His sweet-faced baby brother stepped into the centre of the group.

Iqbal's heart swelled in joy. He reached forward and gripped the hand of Rooksana Vawda's father.

'I want to marry your daughter, Gora Mota,' he said.

Muhammed Vawda recoiled. He pulled his clean hands away from the hands that were soiled with blackness and blood. His mouth twisted into disgust.

'No. That will never happen.'

Aapro waalo nee malle …

16

Jumbo Susan Berdie-Bird

IN THE BOOK THAT THE HOLY MEN WROTE, IT IS SAID that if you eat olives when there is a baby inside you, your baby will be born with dark skin. And in the book that the holy men wrote, it is said that if you eat papaya when there is a baby inside you, the baby will die. This is Meera's third. Papaya. For the day.

Horrible, ugly, lying, filthy woman.

Said her husband to her as he smashed his fist into her face.

And there is a grape stain, spreading on her skin. Her dark skin. Grape on dark brown. It spreads too fast.

He hit me today. Yes, he did. Blue-purple, large-purple, spreading-grape-purple, my purple.

I cried. Yes, I cried. A silent cry that sounded like a hum. I cried. But then I had to stop. The baby butterfly fluttered over inside me, and the baby butterfly smiled a toothless smile.

She cradled an egg in her palm full of lines. A warm egg, room temperature, brown and smooth.

He hit me today.

And then the egg got cracked by her palm full of lines. Slippery, oily. Something comforting and ugly oozed onto brown Formica. Shells swam and laughed in her face.

He's not here, don't worry. He'll come back. He must come back.

Yellow got spoilt, it broke into white; that's not really white anyway, it's clearly murky.

Al-bee-you-min.

'Cook it!' A good resounding voice. 'Cook the bloody thing, doll!'

Who are you?

'Susan, pronounced Soo-zun.'

She cannot recall exactly when the hallucinations began. But here they were … a white woman in her mother-in-law's kitchen!

What are you doing here? What do you want?

Are you real? Susan, are you real? Am I losing my mind?

'I walked out of the walls, love.' Stands on the dirty floors. Sniffing at the dust.

I'll clean them tomorrow.

'Cook the bloody egg, doll!'

I … It's spoilt.

'It's fine. Pick out the shells. Cook it. Eat it. Listen to me, I know. Cook it!'

A warped frying pan creeps out of the cupboard. Did Ma see the cobwebs in the back? Maybe she didn't.

I'll clean it. Later, I will …

Oh, yes, the egg. Cook the egg. Cook.

Scoop with a palm of lines into a smoke-coloured bowl. Pick and pick out shells, the way babies pick at dirt on the floor. Not knowing that it is dirt after all.

Hot warped frying pan creeps onto a stove that needs a scrubbing and a beating.

'Just pour in some oil, will you!'

Susan again. Formidable blonde white woman.

Short hair. Why do they love their short hair?

'Don't cook it! Bash his head in with the hot frying pan!'

Another voice.

Who are you?

'Berdina Garcia Marquez, pleased to meet you. What's that music you playing there?'

I … what are you … it's Chaurasia, an Indian flautist.

'Oh, like yoga music, hey?'

Not really. Not really at all. It's called a raga, *if* you must know. It's like a collaboration of sounds, informal, like a conversation between lovers. Not formal, like a concerto. Informal jamming.

'Ja, I've always liked jazz, hey.'

It's not … jazz. It's … it's … it's jazz.

'Cook the egg.'

Why bother to beat it any longer? That egg, I mean. It's already swirled up into a beaten-up state from palm-to-pan transportation. Dump the thing into the hot pan.

Oh, wait, I forgot the oil. I'm sorry. Really I am.

'Use butter, love.'

Berdina, Susan … who now?

Berdina.

'Butter, so much better, hey? Use butter, love. Watch that pan now, it's getting hot. I still think you should keep it on the go, wait for that man to get home, and then bash his head in with it. But fry the egg, if you want to, fry the egg.'

'Leave her alone.' Susan crosses fleshy arms over big bust. Stepping forward. Protective.

Berdina takes a step forward too.

Now what?

A white-woman cat fight in her mother-in-law's brown-beige kitchen. How would she explain fatalities? But then she can explain bruises well, so fatalities … easy.

'I said oil!' Susan says through clenched teeth.

'And I said butter!' Berdina brunette, pretty girl, nice teeth. Nice lisp.

Stand-off.

Oh, I'm sorry. I'm sorry. Don't fight. I will … please don't fight.

Both turn, whip. Whiplash. Eyes roll. Blue pair, brown pair. Roll. Heads shake. Blonde shakes so much better than brunette.

'You Indian women! You all are so subservient.'

I am … I'll use half oil and half butter.

'That's just what I said, love, you Indian girls … so placatory. Always middle ground, huh? Appeasing girl, you.'

They unite. Against her pacific state, the White Girls unite. Berdina holds Susan's hand, crêpey skin, fresh young skin. Same message. She is just the Indian in the corner. Butter and oil it is.

'Well!' huffs Susan, clearly the alpha female. 'You should've chosen one.'

Too late. Butter blob melting fast in hot oil, egg in, egg out, egg on plate.

'You should put a steak on that. Bruise. Got any steak? Let me check that freezer, hey.'

I don't … I am Hindu … we are forbidden to eat … cow.

'Forbidden?' huffs Susan. Twitching batwing arms. 'Forbidden indeed. Are your men forbidden to hit you, then? Well, are they?'

'What?' asks Berdina, rummaging through the freezer, clearly not following the barrage of words.

'These Indian women and their forbidden this and forbidden that.'

'Oh, like yoga music, hey, mystical!' says Berdina, pulling out a packet crusted with ice.

Not really. Not really like yoga music at all … We are forbidden to listen to music too.

Huff. Puff. Rolling eyes. Forget the steak. Peas in a packet it will be.

'Oh, let's do a pot of tea then,' Susan bosses, and nods Berdina in the direction of the kettle.

Peas in a pod, then.

Mind your peas and queues then.

'Ja, but you Indian girls, you just take too much from your men, hey.'

Blonde, brunette ... heads nod.

Yoga music drifts into and out of the frame ...

I am not going to tell you, Susan, about onions and how chopping them makes you cry, because Susan, Berdie ... it is not these onions that are making me cry. It is not my papaya dreams that are making me cry.

He gave me the book that the holy men wrote, and he trudged up the passage to her kitchen. Her hands rolled dough so softly. So practised. She smoothed the hair off his thirty-three-year-old face, flour making his black hair grey. A mother, smoothing the skin of a fair-skinned boy, leaving flour trails on his brow.

And he said to her, 'Wife, you are going to make me go grey sooner rather than later. Teach her how to cook, Ma. Teach this girl all your secrets, Ma. This girl does not know how to cook for me, Ma. Pasta! What's this pasta? Really?'

I am going to tell you Susan, Berdie, about standing on a bridge in the middle of an African summer, heat melting off a beautiful face. Summer. Durban. I was so young then. Twelve, maybe thirteen.

I know summer is aching to burst out from inside God's chest, hanging back like the debutante at a school party. Peeping from behind a thick fifteen-year-old fringe, waiting and tapping her foot to the music that hasn't even started yet. Will she be asked to dance tonight?

Will she, Susan? Berdie? Are you there?

She is standing on a bridge; her hair is windblown and wild. She is laughing. She has the remains of a lunch, a half-bitten bun and a Spanish orange in a cloth bookbag.

She is laughing. Dearest ... She is laughing. But standing on bridges for hours, and not taking steps to and fro, has brought her here. Into this frame. Standing in a kitchen with a rolling pin in her hand, and a rolling chamber in her heart, ventricles bursting, swelling and contracting. Ventricles.

'Teach this girl how to cook, Ma. Teach her your culinary secrets. She is a bad cook, Ma. She is yours. You can have her.'

She reaches for a papaya. Unripe, but fleshy. Knife poised, she looks into the blue eyes, the brown eyes. Susan, Berdie. Refuse to abscond from her kitchen.

'Leave it!' they instruct.

Leave it!

And she is standing again on a bridge, but in her hands is a rolling pin, and there are spices floating around her face like dragonflies. Cardamom, cumin, coriander. Elachie, jeera, dhania ...

I will learn. I will learn. I promise, I will learn. She sneezes. The belly sneezes and an elbow darts into a ribcage. Or was it a knee? Too soon to tell. It's just a nauseous fluttering butterfly still.

'Chop the tomatoes gently, girl – in a seesaw motion. Don't chop them like you are hacking away at secrets behind closed doors. Marinate the meat in a massaging rhythm, girl, with yoghurt and well-roasted garam masala.

'Don't poke and prod at it like you are picking at bones and prodding messages from your God. Stir gently, girl. Don't stir that pot like you are stirring the pot; knead the dough with energy, girl. Don't push at it like you are pushing for answers.'

Yes, Ma.

He will arrive soon, the cobwebs have not been cleared

away in the back of cupboards, the dishes remain in pageantry in the sink. Peels of oranges, potatoes. Leaves of cabbages, stalks of beans. Adornment of a kitchen. Oil is spilled, flour, sugar, salt … throw some over your shoulder.

He will arrive soon. He will frown. He will say, 'Take this girl, Ma, take this girl and teach her your secrets, of how to cook, of how to wipe. Away tears and countertops. Teach her to pray, Ma. Dirty girl.'

Susan, Berdie … are you there? He will arrive soon. He will eye the room. He will see olive pips and look deep inside a fluttering belly that is heaving with morning nausea.

I don't want this baby.

I have to have it.

What if it's a girl?

I don't want it.

'You Indian girls!' huffs Susan, tea forgotten.

The teapot made of stone and bone smiles sweetly, and says, 'Watch that man. He will throw stones at you; he will pick your bones one day.'

Susan, pass the peas. Mind the queues. The bruise-purple, my-purple, grape-spreading stain weighs heavy on my skittish heart. Pass the peas. I want to be on the bridge today.

Susan blonde, Berdie brown … prepare to open a bottle of fine Chardonnay, and settle their frames on a dirty couch, not dusted in days, picking at breadcrumbs like beggars.

'Hit him back!'

Susan puffs on a cigarette. Berdie sips green-gold Chardonnay, sips uncomfortably from a dirty mug of green-hued, half-empty unhappiness.

'Girl on the bridge. The bun was half eaten. Orange was days old. You were laughing that day. Remember?'

I remember, Berdie. I remember.

'Leave this place!' Ma enters the frame. Arduous, astounding Ma. She places her large rolling-pin hands on beautiful hips that bore fair-skinned boys, those hands that fed soft, buttery rice balls into their waiting bird mouths.

'She will learn. This wife of my son, she will learn. You White Women. Leave this place. There is work to be done. Chopping, frying, stirring. Rolling. With a light, light hand.'

'Ahem,' says Susan. Berdie nods her head. 'Ahem! A light hand indeed! Like the light hand he used on her face?'

'Out! Get out! White Women. Out! She is my son's wife. We all endured. Beatings. We all did. That is just the way our lives are. Out.'

Susan, Berdie ... Brave, brave girls. Sit with crossed legs on crumbed sofas, refuse to move. Sipping wine, smoking cigarettes. Munching on olives.

Ma exits. White Girls fade away into whitewashed kitchen walls. Exit. The frame of reference. All but her. The dirty girl with a secret in her belly.

The girl on the bridge. Smiles. Pops an olive into her mouth. Spits out the pip. It lands on rotting papaya peels.

He returns. Girl on the bridge pulls a soft pink sari over the bridge. Of her nose.

The frying pan. Fills with oil. It boils.

She stirs the boiling oil.

She stirs the pot.

She talks to cousins. Clean boy cousins.

Let's run away from home, Jumbo. Let's do it, Jumbo.

'What are we going to eat?' Jumbo asks, true to his name. But a valid question. Sustenance needed. Even at towers, where you can look for sugar-cane fires. Okay, let's just see.

Potatoes. Perfect potatoes. Dusty ones. You steal it, Jumbo. I'm scared of Small Dolly, Jumbo. You steal it.

'No problem. Potatoes. I can steal potatoes. Wait here.'

Wait and wait and wait. Sugar cane rolls and boils. Not good weather for running away, Jumbo. But let's do it. No jersey, no socks. Just us farm-child feet. You and me, Jumbo. Bring the potatoes. I'll meet you behind the chicken run.

'Smelly there.'

Just bring the potatoes. I'm scared of India Swami. Meet you behind the chicken run. Now run. Go bring.

Dusty potatoes. Jumbo hands clasping. Packet. Put it in. Sugar cane boiling again. Looks like a fire tonight. Looks like someone will start it. Let's run, Jumbo. Thanks for the potatoes.

'Shoes, I need shoes. Where are my shoes?'

No need for that, Jumbo. Let's just go.

'You sure I don't need shoes?'

You won't need the shoes, Jumbo. Let's go. Courtyard slinking, chillies drying on aluminium pot lids. Dry dhal lying on screed concrete. Sun chases weevils. Watch them scurry away. Invisible weevils. Running from sunshine. Away from dry dhal pieces. Towards chillies on pot lids, frying pan into fire, weevil. Never mind, let's go Jumbo.

'Oh, the potatoes! I got them.'

Into your pocket, Jumbo. Into your pocket. They said they'd set fire to the cane later. We can go to the tower. Tower Man won't be there. He went away. We can go inside.

'And cobras, what about cobras. Ricky said there's cobras in the cane fields.'

No cobras there, Jumbo. Are you coming or not.

Fat boy. Slumps. Holds his knees. Twists his fatty self, looking for cobras. Okay, potatoes into pocket. Hard to walk you know.

'I'm coming. I'm coming … but what about … guinea pigs? There's guinea pigs there in the cane fields. Shilpa said they can bite you inside there. Guinea pigs?'

No, no guinea pigs there, Jumbo. I'm going. You coming? Or what?

'Okay, you sure there's no guinea pigs?'

Frown. Looking with angry eyes. Chillies rustle on pot lids. Sugar cane still boils. Someone gonna set fire to the cane tonight. Move it, Jumbo!

'Oh-kay … if you waaaaarnt. Okay wait for me. Wait, I'm coming. Waaaaait okay man.'

Juggling potato pockets. Dusty feet. No shoes. Run into cane fields. Two cousins. One jumbo sized, one too thin. I hate curry. Don't give me curry. I hate it. I don't want food. I don't want food.

'So why were they brushing Usha's hair this morning? So why was she sitting in the sun?'

She got nits. They said. They said she took something. Tablets. They said.

Her green dress, it was nice huh? She is pretty huh. Usha?

'She's fine. She smells. Can I eat the potatoes now?'

No, Jumbo. Stay in my mind. Sugar-cane fields. Tower. Then potatoes.

Drag feet. Drag feet. Dust unsettled and guinea pigs start showing their faces. Tower. Tower. Before they set fire to the cane. Move it fat thing!

Tower Man! Tower Man! I can see him. Run Jumbo. Run Fat Thing! He can see us. No he can't.

India Swami is a very holy man, tells Usha she is too pretty, says her eyes are naughty eyes. Touched her. Saved her Jumbo. Cleansed her. Touched her in the smoky prayer room. Tablets. She took. Too many tablets. Run with me, Jumbo. I don't want to be too pretty and dirty.

Never ever go into the cane fields alone, you children. You hear me? Never ever do that. Scary things happen in cane fields. Fire being the least scary of them all. Can he see us? No, maybe, no maybe, No! He can't.

Breathe Jumbo. Deep breaths now, fat boy. We okay for now. Tower Man won't see us here. Under the tower, don't rattle the ladder you idiot.

'But I want to eeeeet.'

Sit here. Right. Okay, eat then.

Bite. Raw potato. It's not that bad after all.

'This is horrible. I can't eat this.'

Eat, fat boy. Eat!

'So why did they call India Swami today? Who was whispering? They can whisper, you know. Is it for Rosh? Or is it for Usha? Shalini maybe? This potato is bad. Rotten one I chose.'

Priest. Maharaja man. India Swami. Blue eyes. Dark skin. Books and books in suitcases.

Sugar-cane dancing and making love. Jumbo chewing noisily. Raw potatoes. That boy would eat anything. Chillies scurry away from pot lids. Weevils become agents. Guinea pigs start coming towards you. Shilpa was right. They bite you there.

'Is he here, Maharaja man? India Swami?'

He is here, Jumbo. Fat lovely thing. He is here.

I can see him.

Susan slides into the walls, out of the walls. Back again.

'Change your life, doll. Get rid of that man's parasite. In your belly. Do you really want his child? What if it comes out dark-skinned, like you, doll? Think about these things, hey. What if it's a dark-skinned girl?'

How? How do you change your life? How do you eliminate dots on screens?

You may stand for hours in lines to change a fragment of who you are, that face inside a green plastic book – the name you were born with, the name of your father, the name that was smeared then into your hairline one day.

Meera has always seen dots, motion, atoms, electrons, racing towards each other, repelling each other, bouncing and bouncing against each other, then bouncing away.

Susan, it's not that I don't belong here. I was just born here, after all. In a line, waiting for hours with fetid humanity, all waiting to find identities, to change identity. Documents. Names. That is all.

Telephone line clicks. Crackles. Connects.

Fragments of conversation settle on her shoulders like snow from a northern place, the words from a two-way radio. Fake snow in a rented apartment in an industrial playground in deepest Detroit.

'They spray the shop windows here,' Jumbo told her, big man now Jumbo with a job and an aeroplane trip and a possible green card. 'They spray with fake snow from an aerosol can. In mid-July.'

He says it's because people expect a White Christmas fairy tale every part of the year.

'Especially you people, foreigners I mean. You expect too much from snow. You think it is a cleansing thing because it is white and because it is cold. You want red, white and blue; we give you red white blue, Bing Crosby, fake snow in July. You don't expect smelly gas heaters and deep fat fryers and obesity and oily coffee. No mosquitoes. You think we don't have mosquitoes. We have mosquitoes. It's our land of the free.'

South African, cool man. Like Nelson and all that, Tutu and Ladysmith Black. So, what's with your hair, man? It sure don't look Afro to me.

Indian! Oh, yeah man. Like Mahatma and all that. John Lennon and his Guru and all that? Bollywood, I like Bollywood, man. Dances and swirly skirt things, shaky heads, cool man.

No.

So, like who are you, man?

None of the above. A mixture of the above.

I don't get it, man. I mean, you can't be like both, man. You are one or the other. Indian or African? What is it?

Just shut up and play your guitar, okay.

'Jumbo, I need to talk to someone. You. Can you hear me? This line, it crackles.'

'I knew this girl once,' he said finally. 'She got addicted to standing in lines. Strange, huh? So, I mean, she'd get up every morning, shower, dress, then go to the busiest place in the busiest part of town in the busiest part of the year – Christmas maybe, white snow and all that, and pick the longest line and stand in it for an hour maybe if she got lucky. And she got such a high, when she reached the cubicle or the cashier or the lady, man, at the end of it all, then she would turn and walk away to the back of the line. Maybe a few times a day in the same line, waiting, reaching, then walking away. Except once she didn't walk away. Ended up with forms for an American citizenship. Maybe she filled them out. Maybe she didn't. I don't know, we lost touch after a while. I don't know. Maybe she found the longest fucking line in the world and she's standing in it right now. Hey, this is a true story. It is.'

'Jumbo. I need to talk to someone. He hits me, Jumbo. Do you remember how they married us all away? Us girls? Do you, Jumbo? Do you remember how dirty we were? India Swami?'

'Yeah, like I saw this girl once at the Department of Immigration. Looked like she was from Bangkok or something.

Oriental, pretty like, you know. Spaces between her teeth. Sucking at those spaces all the time. Bleached her hair, like you know when people with black hair try to bleach their hair, it ends up orange, man, I mean orange, carrot orange. Yeah. Thought of chatting her up, you know. She seemed nice in an aloof kind of way. You know me huh, I like aloof. Squatting on the dirty floor filling in forms on her jeans thigh. Looked like the zip on her jeans had burst, you know. Like she had it held together with sticky tape and safety pins. She wrote fast. But, dirty nails. No polish. Thought of chatting her up. I saw her yesterday too, walking up Lafayette Street, with a purpose in her move. Yeah, she looked good. She was wearing pink lace sleeves, you know, that stretch lace they reserve for lingerie. Only the sleeves. The rest of her was all T-shirt. Same old jeans, man. Held together with sticky tape and safety pins. Saw her. Two times in a row. Boy, that's got to be something, huh? Maybe I should've chatted her up. Maybe I should've. So why're you calling me, Meera? What's happening thin girl?'

Make me some tea, Jumbo. Don't tell me more about your adventures, and your women. Don't ask me why I called you. I don't know. Maybe to ask you if you remember running away with me to the Tower on the sugar-cane farm. I don't know. You were lucky, fat one. You were lucky. They didn't marry you off. Because you didn't have naughty eyes. Lucky fat thing. Boy.

Boy you. Girl me.

'Hey, man forget all that shit, man. You're happy, right? You don't sound happy, but you're happy. Just accept it, man. Remember the marigolds? So many damn marigolds at the weddings and funerals and prayers. I can still smell marigolds, man. All the time. Whatever happened to Usha, man? I don't know, we lost touch. Shilpa, Ricky, Raj, Shalini, we all just went our separate ways like that. You got married, I came here. But you sound good, man. Sound good. Hey, the closest thing to roti here is like this burrito thing. Almost, you know. Almost. The same. Take it easy, man. You sound good.'

'Jumbo, do you remember India Swami, Priest?'

'No, man. I don't. Forget it, man. Forget it. All that is over now. We got lives now. Gotta go, sweetie. Working tonight at Wendy's. Oh, and it's not Jumbo any more cuzzin. It's Jamz. Okay? Jamz. See you around. Forget it all, man. See you around.'

Jamz.

17

The Beehive Comes Undone in the Wind

SO, WHAT DO YOU DO WHEN YOU COME HOME FROM buying fresh vegetables at a market and you find a white woman coming out of your oven?

You think of the day your mother's beehive came undone in the wind. Your mother's wedding day. Your twenty-five-year-old father, face screwed up because beach sand gets in his eyes. She lowers her eyes, those seventies eyes, those kohl-lined eyes, the beehive unravelled to reveal scalp and hair. Cover up, he mutters. Moustaches twirl. Cover up, girl child. Woman. What are we doing here on this sandy beach?

It is your mother's wedding day. Bees swarm over the ocean. She looks to him, he looks away. She covers and covers, and the pins stick into scalp. Silky red sari, no she wore green. Defiant, flowers in her hair, San Francisco.

'I used to drive a Chevy,' she whispers, and he looks away.

'I used to go on boat trips,' she persists.

And he looks away.

A ritual must be done at a beach, after the wedding has been performed; perfumed incense hangs in the air. Wash away your old girly girl into sea water. Now you are mine. Set that beehive right. Girl. Woman. Bride.

They had such fun at the beach that day. You watch it all unfold on a white wall, before which a projector whirrs and clicks. Good times then. Not now. Now, you are only eighteen, you are married, you are beaten, you are alone. You think that day on the beach they'd ever have guessed their eldest child would be using cheap make-up to cover purple stains, and scrubbing floors at five in the morning? Not really. They were so happy that day.

White woman sliding out of oven, stands squarely in Meera's face.

'And you?' she asks. Her non-existent white-lady eyebrows are fuzzy things, Meera's are caterpillars. 'Are you Happy?'

No …

'What you gonna do, dollface?'

I decorated my hands with henna. Patterns to show me the path to my pulse points. They engrave your beloved's name, hidden somewhere among paisley and dot patterns on a palm, they cover your lines with thick mud-like henna.

Bangles! Always wear bangles. Always wear lipstick. He won't see the bruise if you wear lipstick. Kind of distracting, that red lipstick.

'So, he hit you. The henna hadn't even faded and he placed a palm on your face, hard palm. Young bridegroom.'

I sneak into his mother's prayer room. I sit on the floor. I look at all her effigies; I look at all her offerings. Her sons. Big-shot doctors.

'Pray,' his mother instructs. 'Don't you know the ancient texts, the songs and the clanging of cymbals? Put your hands together, pray, you bad-luck girl. Pray.' Fire approaches her heart. Mother holds a brass tray with piles of burning camphor and non-popping cloves. What's she trying to do now?

'India Swami said you were a bad-luck girl. Bad for my baby boy child. He said I have to cleanse you. Bringing your dark face into my home. But we took you. We are so kind. Eat this lime, break this coconut, light this flame, turn around twice, tie this thread, bang your head, drink this water, eat that leaf, wipe your tears. Now you are ours. Bad luck … wear some lipstick at least.'

White woman that arrived from my oven – let me sort out these vegetables. Then I will go into her prayer room. She wants me there. She says bruises and all that are just part of life.

'Sort out your brinjals, girl. But sort out your stuff too.'

How?

'Leave him. And his black dot on white screen. Erase dark girl. Erase, and then run.'

World is at a standstill. Beehive comes undone in a wind of thoughts.

Leave him. Leave him. Leave … No, yes, maybe, yes … No …

Dot?

So, thoughts of leaving enter her head. Susan packs her bags. Berdie hands her her dressing gown. But Meera, afraid, softly stows them back in the dark cupboard that they came from. It will be a while – years – until she even thinks of taking them out again.

Where will I go? Back to the farm, bad-luck girl?

India Swami said she had naughty eyes. Marry her off soon, Papa. Leave her, and then she'll be wanting to read books and all. We got a good boy. Doctor he is. Soon specialist … But, er … excuse me if I have to be so helpful, shall I check her out first? Just to remove the bad eyes, you know.

Into the green-apple childhood scabby-knees prayer room she is terrified to go.

Into the chaotic kitchen she goes. And stays.

Yes, Ma.

18

Spread Your Legs, Girl

It's actually easy. Three, maybe four white pills, and they poke your insides, check how many weeks along. Don't even bother with any drug to numb it all. It's so bloody damn easy. Swallow, swallow, and swallow. Now wait. Come back tomorrow. If you start bleeding, come back straight away.

Scan? No need for scans. These pills will sort it out. Did they counsel you? No? You refused? Your choice. Pro choice. Not legal. Not legal at all. But necessary, after all.

Signature of 'mother' … signed. Tick box.

Signature of 'father' … she fakes it. Tick box.

You fraud!

'I don't want this man's baby inside me. I don't. Take it out. It's just a six-week-old, seven- or eight-week-old dot. Take it out. Nurse.'

Round black woman, looks at the girls waiting in the line. Girls who don't want dots. They look at floors, they play word games in old magazines. They don't look at each other. They know that they are in a place that is on the backstreets of life, a place that fronts as a family-planning clinic, a place that tells pregnant, fearful girls that it's a home for unwed mothers, a home where their babies could be adopted eventually. But everyone knows it is a place that feeds you pills and then sucks the blood clots out of you, sending you quietly back to the uncomplicated life you arrived from.

A myriad shoe prints on a carpet patterned with threadbare orange flowers on green hills. Ugly attempts at being cheerful. Sounds emanate from behind closed doors. Surprisingly no horror sounds, screaming sounds, howling and wailing sounds. Feminine humanity, murmurs, paper clips falling on floors. You could have been at the dentist, extracting a tooth.

Black man, shiny lovely face. Perhaps a doctor with degrees on his wall, perhaps not. Teeth so dazzling. He's been to a dentist. Big smile. Lie yourself down on this table, Mrs … Miss … Mrs … er … Miss …

Legs up now. Let's just see, shall we. Hmmm.

Nurse hovers, instruments in hand, yes doctor, no doctor, okay doctor, I love you doctor. Afro, sweaty, shiny. Yes doctor.

No platitudes. Clinical times call for clinical measures. Snap of the gloves, and a taste of blood in her mouth, she is biting her own lip, wondering when a soul becomes a soul. Don't ask those questions now, girl. It is time. Time to erase.

'I don't want this husband's baby. I don't want his punches, and his slaps, and the morning when he kicked me clean on the arse. Get it out. It's not wanted here.'

Lying there on that table, she turns her head to the wall, and sees a poster there, on the cold white wall, a peeling montage. How to wash your hands. Scrub here, then rub there, then wrists, then interlock your fingers, pray for a second seeing that your hands are joined – it is an opportunity after all. Soap. They instruct in English, Zulu and some other African language. Use soap! Isn't that pretty obvious?

Doctor Mabongo. Snap-snap gloves in place. Did he wash his hands? Who cares, those two fingers are deep inside now.

'Sister, cervix is soft.'

She is happy. At least one part of her is soft. Those bones, flesh, tendons, heart … all hard as hell. A movement. Sister

Afro moves to her face. She speaks close into her mouth and nose; her breath smells of no breakfast. Meera attempts to not gag. The attempt brings hot stinging tears to her eyes. Nurse pats her head. Puppy dog coming in for rabies shots.

'Never mind, Sisi. It will all be over just now, okay.'

She wants to scream out to Sister Afro that these tears are not because of sadness or fear. She wants to tell her to get some chewing gum, breath mints.

She can't look at the peeling hand-washing poster any longer. A turn of the head in the other direction and she is faced with a network of amazing metal.

'That is going to be in me, Sister?'

Nurse sucks at her bad-breath tongue. Uh huh! In you. And then out again. So keep it together.

There are girls on other beds too. She's the only Indian girl. There are no white girls. Maybe two coloured girls, the one who was doing the crossword puzzle at the back of last week's newspaper in the waiting room, the one whose hair has been straightened into a stiff bob. Can she lie on that table properly with that helmet?

The black girls chatter. In tongues she barely understands. They seem happy. Like girls at a salon, waiting for a manicure. Legs in stirrups, waiting for a man-i-cure.

The coloured girls, one called Geraldine, or is it Ameline, or Anneline … looks across at her, meets her eyes. She looks away, then back again. Maybe they could become friends. Her eyes are gone, looking at hand-washing charts. Too late.

It was pretty easy to do this after all. Just got the telephone directory, looking for 'abortion clinics'. Found nothing in that fat yellow book. Abortion is illegal in this country. 'Feminine clinics'. Nothing. Called the gynaecologist's rooms. The receptionist bristled at her halting question, her whispering from the only place she had the privacy to make the call, his mother's prayer room.

She put the phone down on me, that receptionist. So, who do I ask? I know no one.

Lucky is as lucky does. Newspaper. Classifieds.

'What's this? You reading the newspaper now? Hehhee-hhe! Look Rajesh, your wife is getting into politics and all. Maybe she wants to work for PW. Hehehehe!'

Found it. Small, tiny posting in the Personal section of the classifieds in a community newspaper. Stuffed between personal-loan shark advertisements and a large advertisement for a miracle cream that guarantees penis enlargement by a famous Malawian doctor, Rahim. A place for secret advertisements.

Pregnant and afraid. Call us!

She calls the number, again huddled in a corner, whispering. The woman on the other end of the line pretends to not understand the request. The request to delete the dot on the screen. The woman whispers into the telephone, come here, come to us. We will sort it out. Don't tell a soul, about what we do to souls. Don't tell. Pay us. We will delete.

'I need you to breathe, deep breaths now. It is going to be sore. But Sister will hold your hand.'

It is. Very painful. Don't let anybody tell you otherwise.

'Suction, sister.'

Done.

And then it's bye-bye chicky, back into the crowded West Street throngs, fat maternity pad stuffed between your legs, you worry about bleeding onto the seats in the minibus taxi that will drive you to another minibus taxi, that will drive you for two hours back to the large sprawling mansion near the sea and the sugar-cane fields. Doctor's House.

But these seats of minibus taxis, they've probably seen more blood than you could emit.

It's over. Do stop romanticising like the dot progression to abhorrent infinity.

Dot Gone.

'Where have you been, girl?'

'I went by bus to the farm to visit Aisha Vawda.'

'Bloody Muslims. You keep away from that Muslim family, you hear.'

Susan. Get out of the walls and talk to me. It is three in the morning, the blood and clots are calling out to you. Dot gone, Susan. Dot gone.

19

Big Dolly, Small Dolly, Ripe Red Mango

THERE WAS SILENCE ALL AROUND HER. PURSED LIPS and whooshing silence. Until the day Big Dolly asked the question that everyone wanted to ask: 'What you gonna do with the dee-vorsh-ed girl now?'

A valid question indeed. What now?

It was a ripe red mango that had done it. A fleshy fragrant summery mango that sat at the top of a pile of green apples in the frosted-glass fruit bowl on the dining-room table of the farmhouse.

Big Dolly had seen the mango first. When she entered the house, and stepped lightly around domestic worker Beatrice's head. Beatrice had been shining the floors with wax, lavender-smelling wax. And as she moved her arm in widening circles, she hummed a Sotho tune out loud into the too-empty house. Big Dolly, heavy-footed and wearing a bright-green Punjabi suit, had almost knocked into Beatrice's head, and by serendipity had missed trampling her black hands with all the weight that Big Dolly carried.

'I will eat that mango,' Big Dolly said to herself before loudly cooing her namastes to whoever was home. She eyed the plastic-covered lounge chairs in all their rosy splendour and wondered how nothing much had changed around this place. Yet, so much *had* changed around this place.

Big Dolly and Small Dolly were sisters. Big Dolly was loud and harsh in her words, tactless, senseless. Small Dolly was ratty and conniving, manipulative and whispery. Together they made a perfect pair of dollies who always found time to come to visit. At the right-wrong times always.

And now, what a perfect time to visit the main house. Big Dolly had clapped her hands in glee. Perfect timing. Rubbing her fat hands together she conjured up images of how her brother's wife, Meera's mother, would squirm under her persistent questioning. And she deserved it, she deserved to squirm.

How smug they had been when that dark daughter of theirs, the thin, quiet one, had landed Doctor Rajesh Maharaj as a groom. How plush and elegant and ornate the wedding had been. Her sister-in-law would smile to herself and answer questions about how well her daughter was doing all the way in Millionaires' Row. Smug. That's the way the Dollies saw it. Must be cut. Down to size.

Small Dolly hadn't been able to come. She had her monthly appointment at the local eye clinic, where the doctors had to convince her time and time again that she didn't have cataracts, even though she insisted that she most certainly did.

The chance to throw mud in her sister-in-law's face over the 'scandal' of her daughter's divorce was tempting, but more tempting was the chance that maybe today a fresh young doctor would find some cataracts, and book her for an opper-rayshun ... the best word in the whole wide world ... opper-rayshun.

Small Dolly had waited her whole life for one thing and one thing alone – the chance to have an operation. She felt that having one would complete her, make her beyond other people who had not had them. Most of all she knew that having an operation meant you were spoilt, fawned upon, and taken care of like a little broken bird. Small Dolly tried everything possible to have an operation. But even her chances of a caesarean section were thwarted by four children who came swimming perfectly out of her womb. No operation needed. So Small Dolly had decided in favour of the Eye Doctor, instead of going to the main house to collect information about 'that girl'.

She had warned Big Dolly before her visit to the main house that she must be tactful and conniving in asking Big Questions about what had happened. She told Big Dolly to hold back and let them speak – let them trap themselves in nets. For Small Dolly had an Agenda …

Small Dolly had no allegiances. Not to her family nor to her husband's family. To her children maybe, but that's where it stopped. She was the type of woman who would collect information from you without your even realising it, and, with a swish of a fast hand, deliver that information to your deepest, darkest enemy.

You didn't know who was more dangerous: Big Dolly in her brash tactlessness, or Small Dolly in her secretive manipulation. Together they made a formidable pair, and prided themselves on this pairing.

One day, when Small Dolly was at the local fruit-and-vegetable market, she had bumped right into Anjali, the Boy's Mother. Anjali, whose round green cabbages went rolling to the ground, had stared at Small Dolly and her eyes began to glitter. Small Dolly had reserved her judgement, been quiet and unassuming, but slowly Anjali had started talking.

'Your brother's daughter … ruined my son … ran away … packed her things … everyone is laughing at my son … his wife ran away … what to do, what to do. I am a mother, what to do?'

Small Dolly had listened with a small cocked head, like a mynah bird on a fence. Nodding once, maybe twice.

'If only I knew some inside information …' Anjali continued. 'For the respect of my son who is so deeply affected that his wife ran away in the middle of the night. Maybe if I knew how the girl was doing, what they were plotting in that filthy farmhouse … if only …'

Small Dolly had shrugged and dimpled her cheeks. This was no business of hers. What could she possibly get out of this? Nothing.

Something …

'My son, Doctor Pranesh … his friend works at the eye clinic. Op-per-rayyyyy-shun … Maybe if you can find out … maybe that ugly girl left my son because she was having … an … affair …'

Anjali's suggestion. A rumour began its rounds. A rumour to sully the wayward girl, to absolve her son. To ruin and destroy a girl's life.

Small Dolly had lit up like a Christmas tree in July.

'Oh dear sister, I can see how much you and your son have suffered at the hands of that pagal girl. Don't worry, my sister, I will go and find out how that stupid girl is living, or maybe she is dead. She should be dead, the pain she has caused you. Affair! Yes, affair … it's the only explanation. And your wonderful Doctor son. What a tragedy and all. Don't worry bhabhi-ji, leave it to Small Dolly.'

But the appointment at the eye clinic had arrived, and Small Dolly had ulterior motives. She would send her sister Big Dolly there first. She knew her sister-in-law, and that mad girl trusted Big Dolly more than Small Dolly. Big Dolly would open the road for her to go in and see what was happening at that house.

And what was happening at that house?

Times had changed. Brothers who had lived in that huge farmhouse as extended families had gotten married and moved on to live in places like Phoenix and Chatsworth where semi-detached houses with thin prefab walls made for exciting listening pleasure. The large house howled with empty voices, its thirteen rooms, plus prayer room, vacant and spooky. Meera's father had remained. He hadn't had the heart to leave the house his father had built with his own two hands.

His father who had arrived on this Dark Continent, Africa, as a labourer, and through his own sweat and toil had built a farming empire. Her father still had visions of grandeur, where he and his brothers would resurrect the heyday of the old farm, ploughing through clumpy brown earth, watering dry dusty soil and planting seeds that would burst out of the ground in green splendour. But nothing of the sort had happened.

His brothers had fallen to the allure of the Big City, preferring jobs in clothing factories and large stores owned by Gujarati tradesmen, stores that sold saris, prayer goods, cassettes of the latest Hindi movies, and magazines that flaunted the latest Bollywood stars.

He remained at the farmhouse, occasionally walking out into the fallow sugar-cane fields, and taking large handfuls of mud in his palms, dry cloddy mud that had seen its day. Nothing could grow there now. He recalled the days when rows and rows of the best vegetables grew. The ladies would sing as they weeded and harvested. He recalled a day when the sweetest of sugar cane grew there.

The large sugar-cane truck would come wheezing up the hill, after they had set fire to the cane. A thick molasses smell would permeate the air. Too-fine black ash would settle on everything in the house, the washing on the line, on your eyebrows and eyelashes. The men with dark-black backs, sweaty and glistening, would use the implements called cane cutters to swiftly slash at the stalks of burnt sugar cane. Other men, also shirtless, would bundle up the cane and place it between the chains of the sugar-cane truck. Those days were glorious for everyone.

The smell of burnt cane lingered like a perfume in everyone's noses, and it made you want to celebrate. Meera's father recalled the successful delivery of a large crop of sugar cane to the Hulett Sugar Mill, about twenty kilometres away, and he pictured the lush cane that came from his father's land being crushed into the sweetest of sugar, finding its sweet ways into the teas and the cakes of rich white people, the type of people who went to the Hulett Maidstone Club to play bowls and cricket on the manicured lawns before high tea.

And the days when the sugar cane was burnt, chopped and delivered were the best days for the family, who rejoiced and ate and drank for days on end. They would celebrate the cutting of the cane as they celebrated weddings and births. Another successful crop, delivered.

But the magic was not to last. Meera's father's brothers began to look to the Big City, Durban. They took surreptitious trips into the Big City, hiding from each other as they did so, not wanting to be the first to make the move. But the lure of the Big City was indeed great. It didn't matter to them or to their wives that they would live in tiny prefab houses whose rooms were half the size of the ones in the farmhouse. They didn't care that there were no large, open farm spaces, rolling green hills, big happy trees to sit under. What mattered was the chance of a job that paid.

They slowly began to make their way out of the farmhouse in passive but sneaky ways. It began with the fighting of the wives. Everything always began with the fighting of wives. The sisters-in-law who had lived harmoniously together for so many years – had lived through each other's triumphs and tribulations, births and deaths – began to bicker over trivialities like tiny little insects that crawled on their skin.

'Too much salt.'

'Not enough salt.'

'I washed the dishes yesterday. Today is Her turn.'

'Tell her to keep her naughty children away from my zinnia bush.'

Eventually, to keep the peace, one by one the brothers had moved away. The sisters-in-law had hugged each other and cried as large trucks filled with jagged-shaped belongings went sliding down the hill.

They reached their tiny prefab houses. Their children went to Big School. They went shopping in actual supermarkets. And they never looked back.

Never looked back at the old farmhouse that sat next to a fire tower, on the top of a hill.

So only Meera's family lived there now, like ghosts in the massive farmhouse, the place where things had changed. And her father still ran the cloddy earth between his fingers, hoping to plant seeds.

It never happened. And he grew old and despondent. He was forced to rent out large sections of the house to strangers, for an income. He swallowed angry tears as he used wooden boards to partition what had been his mother's sewing room and his second brother's bedroom into self-contained units. He grew uneasy and irritable as his tenants arrived from all spectra of society. He ignored their crosses nailed to his walls, he ignored their slaughtering of goats on Eid Day. He lived off their rent. And grew as bitter as gall. This was his father's house. His father who had come from the purest of castes in India – the traditional goat-herder caste. Why, even Lord Krishna himself had come from such a caste.

He grew attached to the house as he grew older, prodding and poking anyone who dared alter its image. If the children from the Muslim family in the back portion happened to draw on the outside walls, he would fall into a rant that scared the children and the adults alike. This house was his house. And it was perfect in every single way. Partitioned, but perfect in every way.

They didn't have running water yet, but they had an orange kitchen with a sink. The toilet was still an outside toilet, but still, it had been tiled at least. The voices of all the children who had grown up in the farmhouse next to the Tower echoed in the walls. The prayer room had gone dusty and unused; India Swami had strangely disappeared one morning with all the money the family had been collecting to drill a borehole, and some of Meera's mother's jewellery, including the large Krugerrand that her mother-in-law had given her.

Some say India Swami had taken this loot and gone back to his village in India. Others swear that they had seen him, trailing a stiff white dhoti, chanting and bringing civilisation to another village near Port Shepstone. Who knew? Everyone felt foolish for the 'India Swami' days. But most didn't know the sinister extent of those days. Mostly they tried to lie to themselves that India Swami had ever existed.

Meera had arrived, running away from her husband's house to the ghostly house of her father, and had added to its ghostliness. Her father had ranted and raved about the scandal she was causing and how much he had spent on her wedding and what he was going to do with a divorced daughter on his hands.

Her mother simply pursed her lips and wrung her hands and said nothing, bottling it all up till it boiled over into an attack of the worst psoriasis anyone had ever seen.

Meera was certain. She would not go back to that godforsaken house, with its Fair Ones, its swags and chandeliers, its swearing parrots and its prayer room. She told her parents nothing of the beatings and the abuses. She spared them that much. But she told them, firmly, that she would not go back. They could kick her out onto the street if they wanted, but she would not relent.

Her father had consulted his brothers. There was no India Swami to consult with now. His five brothers agreed that she should be allowed to stay away from her marital home for a little while, but after a time, she Must Go Back. A cooling-off period. They all were adamant: divorce must never ever be allowed. Under any circumstances. They would not suffer the embarrassment and shame of having a divorcee in the family. They called it *separated*, never using the word *divorce*. A trial separation.

Meera stayed on. But a few days became weeks, and weeks became months, and soon a full eight months had passed. She wandered about the empty house, silent and soft, lightly touching the walls, breathing in the scent of lavender floor polish, conversing with Beatrice as Beatrice washed windows, and staring languidly out into the hibiscus trees in the front garden. No one asked her any questions. Her father gritted his teeth and stopped attending family gatherings. He stopped going to the local market for vegetables. There would be too many questions to answer. Once he tried to broach the subject of Meera's returning to Rajesh's home, but she had flown into such a fit and refused food for so many days that she became thin and wraithlike. He feared for her life. Her younger brother and sister didn't know how to behave around her.

She seemed as brittle as glass. Brittle but happy. Nobody knew quite what to expect when she was around.

But the Big Red Mango did it!

Big Dolly had come in search of information, which she would relay to Small Dolly, who would sidle up to the dyslexic-spider paisley gates on Millionaires' Row. And Big Dolly had sat with her sister-in-law, Meera's mother, at the kitchen table, eating a hearty fill of what was for lunch. The subject of Meera was not broached at all.

'Be conniving' is what Small Dolly had taught her – Big Dolly, whose errant tongue was just waiting to unleash a torrent of questions.

After lunch, Big Dolly felt she had done very very well. She had observed restraint and not asked anything about the girl at all. She told herself she would tactfully ask now.

As she sat at the kitchen table, her eyes caught a sight that made her blood boil and bubble as it had never done before.

Seated in the courtyard on an old patio chair was that mad girl Meera, drying her long hair. And in her hands, soft, juicy and bright, was the Big Red Mango. Big Dolly watched as Meera sucked at the juiciness that dribbled down her chin and pooled onto the floor of screed concrete.

Big Dolly's mouth watered as Meera devoured pieces of golden mango – a mango that Big Dolly had reserved for herself.

Her anger knew no bounds.

How could that mad girl dare to flaunt herself in such brazen ways, sitting with open hair, toes painted, sucking at the juices of a mango meant for Big Dolly?

She should be cowering in a corner, crying till her eyes grew red, atoning for the sin of running away from such a prestigious marriage, for daring to leave such a boy, a doctor, after all. As Big Dolly observed, the girl looked positively ... happy.

And Big Dolly couldn't stand this happiness. The girl must be punished.

She got up clumsily from her chair and charged into the courtyard, reaching for Meera's long damp hair with fat ham fists. Yanking the hair backwards, she delivered a hard whack of a slap to Meera's face, and roughly pulled her to her feet.

'Look at you, you pagal witch,' Big Dolly shouted. 'Like a prostitute, you sit here in your father's house, with painted toenails and wild open hair. Don't you realise what you have done, what disgrace you have caused your family? Look at your parents – they are broken people, all because of you. Little witch! Can't you see, you have shamed us all! You think your younger sister will get a good marriage now? After what you have done? All of us, we bow our heads and walk in the village, all because of you. Now, you promise you go back to your husband, you hear. You go back!'

Meera had stiffened her neck as her long hair was yanked by the ranting woman.

'Never, I'll never go back there!' she screamed back in Big Dolly's face. Her mother circled the two, wringing her hands and fluttering, begging them to stop.

'You bloody female dog witch bitch!' Big Dolly was relentless. 'Let me show you what girls like you should end up like.' And she had dragged Meera by her hair through the courtyard, Meera's knees and ankles grazed and bleeding, into the kitchen, where she grabbed a large pair of dress-making scissors, and, holding the massive bunch of Meera's hair, promptly cut it off as close to the head as possible.

'There, you see, you prostitute, bitch, this is what happens to girls like you. They end up selling themselves. You think you're so great, not going back to that family. That family is one of the most prestigious families in our town.

You think you are so great that you can turn your back on them. You have no shame, you're a disgrace. Bitch.'

Meera's mother had stopped fluttering around the pair. She was on her hands and knees collecting the hair that lay there.

'Look at your poor mother, on her hands and knees like a beggar. All because of you. Look at her skin. Peeling, whitening, losing all colour, scaling and bleeding. Your mother is paying for your sins, bitch girl. Now, you don't want to go back to your husband, the man you married under our God's grace, fine. But live your life like a prostitute, because no man will want you now. They will use you, but no one will marry you now. Live like that, fine, you bitch. But watch how your mother, father, your younger sister suffer because of what you did.'

Meera lay panting on the floor. She reached up and felt the uneven stubble on her head. She saw all the hair surrounding her, and her mother on her hands and knees, frantically collecting the beautiful mass. And she knew.

Big Dolly was Right.

Big Dolly was Right.

She couldn't live in her parents' home like an exile forever.

Something needed to be done.

And that night as she lay on her pillow, scratching at the stubble on her head, she began to think of Possibilities. What few there were. Susan sat at the edge of her bed, and helped her scratch her itchy head, saying every now and then, 'What now, dollface?'

The half-eaten Big Red Mango got kicked into the drain. Where the flies feasted.

20

Baboo(n) Did It

BABOO. N SILENT BUT NOT DISREGARDED. DID IT.

The final straw that convinced Meera that it was time to consider all her options. It was not the verbal lashings and the long-hair-slashings of Big Dolly. It was not the sadness and pallor of her mother, or the silent, boiling anger of her father. It wasn't the outcast state that she lived through with every passing day. It wasn't even the rumours doing the rounds that she had left her doctor husband because she was having an affair.

It was Baboo. She had always referred to him as Baboon. He looked like one. He certainly behaved like one. She had always steered clear of him, not trusting the unibrow and the large forehead of him. Baboo's father owned the farm next door to Meera's family. They farmed vegetables, which Baboo would take every Saturday at dawn to the early-morning market in neighbouring Verulam. There he stood with his eyebrows overhanging his eyes, his knuckles almost dragging on the vegetation that littered the floor, grunting out prices to keen customers.

Baboo had managed to secure a marriage. Someone had actually consented to lie in his bed. A fat farm child, from the sugar estate in Stanger. They all called her Annie, although that was not her real name. Annie was quiet and silly and giggled when spoken to, and carried the baby that had developed out of that strange union on her too-fat hips, crooning old Lata Mangeshkar songs to the child as she wandered the farm.

It was during one of those days when Annie and Baboo

had come over to Meera's house for a prayer that Meera realised: the time had come.

The priest was intoning loud Vedic hymns (the real ones this time, not the fake ones of India Swami). Meera's father had decided it was time to begin praying again. Meera had been forewarned not to come out of hiding, not to flaunt her divorced unfaithful self in front of the priest and the neighbours. So she had stood behind the water tank looking at frogs. And sniffing at the fragrant prayer fires. And scratching at her almost bald head hidden under a pink chiffon scarf.

Suddenly, Baboo appeared in her line of vision. Dragging his knuckles and slumping his shoulders, he stood before her in a bright-yellow mesh muscle vest that showed all of his back hair, chest hair, arm hair, and face hair.

Baboo(n), thought Meera, and continued to look at frogs.

'Give one kissss,' Baboo hissed.

Meera jumped back from his hairy attempt at an embrace.

'What?' she shouted, knowing surely that the people praying in the courtyard had heard her.

'One kissss,' Baboo hissed again. And lunged for her.

'No, what is wrong with you. Get out of here,' Meera hissed back, and pushed the squat body away.

Baboo's eyes grew dark and heavy beneath his unibrow. His mouth twisted, and then he bared all of his large teeth. Baboo(n).

'You're a prossie, that's what my father says,' the spurned Baboo said, and reached again for Meera's arm. She yanked it away. 'You divorced ones are just dying for it. You're a real hooker. You had an affair,' Baboo said, and lunged at her again.

'Get out! Out of here! Leave me alone, Baboo, or I'll scream,' Meera threatened.

'Scream then. Nobody will believe a prossie like you. Sies! Divorced, sies!'

He spat. At her.

Meera had stumbled backwards, reeling from the look in Baboo's eyes. Venomous, lusty, disgusted, wanton – all at once. And she had realised suddenly: this is how all men saw her. Prossie! Divorced and dying for it!

She scampered over the frogs and ran as fast as she could to the fence that surrounded the farm. Baboo didn't even bother to follow her. He spat again and walked away.

She collapsed against the wire fence and hot fresh tears came rolling down her cheeks. She had endured Big Dolly's hissing and Small Dolly's spitting. She had endured not being invited to family prayers and weddings. She lived out her days quietly in her parents' house, resisting with all she had every month or so when her father would storm at her and tell her to return to Rajesh's house. She had even endured the pain and humiliation of Navin …

Navin Ramdin was her childhood friend from school. They had grown up together, playing on each other's farms till the twinkling fireflies came out. But they had grown apart as teenagers: Navin had been sent away to school in the Big City, and Meera had simply accepted that he was gone. But one day, after she had left Rajesh and returned to her father's house, she had met Navin on one of her rare outings to the local supermarket to buy bread.

Navin, who had just returned from studying law in Johannesburg, looked at Meera as no one had ever looked at her before. Her shorn hair had grown a little longer, and she had a certain presence about her that men found attractive, though they didn't know why. Her skin was almost the brown nutty colour of almond skins, her eyes were large, and her smile was rare but brilliant. Navin had found himself quite taken. He had asked for her phone number, and she had forgotten her limbo separated-divorced state and given it to him.

Navin had called her the next day, and the day after that, and the day after that. Her mother pretended not to listen to the way Meera giggled and softly cooed into the telephone. They spoke of many things. Mainly Meera was hungry to hear about what Johannesburg was like. Navin would ply her with his interesting tales of Zoo Lake and Sandton shopping centre.

Meera slowly became enraptured by the handsome, bookish-looking law graduate. Her mother, who knew of these telephone calls, simply pursed her lips and shook her head. This was not going to end well, of that she was certain. But she didn't have the heart to stop her daughter, whose face had come alive finally after so long.

And it did end badly. A short sharp phone call from Navin's mother to Meera's mother, and Meera had realised the full extent of her state.

'I will not have a divorced woman chase after my son,' Navin's mother had roared, aggressively telling Meera's mother that Meera should stop her pursuit of her lawyer son. Meera's mother tried to tell Navin's mother that it was actually her son who was doing the pursuing.

But the woman would hear nothing of it. She was furious. She called Meera names, which her mother tried to muffle over the oh-so-loud telephone line.

'We don't accept rejects, second-hand girls from the Maharaj family, Mrs Narain. Keep your wild daughter away from my innocent son.'

And that had been Navin. He had never called Meera

again. She saw him once, again at the local supermarket. He looked sheepish; he cast his eyes downwards as if in shame. But with him, on his arm, walked a beauty with the fresh red powder in her parted hair, the powder that indicated a new bride.

It had been a sore and heartbreaking time for Meera. She had no one to whom she could talk about Navin. She sat alone, quietly, on the large veranda, watching day turn to night, wondering what would become of her. Living in limbo.

Rajesh had promptly refused any divorce. His revenge against her walking out on him was to tie her in knots, where she was neither here nor there, living like a sylph that glided between worlds, hidden from all eyes. Talking to no one. Participating in nothing. For how long could she live like this?

When the hirsute Baboo had tried to kiss her behind the water tank, when he had dared to call her a prostitute, it shook something deep inside her soul. This was no place for her. She would surely become invisible and die here. But going back to Rajesh and his beatings, his mother's rantings and ravings, was not an option.

At night she would lie in bed, her head cradled by the white woman Susan, and talk late into the night of all her plans.

Maybe Johannesburg, she thought, and began searching the papers for a job there. But she was trained in nothing at all. She hadn't been allowed to go to college.

Maybe stay in Durban, jobs are easy to come by here, she suggested to Susan, but Susan reminded her again that she bore no formal qualifications at all.

In misery, Meera began to sink into a deep, dark depression. Rejected and outcast, she lived out her days wondering what was to become of her. Her society and family had kicked her out. She couldn't go back to her marital family. She existed in a no man's land, a place where a thousand Baboo(n)s could accost her and call her prossie. She saw how the men in the family and on the street looked at her. With judging but lusty eyes. They would remain married to subservient fat wives, but their eyes would stray to Meera.

Even Navin. One day she had met him at a large Village Prayer. The annual Kavady Festival, where devotees went into such trances that they pierced their bodies and tongues with fishermen's hooks, and hung fat limes from their skins with thick piercing metal rods.

Navin had cornered her, and, before she could run away, he had held her hand. His hand in hers felt so good. So warm.

'I'm sorry, Meera,' he'd said with a deep sorrowful look in his brown eyes.

'Forget it, Navin,' Meera had answered and attempted to move away.

'Wait, just wait. Talk to me for a minute. I'm sorry it turned out that way. I was forced to marry Kajal. My parents heard I was speaking to you, and they quickly found me a girl.'

'Do you love her?' Meera asked.

'I … I do, now. I've learnt to love her, to love my baby boy. I'm content.'

Well good for you, Meera thought.

'So what do you want with me?' she asked.

'Meera, even though I am married, maybe we, I mean maybe things can still happen between us …' Navin whispered and moved close to her, smelling her perfume. Hotel room? In the Big City?

Meera had been disgusted. She had reeled backwards, twisting her lips.

'What? So I'm not good enough to be your wife, but I'm good enough to be your mistress? You disgust me, Navin. Never.'

Navin's face had changed from a soft one to one seething with venom.

'Oh, I see. Well I'm sorry to inform you, Meera, that's about the only thing you will be used for … some man's mistress. No one will marry used baggage, so you'd better get used to it.'

Handsome advocate now, Navin told the truth. Not all lawyers were liars.

Navin's words had hurt Meera to the core. She knew that no matter how venomous, they were the truth. She knew Rajesh would never let her go, and she would remain as a fallen woman in the community forever.

Almost two years had gone by; Meera was now almost twenty-four. And her life had come to nothing.

She would have to think of a plan. And in her silent words with strong, brave Susan in the middle of every night, a plan began to form. A good plan. A strong plan.

She heard through the massive intertwined grapevine of the town that Rajesh had developed a penchant for Muslim women and had started spending all his time with girls with rose-scented names like Shenaaz or Saadiya. But he refused to give her the divorce she desperately needed. That was Meera's punishment.

Dublin

21

Dublin International Arrivals Terminal

She arrived in Dublin on a grey day in April. A soft day, the taxi driver told her in his melodious Irish tone. Clutching a rusty-red beret with half a pompom and a shawl to keep out a chill that wasn't really a soft chill, out of the aeroplane with businessmen. Aer Lingus, bright-green orb in the sky, expelled her body onto the tarmac and made her walk into a too-bright airport thronging with nobody in particular. Who arrives in Dublin at six in the morning, anyway? Businessmen and spinsters on matchmaking holidays.

'Where to, love, and would you please put out that cigarette. No smoking in my Škoda.'

'1146A Heron Street, Palmerstown.'

'Where, love? Don't know any Palmerstown.'

'But, but, but …'

She looks down at the piece of paper, a letter from an agent called Siobhan, confirming her arrival at a Home in Palmerstown, Dublin 12. Try another taxi driver, this one's a mad man, she thinks.

Two drivers later, one that doesn't particularly care if she smokes – an old squat gentleman with eyes that disappear into creases.

'Climb in yer lassie,' he says and opens the door with a flourish. Bags safely stowed, reeking of incense, she settles into the back seat of a car. Meera does not recognise the brand of this car.

'Palmerstown, huh?' The taxi driver jolts a conversation into her brain, her terrified, terrified brain. 'What you gonna do there, love? Should rather be staying closer to the city, go to Temple Bar, young girl like you. Palmerstown, now that's a place for no angel.'

He appears to flirt. He asks her if she is Italian. Maybe the skin tone, maybe the darkness. She shakes her head, choppy wild hair flying in soft weather days.

'To work. To work,' she replies and falls silent again, not trusting her voice, not trusting the actual green-and-grey landscape that passes her. It depresses her already, this lack of any other colour, the service stations with their bright neon lights, the warehouse selling garden furniture, the corner shops. Depressing. Scary.

'What kinda business has anybody in old Palmerstown, love? 'Tis a wasteland, that. Houses only. No businesses.'

'St Joseph's House of God,' she mumbles, and she almost sees his ears, filled with wiry hairs, twirl in her direction.

'Jaysus, girl, what would ya be doing in that godforsaken place? That's a home for the idiot savants. Not-so-right-in-the-heads. No place for a young lass. Gotta see the sights, get the craic. St Joseph's … pssssh …'

He shakes his head, his true unstylish poor-boy cap going slightly askew.

'I'm going to be working with the … Savvvv Arnts, Sir. Autistic children. Caregiving. Taking them for walks, giving them pills, cleaning their dirty arses.'

He regards her in the mirror and decides that it is time for silence.

'Light up, girl,' he says, and hands her a lighter with the Queen of Hearts on its flank. A green lighter. What else? An evil Queen of Hearts, staring into her lying eyes, as the flame hisses to life, smelling too strongly of butane.

The old manor house looms. Large walls covered with ivy, from a long round tower next to an automatic teller machine and a bus stop, opposite a construction site and a lone hairdressing salon. The taxi driver waits at a red traffic light, waiting to turn into the private road of the badly placed manor house.

'I'll get out now,' she says, and he appears stunned and affronted all at the same time.

'I'll be driving ya to the doors, love, settle in now.'

'I said, I'll get out now. How much?'

Money changes hands. She realises as he brushes her hands while giving her a fifty-pence piece in change that this is the first foreign hand she has ever touched in her life. This is the first white person's hand she has ever touched in her life. It feels dry. It feels soft. And she feels liberated, as if she has crossed a Rubicon into a world that will involve touching. Brushing up against strangers on buses, on streets, in nightclubs, rubbing your senses and body against theirs. All of humanity, touching and touching, and feeling how you are able to love only when you practise the sense of touch, to know that love grows in touch.

She comes to enjoy the smell of closeness, the human sweat of a day's work and poorly made perfume, cheaply bought from the one-pound store near Liffey Valley. She will make a habit of touching shoulders when she talks, touching baby fingers when she passes, running her hands along jackets stuffed with fat arms, even one day daring to touch a lady's stockinged leg while pretending to look for a coin on a crack in the pavement.

Stepping out of the taxi, she knows she will never forget him, her Irish taxi driver, shocked that a young girl hopping out of a green aeroplane would actually choose to drown in a donated manor house filled with crazy, raving people. Rather than simply go to a pub filled with crazy, raving people.

She passes the hair salon, seeing a matriarch hobo stuffed

into a chair having her fluffy hair chopped by a dumpy girl chewing gum. The smell of hair dye and chemical perming lotions accosts her and stings her eyes, sulphurous, acrid; long after she has passed, the smell of burning hair stays with her. A yellow Caterpillar digger glugs slowly down the street, and before she turns into the private road, dragging a suitcase behind her, the man leans out of his Caterpillar box and whistles. Butterfly. Whoop whoop. Hot thing. Sexy thing. Come on, sit in my lap, while I dig up dirt. She ignores him, and he picks his teeth. He's used to this game.

A suitcase and a knapsack, a shawl and a beret, all her worldly possessions. She crosses the street and looks for a sign. The gates of the house, large and looming with the faint possibility of gargoyles, remain shut to her face. What now?

She lingers for more than a few seconds, forehead pressed to wrought iron, enough time for the imprint of a leaf to appear on dark, pressed skin, her knuckles whitening as she clutches the bars of the gate. Let me into this prison. Let me out of this world.

The imprinted forehead and the impassioned grasp at iron straws seem to have worked, and her body is jerked forward by the slow mechanical opening of the gates, inwards, creaking. Someone, an eye in the sky, had seen her begging there. Someone had let her in.

The old suitcase does not travel well on cobblestones and chugs along in staccato hops, lurching into her calves as she tries to navigate a snaky driveway, looking only at trees and green manicured lawns. Not a person in sight. She gives up, she stops and sweeps an angry mop of wild hair from her eyes, and, despite the softness of the day and the faint hiss of drizzle, a sweaty upper lip appears. On the backs of her knees, the nape of her neck, the sweet smell of sweat. Someone could be looking at this figure from one of the many gabled windows of the manor house that looks more like an abandoned castle housing a petulant lord than a world filled with children.

Where are the child voices, the laughs, the cries, the playground screams of roundabout delight, the swish of a swing, a child's shoe dropping onto the ground in mid-air? Nothing but silence, nothing but green, nothing to hint at a home. Somewhere inside this groaning concrete there is probably a rainbow of babies, sobbing and grasping and asking and dribbling.

She wouldn't know where they were, where they were kept hidden. She could never know anything about them. She has never actually seen a child like that in her life. But on her application form, she lied. Not told the truth. Lied.

Caregiver Wanted. Home for Autistic Children.

All she saw was a foreign address, a country so far away from her own that she filled out the application form with lying fingers, and waited, and waited till a distant letter from a country she had barely heard of told her she was the lucky one.

Did a course in childcare, she had written, not entirely lying, remembering that she had enrolled for one through correspondence but had not actually done it after her father forbade it.

She doesn't care that she had lied, that she forged and frauded. She cares that she was out of there, out of that place, that world. Thrown like a fish from the warm waters of Durban onto the icy sandy beaches of Dublin, like a liar fish lying on its side, opening and closing, opening and closing its mouth, gasping for a way to drown.

The sound of high heels on cobblestones tells her that someone has seen her approach, and she looks with screwed-up eyes as a woman in a navy skirt and a grey office blazer walks with purpose towards her.

'Maura Sweeney,' she says, extending a hand, a dry perfumed hand, and the smell of Gaultier's latest range assaults Meera's aeroplane smell.

'This is the Clinic, this is the School, this is the Office, this is the Gym, this is the Swimming Pool' – pretty obvious that one – 'these are the bungalows where they sleep, this is the Maze and Zen Garden' – pretty obvious there too – 'this is the Library, this is this is this is ...'

Maura is a professional. No pleasantries. No how was your flight, how is South Africa, nice to see you, nice to meet you. Nothing.

She could easily have been a robot, or a secret agent called M for Maura.

Isn't that a sweet coincidence? 'I am M for Meera, you are M for Maura,' she probably would have told Maura, had Maura developed eyes, and a smile.

But Gaultier attacks Meera as she walks from empty corridor to empty corridor, poking her head into halls and rooms and gyms and strange-looking alleyways. Everything is painted a pale, verdant green. An attempt at calm that just appears sterile and untouchable.

Her suitcase is still on the driveway. She ignores that fact, and then wonders if there are thieves here in Dublin. In South Africa, the suitcase would have been ransacked, and all its ugly contents stolen, and the suitcase itself probably hacked into pieces with a broken beer bottle.

'Where are the children?' she finally asks Maura, who looks mildly offended that her artfully prepared, probably a-million-times-delivered monologue has been interrupted by an accent.

'Today is Awards Day, they are all off to the town hall in

Chapelizod for a ceremony. The Mayor's probably coming. Heard he was probably coming,' Maura says, pausing before a door that says simply *Josephine*. That's it. Just Josephine. On a white piece of paper with peeling edges printed in fading ink, *Josephine*, stuck to the pale-green door with sticky tape.

Josephine, it turns out, is the Staff Liaison Officer (so who or what is Maura)?

Silently, in well-used Hush Puppies – brogues (as in Irish) – Josephine pads around a carpeted room filled with files, paper clips, and officey-looking implements. Sign here. Done. Like Maura, the rotund Josephine has no time for pleasantries. Meera realises they are so silent and grouchy because they do this all the time. Welcome strangers from all over into their disconnected, crazy world. People don't want to work in this place, it attracts runaways from all over. Maura and Josephine have seen aeroplane eyes before. Nothing is ever new, or nothing that happens has never happened before.

She had arrived in Dublin. She was a working girl. There were probably hundreds like her right there at the manor house.

'Let me show you to your room. You share a bungalow with two Australian physiotherapists and a Spanish occupational therapist.'

Bye bye now …

Exit Josephine.

An empty room in a decent bungalow, furnished in peach chintz, unfashionable, seeing that it went out in the early eighties, but nevertheless, pictures of orchids on the walls.

She thinks of going in search of her suitcase, probably sitting like a lonely boy on the cobbled driveway, waiting for a mummy, spreading incense on grey and green lawns with each wafting breeze.

It is 8:15. It will be at least five more hours till anybody arrives back from the awards ceremony. She decides to sleep. She needs sleep desperately. And she sleeps. Aeroplane alcohol and dizzy heights, the robotic Maura and the smell of dust, drowning in a peach patchwork comforter.

She sleeps.

The suitcase will still sit and wait on the driveway. For hours. Till somebody kicks it into the hydrangea bushes.

But she sleeps.

'The day I arrived here, Ian, it was a soft day. Rain like mist on your skin.'

'What's this all about?' impatient Ian asks, pulling her frame into his.

'Nothing you can understand. Touch me. Touch me.'

'Where?'

'Anywhere, Ian. Anywhere. Show me the places where I am alive. Show me the skin that survives.'

'Hmmm … spoons … let's do spoons …' Ian mumbles.

'No! Bite that ear. Wobble that thigh. Skim the surface of dark skin with your sticky tongue.'

'You girl. Wobble? You're all arms and legs. Grasshopper … Daddy-long-legs. What's that insect called? The one that prays?'

'Man-tisssss …' Her gravelly voice hisses into his blond head. Meera bites a tuft of shampoo taste.

Nice.

'Roll me over, and then over and then over, Ian.'

'Meeee-raaaa … stop this now. We can't. We should stop now. My boy … is all I care about. I want to leave a place for my boy in this world. I want to leave my boy something. I can't be consumed by you and your madness. You're eating me up, you hungry hungry child.'

'No, forget all that, Ian, feel this softness and this wetness. I am alive, Ian. Forget all else but never forget me.'

'What's this then, you exotic dark thing? A beauty spot?'

He runs a thumb across a spot on her exposed hip.

'Just a spot. Just a spot. Kiss it, Ian.'

'No.'

'Please.'

'Oh come on, let's do spoons. Gotta leave in about five. Got an overnight to Galway. Dutch tourists waiting. Gotta put on the uniform, practise the craic, pick my nose, gargle my mouth. No time, Meera love. Let's just do spoons. By the way, when's the last time you washed your hair? Smells of pillowcases. Meera, we need to stop all this now. My boy. My boy. He needs all of me.'

'I need all of you, Ian. You make the voices stop, you know.'

'Jaysus, woman, you're a complicated one, aren't ya?'

'Ian, hold me and bite me. Twine me, vine me and roll me, twist me and squash me. It's the only way I know.'

'Five minutes, Meeee-raaaa. Then I got to go. Pick up Stewie from occupational therapy. They make him play with foam. Wonder if it helps. Make him roll snakes out of Silly Putty. He can't do it, Meera. He can't roll a stupid snake out of lime-green Silly Putty. My boy … Okay, five minutes. Five minutes more.'

'Give me more. Time. Ian, give me more. I am hungry.'

'I said five, okay fifteen. Roll over. Angle that hip. That's right. Your feet on my back are cold – keep them off. In the air. Limber girl, you. That's better. Oh, that is so much better, Praying Mantis Girl …'

22

The Twisted Twins

ALICE AND ONYA DOYLE ARE IN THE ARMS OF THEIR father. Strong man Brendan Doyle carries them like sacks of potatoes. They hug each other. They do not hug their father. He enters the place everyone calls the School. A euphemism for a Day Care Centre, a place where frazzled, depressed parents deposit their broken children every day, hoping for some respite. It is not a real school at all. Although the classrooms boast alphabet charts and educational wooden blocks, no one really admits that the children do nothing the entire day.

A loud CD player is constantly on repeat. Nursery rhymes play into nothingness. Incy Wincy Spider keeps climbing up the water spout. Teachers rush from room to room, carrying fat books filled with the hint of activities. They don't even bother. With papier mâché or sticky playdough. They look like thieves as they smile their fake smiles at parents who have no choice but to keep the antidepressant suppliers in business.

In a large hall lined with spongy mattresses they leave the children on the floor. Each to his own, the children stay put. They lie down in gnarled postures. They stamp their trainer feet, and issue whooping warnings to the confused adults. A lone psychologist comes bearing a suitcase filled with a generic test, an instrument that will place the IQs of the children in neat little compartments. Occupational therapists, who always seem happy, bring finger puppets and trays filled with sand. Everyone tries their very best. To pretend that they are making a difference. When all they're doing is passing time. Waiting for death.

Meera lurks outside an office door. The Head Teacher, Mrs Morrison, a Scottish beauty, loudly shuffles pages. Meera hears the short sharp bang of a stapler. A finger being stapled, and a Scottish swear word. A large file drops with a thud to the floor.

'Enter,' Mrs Morrison commands, and Meera walks shyly into the office lined with ferns. The fronds are new and infantile, giving an earthy smell to the dustiness of shelves. Meera stands shifting from one foot to the next. Mrs Morrison looks up from beneath bifocals and frowns. 'Where's the rest of them?' she asks, and Meera shrugs. The Head Teacher grabs a screeching microphone and gargles into it. 'The case meeting for the Doyle twins has begun. Will the relevant people please make their way.'

In lazy time, a sixty-year-old psychologist called Timothy follows two Dutch occupational therapists and a physiotherapist from Melbourne into the office. They make no apologies. There's no need to hurry. Not in this place. Mrs Morrison indicates for someone to call in the parents of the twisted twins.

A hesitant couple walk like sideways crabs into the room. They seem happy, excited even. They have been waiting a long time in the passage. Meera had stood away from them, watching them wait. Not meeting their eyes. They have finally received the coveted meeting. The big important one with the important therapists and the matriarch of the School. A moment in the sunshine. A place for their woes to be heard.

Mrs Morrison clears her throat, and bends her large red head into an obese file. She reads loudly. 'Alice and Onya Doyle, aged five, were brought to the School six months ago after being referred from St Columcille's Paediatric Unit. They were assessed individually by the Head of Psychology,

Mr Timothy Atchinson. They were then placed in the Profound Section of the School. They are currently receiving physical as well as occupational therapy.'

She pauses and peers over the top of her glasses at a clearing of a throat and a hand in the air. She purses her lips. 'Yes, Mr Doyle?' she asks, annoyed that her soliloquy has been rudely interrupted by the working-class arm in the air.

'I beg of your pardon now, Missus,' Brendan Doyle begins, and Mrs Morrison seems disgusted by his rough, colloquial way of speech. She is a woman who adores eloquence and flourish.

She prides herself on the higher social classes that she admits into her School that is not really a school after all. Brendan Doyle looks sideways at his wife, Margaret, who sits wringing a handkerchief in her hands. He seems not to see the annoyance. He continues. 'Me and the wife … we've been having a hard time of it, don't you know. These lasses are our very own, for sure, but we can see no improvement in them. Are they going to be all right, are they? Will you and your important people be curing our lasses, now?'

An audible gasp runs through the assembled professionals. Therapists sink into their seats. Meera, who had preferred to remain standing, looks from expectant parents to irritated Head Teacher. She knows these girls. She has been their caregiver at the School for the six months they have been there. They are indeed the worst of the worst. They do not speak, they cannot swallow food, they spend their days lying on the floor holding each other's hands and staring into space. What was this father thinking? Asking for a cure.

'Mr Doyle,' the Head Teacher interrupts, 'you have to understand. Your daughters are profoundly disabled. I don't have to be the one to tell you, Sir, that they can barely function in the activities of daily living. We have … done all we can for them.'

'Have you?' Mrs Margaret Doyle whispers into her handkerchief. She looks wildly from therapist to therapist. She challenges their competency with her twisting hand. She stares blatantly into their faces.

'We have, ma'am. We have.' Timothy the psychologist nods, keeping in mind that this is surely his last case meeting before he has to go for chemotherapy for his prostate cancer. He has grown tired of this world. He has been here for years and years. Part of the furniture. He has seen gaggles of anxious parents and every type of child under the sun. He knows somewhere that his job is a futile one.

There is no point. Nothing touches these children. They remain distant and gnarled, and they skim the surface of puberty, fading into their own eventual funerals. They come out of dusty cupboards, from the cottages of grey-green Kerry and the council houses of County Kildare.

This School, their very last resort. The last outpost before they are eventually retired into the stuffy bedrooms of their ageing parents. Nothing. Nothing becomes of them.

Brendan, the father, diminishes in length. He drowns in the fake leather of his seat. He places his hands palm upwards on the Head Teacher's table, a prayer of hope. He beseeches in despair. Meera can stand it no longer. The begging father, the glazed eyes of the mother, her cotton-wool mouth gaping in its antidepressant side effects – it is all such an ugly scene.

One of the Dutch occupational therapists opens and closes her mouth, as if wanting to mumble platitudes. She looks down at her hippy-shod feet, dark-brown Birkenstocks, the thick socks pooling at her ankles. This day, this meeting, is the least favourite part of her job. She wonders if she should have taken the job at Oxfam, the work in Malawi, or perhaps she should have remained in Holland, where she would have cycled around canals and worked at a gym.

'I'm really sorry, Mr Doyle. We're going to have to let them go. There's nothing for them here. They're going to have to leave,' Mrs Morrison announces – the main objective of the case meeting laid bare, finally out in the open. No need for pretences now. The shocked parents jolt in their seats. Surely they had not come here for this news. They had arrived with hope in their eyes, feeling that the saints had blessed them that Wednesday, the day someone would tell them that their offspring would be cured. Wednesday's child is full of woe. And twisted sisters now have nowhere to go.

'We can't …' the mother whispers again, louder this time. She imagines a shift in her world. She imagines her days now filled with those dead staring children from her bloated womb. She knows she will not be able to handle them. They have to go elsewhere. Somewhere. Far away from her – a failed madonna, who likes her mornings free from them, where she can sit in her drugginess, staring at soap operas. No, she cannot have them at home.

'There is no option, Mrs Doyle. The twins are too Profound for us to keep them. We have a long waiting list. We have done all we can to get them to where they are.'

Where are they, Meera wonders. Same place they've always been. Lying twisted on floors, drooling toothy smiles and holding hands. Always holding hands.

Mrs Morrison's words are final. Meera, standing dumbly in a corner, wonders why on earth she has been called into this devastating meeting. Surely this is no place for her. But she realises that it is merely a formality. All who work on the 'Case' must be present. The decision has already been taken.

And the presence of the silent therapists and her own shifting feet means nothing. Just a formality. A by-the-book Head Teacher. Needs witnesses. In case things get ugly.

'When?' Margaret Doyle asks, wiping back tears that run rivulets into her thickly powdered face.

'Now!' announces Mrs Morrison, slicing the air with a flat palm. The knife that kills the hopes of anguished parents. Now.

'But … but, Missus. Where will we take them? They told us at St Columcille's that this was the place for them. They told us our daughters could be sorted out here. A school, where they could learn things. Not large things, mind. Maybe small things like colouring in pages, maybe nursery rhymes. We are not unreasonable people, don't you know. We can see they will never be normal girls at the end of it all. But this was a place that they came to. Every day … Every day …'

Timothy removes his silver glasses. He wipes them slowly with the front of his grandpa cardigan. Slowly he places them back on the bridge of his nose. He begins tasting in his mouth the metallic tastes of chemotherapy. He watches his bodily cells being assaulted by their extra-strong chemical madness. He wonders to himself if he should possibly have tried Ayurveda. Oil massages and potions made of roots and leaves. He grows angry. At these provincial parents with their silly hope, and their silly beseeching. He clears the thickness from the back of his throat. Mrs Morrison looks towards him with expectant eyes. You are the psychologist. You sort this out.

'We are dreadfully sorry, Mr and Mrs Doyle. Dreadfully sorry indeed. But the Board has taken its decision. Perhaps you could get a home caregiver for the girls. Maybe someone who will make them comfortable …'

The parents' eyes swivel towards the current caregiver, the silent Meera standing near the door frame. She looks away, not knowing what they are looking at. All she does for the twins is push them around from classroom to playroom to on-the-floor room to Zen Garden; she cleans their messes and feeds the puréed fruit. Caregiver. She treats them as if they are sacks of concrete. She never speaks to them, croons to them, or, like most of the therapists, shouts loudly and smilingly to them, 'Hello little poppet! How are you today. I am going to play some games with you okay little poppet!'

Loud, shouting. As if loudness would wake them from their autism.

The father puts his flat palms together and begins begging again. 'Please, please, Missus. We have nowhere we can keep them. The wife, see … she is not well. Not well at all. Can't care for these girls at home. She's seeing a doctor in the city, taking pills. Me … I have to work. My work with the Gardai. It's not possible to keep them at home. There is nowhere. Nowhere.'

His voice fades into the steel gaze of the Head Teacher. She appears aloof, she sighs out loud, showing her irritation. She rolls her eyes. The mother begins a mournful dialogue. 'It is all my fault. I know it is. These girls … they lay inside me like stones. I told the doctor, I said to him to let me have my labour. He said, he said he needs to cut them out. I insisted. I wanted to birth my children. Like a proper mother does. I didn't give up, even when they got caught with the cord around one's neck and the other one's head stuck inside me. I wanted to birth my babies. Too late. Too late I said to him, yes you can cut them out. They came out of me, floppy like ragdolls. Such beautiful girls. Such beauties. All my fault.'

'Well, Mrs Doyle, it is a temptation at these times to lay blame. But what happens to each child that is born is only God's plan. His plan, which we must never question.' Timothy decides to issue the God platitudes, the fallback words for tragedy. The explanations that somehow convince us that what happened, and what didn't happen, in this world was never our doing after all. God's Plan. The Eternal Planner He Is.

The mother begins keening, crying with hacking sobs into her crumpled handkerchief. The therapists grow uncomfortable and stand up to make their exit. They prefer not to be around for such ugly business. Their job here is done.

Brendan Doyle watches his wife melt. He hears his silent daughters lying on a classroom floor. He suddenly stands up and balls his fists into a punch, his policeman body knotted in rage.

'This is bullshit. Bollocks, I tell you. We brought them to you to be healed. We gave our children to you. Big, dear money we paid this place we did. And back then you smiled at us, you took our babies. You told us everything would be all right. And now they become your inconvenience and you throw them back at us. Because maybe a parent with a deeper pocket comes knocking at your doors. Don't think I haven't seen through this. It's all about our money, isn't it? This is fecking bullshit!'

Mrs Morrison has had enough. She stands up and squares her stocky Scottish self up to the raging father. She points at the door, and arches an eyebrow into his anger. 'We don't tolerate such violence and swearing at our School, Mr Doyle. There are children here.'

'Children! Yes, Missus. Your School is filled with bloody children who can't barely hear. Don't talk to me about tolerance. You bring a broken child into this godforsaken world, and you watch their pathetic bodies grow into nothing. And then you talk to me about fecking tolerance. Come, Mrs Doyle. Come. Let us leave this Hell.'

Meera shrinks away from the door she is guarding as the couple strides in a mixture of anger and despair out of Mrs Morrison's office. She looks the father straight in the eye, and says, 'I'm sorry, Sir.'

'Feck sorry, girl. This place to the devil's. May the Virgin bless all your condemned souls!'

The parents had left the office. Collected their twisted children, each carrying one girl in an arm, crunching up the driveway towards the iron gates. The girls, who knew nothing of the turmoil of their destinies, held hands across their parents' defeated bodies. The long bus ride home awaited them. This place had spit them out.

'Well,' said Mrs Morrison when tea had been served, 'well, back to work. We are not miracle workers. Back to work.'

Meera had shivered, like a dog after a bath. Shaking some of the ugliness off her. But not all. Never all. She walked dumbly towards a boy sitting on his haunches behind a shelf, staring at an Incy Wincy Spider.

'Gavin,' she said, and the boy stared into space, not hearing or seeing her at all. 'Gavin, come, let's go potty.'

His pliable little body sat on the toilet seat, nothing happening. Meera began making hissing noises, trying to sound like running water. Then she opened the tap at the sink, saying loudly to the slumped boy, 'SoooooSooooSoooo.' Still, nothing happened. Nothing ever happened.

Later that week, Fiona Moody flopped moodily down onto the threadbare armchair in the staff lounge. She threw a folded newspaper onto the piles of two-year-old *Elle* magazines. The newspaper knocked a mug of tea over. Nobody cared.

The Doyle father had driven his family into Rosslare Harbour. With a boot full of rocks. Everyone simply wondered why.

23

Pedro and Phil

'I DON'T KNOW, IT'S JUST A BIT VISCERAL. WANT A JOINT?' Pedro asked, slumping in the doorway, looking both ways.

'Yeah, but of all the fucking places to go, you came to bloody Ireland. I mean … most of us wanna get outta here, and good old Meera brings herself over here. What were you thinking, ladybird?' Phillip's cigarette dangled so Rodney-Dangerfield from his mouth, asking the questions.

'Oh come on, Phil, Dublin's fabulous. Look at Barcelona, we can't get jobs there. We can't speak English, so we can't go to England, so we come here, we learn some craic, we get a job. Packing shelves. Whatever. Not so bad. Want a joint?'

'Drives you a bit mad, this place. Not the weather, weather's too dull to drive you batty. It's just something in the flowers. Something about coming over the Ha'penny Bridge into Temple Bar, seeing a busker vomiting out Jim Morrison knock-offs, watching them boys in checked shirts get off the goddamn bus from Limerick or some other small town. These boys, they look for a pub, right. Some pub they can drink themselves silly in after a day spent pushing ledgers or whatever they call those books accounting people use. I don't know. Visceral? What the fuck is visceral?

'What are you mourning, ladybird?'

'This girl, she's got a mind that is churning. Can you feel it, Phil? I can feel it. Something dangerous in this girl. Hey, girl … want a joint?'

'Nasty times, ya. Why has this dragonfly flown away to hide in fucking Ireland, man? Maybe she's a double agent, hiding out here in Dublin, man, punching buttons, making telephone calls at midnight. Don't you think I haven't seen you do that, ladybird? I've seen you hover around the house phone, dialling then putting it down, ten maybe twelve times at midnight. Who you calling, girl? Meera, who you so afraid to call?'

'Phil, I am telling you, it's visceral, all this. Meera, she's a visceral chick. Feels it in her gut. Can't call her cold-hearted. She just having some issues with some folks back home, that's all. Hey, man. Want a joint?'

'I mean, this is no place for a butterfly ladybird. This place sucks. These kids, they drain the blood out of you. I can't take it any more. Screaming, biting, that's okay. But it's those vacant stares I can't handle. They just look right through you, honey. They just blank. I took the job. Care for them, you know. Just like you did, Meera. Took the job. Care for autistic children. That's what the ad said. Watch over a bunch of kids. How bad can it be? Just a bunch of kiddios, man. But this shit is tough. They give me the creeps. The ones in the Profound Section, you know. Birch Grove, they okay. They just lie there in these rooms watching the disco ball go round and round, their bodies tied up in knots. The nurses tie them down with rolled-up sheets so that they don't lurch outta their beds, hurt themselves, tie their hands down so they don't gouge their own eyes out, man. I can handle them. But these ones, here in the Moderate Section, the school-going ones. They freak me out. They appear out of nowhere. They come straight into your face, man. Say nothing, do nothing, just stare into your eyes. Then walk away. Five-year-olds, six-year-olds. Can't take it. Can't take this any more.'

'Paciencia mi amigo, Phil, it's a job. You watch them. You take them for walks. You feed them yoghurt. You wipe their arses. You take them to the physio. You walk around a bit, get their bodies going, blood pumping. They just kids. Don't take it so serious like. Relarjarse, relax amigo. Then you put them to bed. How hard is that, man? You all want a joint?'

'Pedro, I am telling you. There's something about these kids. I mean, I can handle it when they bite me, but those seizures, fuck me! Those I go nuts about, all those rolling eyes, spitty mouths. I'm saying, I'm gonna look for a job in America. Maybe construction, bricklaying. Something that don't have a pulse, right? I used to work in St James Hospital. As a porter. Just pushing the wheelchair around taking old ladies for their therapy, pushing pregnant ladies to their caesarean sections. That wasn't so bad, no not so bad at all. No.'

'Ese fue buen trabajo, good work. So, why'd you leave then?'

'Got fired. Got caught having a joint on the job, Pedro. Yeah, but I'm thinking right after I got fired and I'm walking out of the superintendent's offices with a green slip of paper in my hands, I'm halfway stoned and I'm thinking, so if you're slightly doped while you're doing this job, yeah, what's the big deal, right? I mean, it's not like brain surgery. You just pushing and pushing a freaking wheelchair around. So why'd they fire me? But I left. I had a lead for a job in Blackrock. One of those fancy guest houses there you know. Valet parking, general maintenance. That sort of thing.'

'So what happened?'

'I take myself over to Blackrock Pedro, right … and there's this girl at the reception. Bloody gorgeous Swedish girl. Legs and blonde hair, that's about all she had, plus this red lipstick. I mean, red lipstick looks shite on pale birds right. But this one, she had that scarlet pout working all kinds of magic. So, I tell her … Mr Phillip Kevin O'Connell … at your gorgeous service. And she looks at me like how all these fancy birds look at me, and she raises that pout and snarls. Man, she fucking snarls. Like a bloody dog, yeah. So, I growl at her, thinking she's like into animal flirtation. Turns out, she's the owner's wife. He's this big-shot property developer in Blackrock. Anyway. Let me not bore you. They kicked me out. Now I'm here.'

'Somebody's not talking, Phil. Somebody's gone all silent on us, Phil. What's up, ladybird, you got a depression? Ojos tristes, si. Sad eyes. Here, have a joint.'

'Leave her alone, Pedro. You and your freakin' joints. It's all shite, that stuff you get from the Rastafarian guy on George's Street. He's conning you, boy. It's probably dried lawnmower grass.'

24
The Tretchikoff

SEX WAS NEVER THE HARD PART FOR MEERA. IT WAS the sex, of it all, that was easy. Minutes, maybe an hour, of contorted pleasure wrapped up in a foreigner's body, enveloped in his scent. Nothing could compare to it. She had made it easy for herself. She made love with a serious detachment, a moment followed by a moment of quiet introspection, a slow, steady wrapping-up within herself.

Ian loved the quietness of her. He enjoyed her subdued sighs, her ability to hide her pleasure behind closed eyes, arms crossed over her chest, arms thrown over her eyes. Something about it made him desire her more and more each time. He was tired of theatre. Of drama and action. Her inert body beneath his felt more real, solid, pliable.

A subtle shyness would come over her once he had spent himself into her. A shyness of crossed legs and a body turned away, a sheet wrapped over her torso and pelvis. She would slink out of the bed and, like a thief, creep towards the bathroom, where he would hear the water running for a long, long time.

She always showered. Cleansing herself. Of him. She would emerge from the bathroom in nakedness then, the shyness forgotten with the washing-away of fluids, and lay her cool body next to his, seeking his eyes in the semi-dark. And it was always semi-dark. Even if they met at her house in the light of a ten o'clock morning, the thick drapes would be drawn. Like a hotel room, stark white sheets, no personal items on nightstands. Just an alarm clock that ticked in time to their movements. And a print of Tretchikoff's *Lost Orchids*. A print peeling at the edges, adding kitsch and cliché to their affair. When he entered her body, the orchid peeled off the wall, came swimming onto her chest, crept into her eyes and blinded her. She came in the quietest of sighs, fondled by an orchid, penetrated by its dancing leaves, violated by its garishness. She fell in love. With orchids.

He knows he should end it. He knows the day is coming when he will. He can already feel the burning hatred of his wife as he slinks into the coolness of Meera's room. He hears her housemates walk down passages, he imagines them looking outside the window and perhaps peering a few houses down the street to find the large green Emerald Wagon parked like an obvious telltale. He knows that everybody knows. Even Teresa knows. Even Stewart knows.

He remembers the day he picked Meera up from Stewart's school, boldly stalking her and ushering her into the Wagon. He sensed her discomfort and her pretence at irreverence as the busy after-school traffic full of parents and teachers watched them.

He remembers taking her to the Emerald Wagon offices in Grafton Street, and how she sidled onto his lap, biting his ear, sullen, eager, wanting. Over her shoulder he could see Stewart playing that incessant video game, the beeping hedgehog jumping over hurdles, the sound punctuating his own sighs.

It was dangerous that day. But Ian had been desperate to be near her. He had braved the stupidity of having his lover and his son in the same room, watching each other like cats in a cage, both guarding his attention, both saying nothing.

Meera made him not care. Meera made him not worry. Meera made him do things he never thought he could do. Like flaunt his love affair in broad daylight, like breathe for the first time in years, like talk, like think. He felt like an idiot. Like a schoolboy at a party. But he looked at his son, staring into the places that Ian could never go, and he felt like a thief in the night.

Stewart had been taught well. The handheld video game calmed his restless energy. It never left his hands. He pressed buttons and stared into the tiny screen with the concentration of a scientist. Meera had showed him how to play the game. And as she played hers with Ian, little boy Stewie played his, occupied, but looking at them with his amber eyes. Ian sometimes had the strange feeling that it was the amber eyes of his son that spoke to Teresa at night, telling her the secrets of the moments inside the Wagon office.

It was strange how they decided mutually not to hide their affair, their affliction with each other open and obvious for all to see.

Perhaps they were worthless lovers. A waste of time. Their ineffectual fumblings belied the dramatic reality of what it meant to be illicit lovers. One imagined heat and grinding snakiness, oily bodies writhing in pleasure. But instead they were an uncomfortable, poor attempt at competence. Why they constantly gravitated towards each other's bodies, each would never know. Ian was solid. His body never fully relaxed into her. Meera was a mixture of shy and angry, a heady mix of distance. But it worked. It always worked. It was never about the sex.

Their affair sustained itself by its ugliness, its silliness, its still moments where no words needed to be exchanged. Meera never touched him. She would undress and lie supine on the pure white sheets, looking out of the window, waiting for his first touch, one that was always on her inner thigh, prising the thighs open with a sharp shove. It always happened that way.

A touch on an inner thigh, a kiss or two on the neck, and the beginning of a jerky dance. He always felt like a pathetic lover. He wondered if she faked her silent heaving orgasms. He was sure she did. She knew she didn't.

And the air turned sour because she refused to open a window, refused to blow the oily smell of sex into an Irish landscape. She would lie on her side like a prawn, curled up into the deepest part of the ocean, feeding her soul on dirt and dead bodies, a stagnant, invasive seeping. He tried to touch her shoulder blade, and she recoiled as if being scratched by reptilian claws. She slowly filled up with a wide gaping hole. A hole that was neither satiation nor frustration.

A hole that told Meera that death was not the man stretched out beside her. Death was the aching need inside her. A need to stop being trapped on an island of self-hatred and disbelief – that this was what her shredded life had come down to. She knew she was incapable of affection. She knew her inertia. Her bubbling rage had rendered her incapable of motion, like a pendulum that had swung too many times in too many directions. She was lucky. Ian did not crave anything more than her body. She wondered what she would have done if he had craved more. Perhaps she would have killed him.

Perhaps she would have caught him at his game, trying a hand at pretence, of love and all things sweet and exciting. Little gestures, little touches of the hand, large garish bunches of flowers. Wasn't that how they did it in the movies? Pretentious love affairs, Valentine kisses and bridges of sighs? But she knew instinctively that she couldn't and Ian wouldn't and that was how it was supposed to be. Catching each other like insects at every available chance, insects in nets. One day he was the catcher. One day she. And the days would pass in the dance.

25

Stolen Watch

IT WAS THE NIGHT THAT SHE STOLE IAN'S WATCH THAT she knew she was beyond redemption. She was too far gone, dredged in him. Obsessed. He had arrived at her house on a rainy Sunday afternoon, not caring about the others who were there. Phil, Pedro, Belinda, all just looked and then looked the other way, then blatantly stared again as he stood, shuffling his feet in the hallway, waiting patiently for Meera to sip her tea, regarding his soaked body from beneath her half-closed eyelashes.

He ignored their stares as he pulled her up the stairs to her bedroom, a mad look in his eyes. His look held a wildness, yet somewhere lingered a veil of weariness that could never be lifted. A look that craved a creation that only Meera could conjure up, which needed only his silent nodding consent to take shape and form.

He had appeared. He had come to her, but it was she who held the wand that would allow the symphony orchestra to play. He seemed, with his drugged, tired eyes, utterly captivated by her, and she spurred him on to deliver the considerable gift of this new presence. Meera ignored the shocked stares, the whispers. She had seen the look in his eyes as she had opened the door to him standing there in the hard rain, and she knew he needed her. The power was hers now. She fed him with crooning, she fed him a warm embrace, and she fed off him, murmuring to him as they entered her bedroom that they were soul mates.

He smelt of the rain, clear and fresh, his head dripping raindrops on her white comforter. She had followed him up the stairs like a faithful dog, like a daughter, but a petulant daughter who knows her bitten bottom lip has got her her way with a once-distant father. And when the door was shut, he sat on the bed and she stood before him, holding his damp head in her hands to her stomach. Tightly protected. Rediscovering him. So much more intense than discovering him in the first place. Better than getting to know him in smelly garages and stuffy buses, where his gaze always strayed to the beeping in the corner.

She forgot everything now, wanting to intoxicate herself with this new development. Ian at her door. In the middle of the afternoon. In broad daylight. But like anyone who tries to drink oneself into oblivion, no matter how much you soak yourself in your chosen intoxicant there is always something lurking at the back of your drunk brain. Lingering in the recesses. That son.

'I'm tired,' he said and she watched his lanky body slacken. She knew exactly what he was saying. She kissed the top of his wet head and breathed warmth into his body.

'I want you to touch me, Ian,' Meera whispered into his ear.

'Don't talk, Meera, all I want is your silence. Your stillness. I love you for your silence,' he said, and he began to scrape away his clothing, his shoes, his socks, until he lay exhaustedly in his pale-grey boxers on the bed. She pulled the comforter down, urging him with her body into its waiting cocoon.

'Sleep,' he said. 'Sleep with me.'

'Touch me Ian,' she whispered again.

'Sleep,' he replied.

Almost as soon as he had said it, his body began to relax into sleep, and she watched him curl onto his side. She wondered what demons he had been battling that day for him to come to her door, to her bed, in this state, demanding no words, just sleep.

The word 'love', with its deeply coveted resonance, wrapped around her body in the places she wanted to be touched. Love. He loved her. And she was soft and tender and convinced that love would never leave her, now that the word had found its way to her.

She pulled the comforter over him and his beautiful glistening naked torso disappeared into a fluffy pile of white and blue cotton. His hands lay splayed forwards, the palms together as if in prayer, and she noticed he hadn't removed his watch.

She slowly undid the clasp of his watch, an old-fashioned one on a leather strap, and left it on her nightstand. Twilight approached quickly. The light from the street came into the room like a thin silver sword, and, with that light, she watched over him sleeping. And she fell in love. Deeply.

She lay beside him, but every cell within her flew to all parts of the universe saying the word, saying the word. The afternoon rain had loosened his tongue, had opened his heart, had spoken the truth. She thought of the old Indian myth that tells of the power of the monsoon rain, the Sawan season, the season where lovers spill over and cannot hold back their affections any longer. On rain-soaked streets, shy lovers come out to dance in wet saris, with drenched heads, using the powerful excuse of the rain to display their love, to out themselves. The rain had untied Ian's heart. It had broken his chains and bonds. And as time ticked slowly on his watch on the nightstand, the rain fell harder and harder outside the window of a tiny house where a faint night light, left on, burnt through the hint of moonlight.

Quietly she traced a line from his earlobe to his chin, stubbly now with the day's workings. And then a tiny feather-light line down the sinews of his throat. She lightly touched his Adam's apple, wanting so desperately to place her mouth there in a kiss.

But that would wake him, and she loved him too deeply in his cavernous slumbering to wake him up. If she woke him, he would leave.

His sandy hair, longer than average, curled under her fingertips as she leant over and took an entire lock into her mouth. She couldn't help herself. He stirred ever so slightly but remained in an easy sleep. She lay down next to him and watched the rise and fall of his chest, the soft dip between his collarbones, the line of fine hair pointing downwards to his navel, the hip bone, barely visible under the comforter. There, but not really there, his lean body inviting a kiss. She dared not wake him. If she woke him, he would leave. And he would never be hers like this again … innocent, desperate, helpless. She smelt his closed eyes, breathing them in, breathing in all that they had seen that day. Taking the goblins away.

He slept so beautifully. She lay next to him in the semi-dark watching his every movement, enjoying him as she had never enjoyed him before. There were times when his breaths were deep and even; as he lay on his back she watched the steady beat of his heart through his thin ribcage. Then suddenly something would catch him in his sleep, and he would begin to fight demons, his eyes flickering, almost opening wide and staring at unknown monsters. He would claw the air, twist the sheet between his fingers, roll his head from side to side. Meera would slowly and with a flat palm call him back to a restful state, rubbing his body in calm, steady movements, crooning, although she didn't even know she was doing so.

Sometime in the middle of the night he had almost woken,

and called out for her, mumbling as he buried his face into her wild hair, as they both lay on their sides like spoons. She was careful and gentle not to wake him as she eased herself up on one elbow, to watch him as he slept, knowing she would never again see him with such vulnerability.

He always retained such composure when he was around her, his mind flashing in a myriad directions, never able to settle. A deep thinker, always darting to different scenarios and situations, people, places, things. He seemed like a bird trapped in a cage, flapping its wild wings at the air in a futile dance. She had been disturbed by his restless energy, been envious of the things that took space in his mind, knowing gravely that those things more often than not did not include her, but included his guilt. She knew he felt the guilt intensely, but still did nothing to hide their affair from the prying eyes of the child.

This was his passive-aggressive dance with the cards he had been dealt in this life. Their affair had started out being all about sex – the blatant carnal attraction between two people. But what the two people had failed to realise was that it never really was lust after all. It was refuge. They had been thrown together like two refugees after a war, and kept coming back to each other like magnets because their internal compasses always pointed at each other. They had survived wars, they had braved typhoons. They had lived through thunder, pain and starvation. And that was why they were drawn to each other. Sex was just ancillary. Meera knew this long before Ian.

Ian fought it. He kept telling himself it was just sex, just physical pleasure that he craved from Meera's body. But things were changing inside his mind. And today, today was different. She could tell. Today, he needed her. Not for sex. But for comfort. And she revelled in all that it meant. His arrival at her door signalled another dimension in their togetherness. Meera smiled. The time was coming. Soon, she smiled. Soon.

She passed the night not sleeping at all. She spent it in glorious time lying next to him as he slept. His deep, peaceful breaths, his turning from side onto back with arms thrown up over his head, the movements of his legs – everything he did was perfect.

She luxuriated in the smell of him, she sniffed at his skin that smelt like rainwater. In the crook of his elbow, in the creases of his wrists, his lips, his eyes, his armpits, she sniffed and drank him. She stroked his shoulder muscles, not strong and powerful but almost frail, sloped, and traced a line invisibly from his shoulders to the tips of his long, ladylike fingers. His bus-driving hands, curled into a loose fist as he slept. He was perfect. Perfect.

In the early hours of the morning, he awoke, with a start, finding her next to him, lying with a protective arm thrown across him. He awoke as if some dangerous creature had chased him from one world into another. A realisation of where he was, who he was with.

Meera.

She was fully dressed but lying next to him. She hadn't bothered to undress. He sat up in fright, and as she jolted awake with him, the man who had come to her last night was gone. In his place was a man who frantically began throwing clothes together, jeans, shirt, socks, shoes … no watch.

Somewhere in the middle of the night as she'd listened to his even breathing, coupled with the sounds from the street outside, she had taken his watch, smelling its metal and leather, running a tongue along the strap, running the face of it along her neck. And she had simply stolen it. She had wrapped it in a scarf and put it into a drawer, to be saved for later, where she would spend her time in its presence, knowing it had once belonged to him. And now it belonged to her. Just as he did too.

He gushed about, mumbling things to her about needing to get back, about his son – but never about his wife. She sat on the bed, not moving at all as he rapidly dressed.

Have to get back home. Stewie … worry … all alone … Stewie were all the words she caught. Even though the son was probably with his mother in their little house, Ian was wildly convinced the child was alone. Abandoned.

Inert, she sat with her legs folded under her, not fearing at all that he was leaving her.

He would never leave her. He had said he loved her. He had said it, and now he was hers, forever. Forever. Soon he would realise it. And life would be perfect.

She almost succumbed to the desperate temptation of begging him not to leave her like that. The lover's song: Please, I need you. Please stay with me. Please.

But she sat quietly. The kind of quietly that he loved. She would not push him away now, by grasping him like a vine. When the moment was right, he would come to her again. And she would possess him forever. Now was the time for silence.

After he had gone, and the dawn was drawing in, she took out his watch from its silky indigo home and held it like a newborn baby in her arms. She sniffed again at its leathery metallic scent, and she felt as if she had returned home. She rubbed the watch between her thumb and fingertips, she kissed it openly on its face, held it up to the emerging daylight and watched its face glow and smile at her. Its tickings became a song. A song she would sing for him from now on. You love me. You are mine.

26

Only the Next Day

THAT MORNING, AFTER DAYS OF SHEETS OF DOWNPOURS, a spring day seemed to have burst forth, flirtatiously toying with the breezes that blew in from Dublin Bay. The flood of light invaded everything from dawn, as Meera threw her body into the day, elated. The beams of early sunlight invited her on an early-morning walk. Although sleepless, restless, she felt peaceful, as peaceful as the pigeons who feasted on crumbs on St Stephen's Green. Meera had been too deliriously happy to go to work. She would go later.

A tall, well-built man also stood regarding the pigeons, and Meera and the man looked at each other as though they had stolen something together. His bright, happy face told of a night that he too had passed, one that perhaps he had been praying for.

'Brian McDermot, at your service,' the man laughed, and Meera laughed with him as she introduced herself.

He wore a brown corduroy jacket and Meera recalled owning a jacket like that, somewhere in the mess of her suitcase which had never really got unpacked. She lived off the strewn clothes within.

'You're very happy today,' he remarked. It was a straightforward remark. It required no reply. And Meera felt glad, for she had no words to say how true his statement was.

'So are you,' she eventually mumbled, and they both laughed into the new sunshine. So pleasant to hear the voice of a stranger, a happy companion who also needed no room for platitudes and dissections.

They stood near each other, looking at the pigeons under the cherry-blossom trees for a few minutes longer. It seemed too sudden to walk away, when all she wanted to do was walk. Walk and cocoon herself in remembering every single moment of last night with the sleeping Ian by her side.

Love.

A singing word. A singing heart. For the first time. Ever.

She felt like a heroine in an old novel, skipping in a gay dress to the bus, heading off to work, where she no doubt would still infuse the day with the joy of it all. So much had changed.

Love.

Coming in late to work, at the Manor House, Meera passed the School, not looking but looking for the click-click boy. She felt strangely that, if she saw his face, she was seeing Ian's. He was not at school. She didn't find it strange. Maybe a sick day. But passing the respite home where parents left their children for a few nights of rest, she saw Stewie sitting on the cold grass, his knees folded under him making the letter z. She wondered fleetingly why he was sitting there alone.

Perhaps wandered in through an open gate that the ancient guard had forgotten to lock? As she passed, Stewie looked up at her, and for one small moment her heart lurched. He seemed to have seen her. She lied to herself that his father had mystically communicated his love for her to this beautiful unspeaking child. And again her joy knew no bounds. She felt the need to talk. To tell someone. Anyone. She was in Love. For the First Time Ever.

She grabbed her cellphone from her pocket, pulling out sweet wrappers and stray hairs and fluff. As she blew the dirt away from the screen, she knew who she wanted to call.

Love.

Meera braved the clicks, the cost of an overseas cellphone call to a home with a courtyard where weevils coveted dhal drying on old tin pot lids and little girls lined the shelves waiting their turn. Times had changed. They went to secretarial college now, she heard. They were allowed brief forays into hairdressing schools and beauty academies.

On a morning like every other, her fingers dialled the numbers, and her mother's voice was manic, frantic, cold. Thick with sleep.

'Mummy,' was all she said. And the silence at the other end was frightening.

'Meera,' her mother whispered.

'Mummy, Mummy. He loves me. I am in love. Mummy. He loves me.'

The line was ominously silent again. And then her mother cleared her throat. And spoke. 'Come back. They will take you back. That man, his family. If you beg, if you plead, confess you were wrong, they will take you back.'

Meera felt a world drop into heartbreak. 'But, Mummy …' was all she could croak into the distant line.

'Go back to your husband, Meera. That is your family now. They will take you back. We will arrange it.' Her mother's voice became hurried and manic.

And her mother's mania became her mania. She felt a loss of control. The control that had kept the voices of white women safely hidden in their homes, and away from the whitewashed walls and ovens of her mind, began to crack.

She felt Susan's breath on her neck even before she heard the South African accent. Even before she saw the flash of a flowery summer dress in an Irish April.

She pressed a bitten thumb nail into a button that cut the long-distance call. Bitterness, anger, grief, rage bubbled upwards to chase the spring away.

'What now, doll? What you going to do, huh?' Susan laughed and glared into her face, blowing smoke rings into her welling-up eyes.

Meera threw the phone at Susan's face. And fresh air laughed.

'What now, doll? What now?'

Ian.

For the first time in her affair with Ian, she called his number. There were no clicks. He answered on the third ring; she knew he was driving. Driving and talking all his rubbish talk about the Rock of Cashel, about the Blarney Stone.

She screamed his name into the phone. Why? He was all she had to turn to.

Ian.

They will take me back. They will torture me.

'I'm on an overnight to Galway, Meera,' was all he said. Cold. He had not added 'with Teresa'.

He hadn't needed to add that name. Meera had heard a loud laugh in the background, a powerful Canary laugh.

'Thought we'd get away. We need to get away,' Ian began to explain, knowing Meera had heard the laugh.

And he cut the call. That easy. That easy for him. Dog! Monster! Horrid Dog!

Meera felt a shudder reverberate off the walls. She stood in the courtyard of the dusty old manor house and heard the howling of little Padraig Douglas, the oldest autistic in the world. Fifty. He howled in his masturbation. She looked at the greying sky, and imagined a smiling Spanish señora clap her hands in glee. She closed her eyes and, in time to Padraig's howls, she screamed howls and howls of her own.

'What now, dollface?'

Fuck you, Susan. Leave me alone. Go away!

Padraig screamed. Meera howled. Susan laughed. And a million little pixel dots appeared in front of her eyes. Hedgehog-shaped pixel dots. Deleted dots. Deleted dots on black screens. In her howls, she foamed at the mouth. No one cared. No one heard the outside-ly howls. This place was saturated with howls of despair.

She dialled his number again. He didn't answer. And again, and again, and again. A feral, senseless woman punching the dial button on a cellphone repeatedly. And repeatedly being rejected.

And then a text message: 'We must end it. It is over. I won't leave her. I have to think of my son.'

That was all. That was all he had said to her. In her greatest moment of need and desperation – *we must end it*. End it all. She filled up with rage, an anger bubbling and boiling inside her, the knots in her stomach gnarled into a movement, a killing, hating type of movement. Destroy him! He has destroyed me.

How?

'Where's the son, then?' Susan whispered in her ear. It became a song. 'Where's Stewiestewiestewieee … Stew? Find him.'

Meera ran towards Padraig's howls. She shoved wheelchair-bound people aside. Children in swing sets stared at her flight. Stewie Stew. Stewie Stewie Stewie Stew.

She found the door. It was not locked. The respite care quarters. She should have known. That ancient guard fallen asleep on a chair with a wide-open gate swinging back and forth in a wind that had picked up. Rusty, swinging metal sounds. Howls. Pleasure.

Now she knew why Stewie was on the respite home's lawn. They had left little click-click child for an overnight stay in the respite care and gone on a honeymoon adventure to Galway. Teresa laughed and laughed, Padraig howled with self-pleasure.

She found tiny boy Stewie with his handheld game staring into a closed doorway. He stared with his amber eyes at the locked door that housed the masturbating Padraig, looking in interest, looking but not really seeing or understanding the pain and the pleasure on the other side of the doorway.

Meera heard his breath quicken with each new howl. She hated him. She heard a peal of laughter and a Canarian turn of phrase, and at the top of Stewie's head she saw Susan's face appear like an apparition, saying things. Saying things …

'What now, dollface? Doll Face. Doll Face …'

The words echoed in the hard places. In the skull of her. In the bones and the heart of her. In the gall bladder of her. And the anger razed all rationality to the ground.

The boy.

'Punish him,' Susan told her. 'Punish him.'

Meera heard the crescendo of Padraig's pleasure reach its slow-climbing climax. It would be a while yet. Padraig took his pleasure seriously.

Punish him. He belongs to her. He is the reason you have lost your love.

Punish him. Ian.

She felt the boy's ribcage move in time to Padraig's howls. With the keys assigned only to her capable hands, she unlocked the door to Padraig's room. His permanent home in the respite quarters. Nobody had come to claim him, to take him home. So he had stayed on in that room, and now he was fifty. Autistic and fifty.

She looked in the doorway and saw Padraig huddled on

his side, his hands pumping vigorously, and she watched Stewie staring, his little hands pumping more vigorously at the video game.

She recalled a day many months ago when a school psychologist had instructed everyone who worked with Stewart Buckley to give him the game. To stop him from clicking his fingers next to his ears. Replace one obsession with another. Perseveration. He couldn't live without it.

Meera looked around. Frantic with the sounds of Spanish moans and Padraig's groans, she found Susan smoking a cigarette in a corner of the empty hallway.

Punish him.

She swung open the door. Padraig stopped his pumping, his large bulk turned, and his wide-open erection weaved dangerously and unabashedly towards her.

Stewie looked up and caught his breath. His eyes. His amber mother Teresa eyes. Meera hated those eyes. Hated enough to Kill. Over the edge of the world she tumbled, seeing free-falling spices, golden arms and white sheets, and Love on its way out the door. Hate annihilated its way through her. The clicky boy stood near her. Into his Teresa eyes she glared, and the gall of rejection rose up in her throat. The laughing Canary mother and the newly reformed Sparrow Father.

'What now, dollface?' Smoke rang in her ears.

What now?

And Meera grabbed his hedgehog lifeline. She threw it into Padraig's room, knowing the beeping and whizzing sounds would drive Padraig to absolute lunacy. She grabbed the tiny shoulders of the little click-click boy and pushed him into the room, shutting the door. Alone with a raging tumescent Padraig, little boy went. Door locked in his shocked face.

Leaning against the door frame, she breathed rapidly. She heard two sounds. Padraig's new screams, and Susan's humming. Susan smoked. Susan smiled. And with the combined screams of a little boy and a wild fifty-year-old lunatic, the people came running to find Meera slumped in the doorway, staring at a corner of the passage. No one could see Susan sitting there in that corner, legs splayed out before her sluttishly in her summer dress.

The keys dangled in the lock. The South African key chain an obvious tell.

They pulled Stewart away from Padraig. Clicky Stewart not clicking his fingers a thousand times next to his ears, saying nothing, only gutturally grunting loudly. Breathing raspily. Dear Padraig had included the frail bird-bones of the boy in his self-pleasure. Wild. Mad. Out-of-control Padraig. The shhhh and the whisper Padraig. The hunchback-hidden-in-the-closet Padraig.

Never, I say Never. Go Into His Room. They had warned everyone. He only tolerated the presence of a large guard called Vincent. He grew violent, violent and scary, if anyone else entered his room. Violent. Especially in his pleasure pain. He had grabbed the clicking angel and flung him like a ragdoll against the walls. Once, twice, maybe ten times.

Until the sound of the hedgehog in the boy's hand had died with a wheezing sound. Howls. No more clicks. Stewart was dead, his tiny body flung too many times against a hard wall, shattering his ribcage, piercing his heart. His fragile bird-bones broken in too many places to keep him alive.

'What have you done?'

A million questions.

Meera answered no one. She fell to the ground, and reached out for Susan's hand.

'Meera, what have you done?'
'Nothing.'
'He stole my keys.'
Lies.

Durban

27

Purple Fanta Grape, Purple Methylated Spirits

THE BARE DARK QUARTERS OF THE ROOM BOAST WEBS the size of dinner plates. The upper cornices string unhappy spiders with a penchant for baby cockroaches into an arachnid Circ du Soleil. The floor is all that is beautiful. Someone, somewhere – the owner of the house, at one time sober perhaps – chose a tile that looks like the tiles that line the inside of a temple. Marble-like. Marbled with sienna-yellow lines and light-grey shadows. A temple floor. An ugly room.

The walls are plastered, not painted. Yet. The owner of the house is too drunk to choose colours. He sleeps in the room next door to the only other room, the one he rents out to nurses. Him, his old wife Basanti and their four grown children, all asleep on sponge mattresses on the floor. Three older thick-plaited girls with flirty eyes, and a teenage boy they call Anthony. A quiet, deep-gazed young lover boy with a smile that is shy but provocative. Meera feels she is in love with sixteen-year-old Anthony. She feels she could fall asleep next to Anthony some day.

A hot January day in the throes of a Durban humid seizure. She feels she could kiss the sweat drop that appears on Anthony's slumbering foetal Adam's apple. She knows that will never happen.

Meera hears the old man rattle bottles. She hears him swear when the rattles reveal emptiness. Dhanraj. His name. He used to be a postman. And the government had bestowed his letter-carrying sack along with a house with a minor subsidised bond in a low-cost housing project filled with unfinished semi-detached homes in Unit Five in Phoenix.

Dhanraj had to pay very little for his place in the world. The government loved Indian people in those days. The days when the government was white and the flag was orange, white, blue. When Indian people were given privileges. When black people were given sickles, spades and concrete hatred. Hatred that was simmering yet singing freedom songs out in the open. Baying for blood. Baying for the right to identity in a country they knew was their soil. But amid their marches, the tear gas and the pyres of tyres, they still had to eat. They still had to work. They worked. For the Indian man. For the White Man.

Dhanraj is a bushy-eyebrowed retired letter-bearing Indian man. A businessman inside his heart. He uses the subsidised house to its maximum capacity. He uses the overgrown garden as a tuck shop.

Here he places Thandi, a thin unhappy girl in her twenties, to sell sweets, paraffin in rose-water bottles, sanitary pads, shaving blades, purple methylated spirits that glitter in the sun. Glue.

Methylated spirits that are used to clean mirrors in rich people's houses. Or to be drunk up by the beggar street children from the bushes near High Chaparral, known to all as the Unit, where you can buy any drug you desire. Even methylated spirits. But there at High Chaparral the spirit is too costly. The torn-clothed street boys walk to Dhanraj's tuck-shop table to buy bottles of it for a fraction of the cost. Methylated spirits and glue. For it is known that drinking methylated spirits and sniffing glue fumes from a paper bag quells hunger for days.

And a bottle of purple-blue foul-tasting spirit or a can of industrial-strength glue is cheaper than a loaf of bread. Bread lasts a day. Glue lasts days. Methylated spirits lasts many more days. Your stomach thinks it's full, your brain thinks it's happy. Fair trade.

Dhanraj has priced it cheaper than cheap. Undercutting the dealers at Chaparral by almost three-quarters of the price. His bony customers come. Glazed and retching, these dirty, dusty boys come like hyenas to hand over their five cents with shivering hands, and receive purple heaven in return. Later, only a year perhaps, and these same boys lie dying on the streets, they can't feel their feet, their legs have given up. Or perhaps if they're lucky they make it to the hospital down the road.

Their insides burnt, they vomit thick black blood before they die, and no one knows, no one cares. Dhanraj knows. Dhanraj doesn't care. He gruffly instructs Thandi to keep decanting the purple fluid from the large wholesale bottle he buys at the Muslim-owned wholesalers into the tiny little nip bottles he collects from the dustbins outside the horse-racing tavern down in Unit Two.

Thandi fills. She closes her eyes to stop the burn and fills the bottles through a funnel made from an empty soft-drink bottle cut in half, placed upside down, its lip fitting improperly into the tiny openings of the receiving vessels. Spirit dribbles down the sides and Dhanraj swears at Thandi for every drop she wastes.

Blind, behind shut eyes, looking into the darkness and the eye worms but smelling the deep alcohol poison smell that only methylated spirits can give off, she fills precisely each and every bottle. And each and every bottle gets sold. Every day. For five cents apiece. A slice of brown bread costs more.

Daily over the makeshift counter, Thandi sighs and picks at the one nail she keeps long and pointed. The one on her right hand, the Peter Pointer. Long and sharp so she can scratch regularly at the scalp, where there are tight braids on her head. Her natural hair pulled and bonded with a sewing needle and black cotton to fake synthetic braids that Thandi thinks look so pretty. But her price for prettiness is a constant headache from the heaviness of the thick braids as they traction her natural hair all the way down to the follicles. And scratch she must. Often. For it itches like hell.

She occasionally straightens the pile of Always Ultra Sanitary Pads with Wings, as the pile keeps falling over. She scratches her head, and with a thumbnail flicks the dry scales from underneath the long nail onto her lap. She steals sweets called 'black balls'. The round hard boiled ones that leave telltale signs of your thievery on your tongue, inside your cheeks. Signs that linger for two days. Black-ball signs that usher in two fat slaps from Dhanraj.

'Chor! Thief! Stealing sweets! I'll show you what your stealing will give you.'

The black-ball-stained inner cheeks smart on the outside, almost red from the slaps. Thandi never stops. She steals the liquorice-tasting black balls again. And again. And soon Dhanraj grows tired of slapping Thandi. He simply pokes her legs with his stick instead and they have reached an agreement. She can eat black balls and he can look the other way. Thandi wins the Black Ball War!

Her boyfriend Gottlieb comes to visit the tuck shop three times a day. He works at the construction site two streets away. The wasteland the government is converting into blocks of one-room flats for pensioners. Six storeys of holes that they will fill with seventy- and eighty-year-olds who cannot climb stairs. Indian pensioners.

Each time Gottlieb comes, he leans on the rickety table and the stacks of sanitary pads fall over. Thandi never touches them in his presence. He buys Zam-Buk lip balm and a can of warm Fanta Grape. Dhanraj hasn't even bothered with a cooler box filled with ice. You take what he gives you. You give him coins. He gives you nothing much.

Gottlieb never pays cash. He never hands Thandi money. On credit, Gottlieb simply grabs the can of Fanta Grape. He feels he is owed that warm sugary can. Dhanraj owes him that much.

Thandi reluctantly enters his lengthening credit record in a book Dhanraj has given her. A tiny black hard-covered book he stole from his son's school bag. Back when his son bothered to go to school. The book bears a teenage boy's scrawl on the inner cover: 'This book belongs to Anthony and whoever steals it will be punished by Anthony. This book is written by Anthony. By order … Anthony.'

The first few pages have drawings done in teenage boy's Bic blue of women's breasts with exaggerated nipples, and rude-looking symbols that look like sex, but can never be sex, for Anthony is a virgin and does not know what goes where and how. He imagines sex in his dreams and draws pictures of it in books, in sand, carved into tree trunks. A long phallic obelisk placed deep inside a wavy-edged oval with a few droplets of satiation dripping off the end of the long obelisk.

A phallic obelisk with a head at one end that looks like the top of a rich man's cane. The wavy, feminine oval is never quite right-looking. It is always too small. The obelisk and its rich one-eyed dripping head dominate too much of the sketch. It displaces the wavy oval and takes over the page. One day Anthony will learn what goes where, and Anthony will learn what size is what, and who dominates whom. His battering ram of somethingess, almost menacing towards and inside a wavy folded-looking hibiscus flower, will learn its dimensions in the real world. One day, Anthony, one day.

Anthony still thinks about his mother's youngest sister, Tina Mosie, coming to stay after her husband Rishi ran off with a coloured woman. An ugly, crass, pockmarked coloured woman with orangey-red hennaed hair and gold slits in crooked teeth.

Tina Mosie often wonders what the attraction was. She imagines the reason was because maybe the coloured woman allowed herself to suck Rishi's dick. Tina never did that. Never.

Anthony finds Tina Mosie one morning after breakfast near the washing lines, chewing at a sweet end of a grass blade and humming the tunes of the latest Rajesh Khanna movie. She offers to teach him how to French-kiss behind the washing tap. Where no one can see them. She whispers like lace into his ears about tongues and cheeks. Tempted beyond redemption, Anthony follows Tina Mosie to the dark cement crevasse behind the outside washing tap. He pouts his thin moustache towards his aunt's fat lips and she comes close enough for him to smell the toast and tea on her breath.

And with Anthony's lips waiting desperately, Tina Mosie almost touches those lips and then she laughs at him and swings away. Throatily laughing, she wiggles her bottom towards him, a bottom clad in too-tight green stovepipe pants, and then she says: 'You dirty boy! Gandhe, Chee! Chee! Trying to kiss your own aunty. Filthy …'

And Anthony stood uncomfortably next to the damp drain, with his arms placed over his crotch, and burnt with hatred. For women. For Tina Mosie. For drunkenness and for hiding under home-made coverlets called 'gudris', till his father fell over soaked in alcohol. And Anthony loped away, back into the house where he stood at intervals next to the telephone.

That telephone – a black frog that sat on a crocheted doily next to a light pink ceramic horse in mid lurch – had become Dhanraj's next source of income. Drunk and reeling, Dhanraj had dreamed up the idea of offering the use of his speaking-listening toy to the public. People would come at all hours to pay fifty cents a minute to use the telephone. Black people. They came. They didn't own telephones. They needed to call far-off places like post offices and general dealers in Bizana and Sigeni, many kilometres from their homesteads.

Somehow arrangements would be made for a mother, an aunt, an uncle (never a father) to be waiting at the telephone at the post office or general dealer for the rare call from their money-food-shelter provider in the Big City, Durban.

Anthony would sit on a stool next to the ugly black frog and keep time with his mother's plastic bedside alarm clock, and then ask for payment after the call ended. He would wait for the receiver to be put down before he would enter into yet another stolen school book the speaker's name and duration of the call. And with his crunchy breaking teenage-boy voice he would ask for the payment that was due. The transaction having been made, Anthony would always feel slightly guilty as the speaker – bearer of good news and bad – shook his head and unwrapped coins from a stained handkerchief or a silky-soft overused telephone-directory page, and handed over what seemed like a small fortune for a large conversation.

Anthony tried not to listen to the one-sided words. He

failed. Talking into a telephone, people who were unaccustomed to doing so shouted loudly into the mouthpiece mundane pieces of information about ancestral dreams, cow-slaughtering ceremonies, mud huts that had been washed away, people who had died and babies that had been born. The shouting echoed off the unplastered walls of the house, competing with the sounds of Basanti assaulting the tin pots in her passive-aggressive rage against her drunk husband, and the scratchy transistor radio on which Anthony's sisters listened to the latest pop songs. Inside Anthony's head, Kylie Minogue, tin-pot concertos and flood-eaten mud huts all became one large orchestra that played on and on, even in his sleep.

Of course, the more secretive and sultry and whispered conversations invaded Anthony's dreams more deeply. For the borrowed telephone also became the place where illicit lovers planned their moves. Anthony knew the cheaters when they entered the door and pointed to the telephone. It was a small community. And Dhanraj knew how to keep secrets. Keep the secrets his drunkenness could contain, as quiet as the night, until he could use those secrets. For money. Money to buy alcohol. Money he stashed away from Basanti, forcing her to find work in a factory where they sewed bras and panties for pennies. Forcing baby Anthony out of school so he could walk the length and breadth of the streets, looking for day jobs. To put food on the table.

There was no good enough reason why the uncle from house number 322 would slink into the house towards the telephone on his lunch break from the hospital to moan and giggle at the listener on the other end of the line. Or why Sheila would come at ten in the morning wringing her hands on her old housecoat to hastily whisper a call to an eager recipient, leaving out of pocket but with a glow in her face and anticipation in her eyes.

Anthony sat on his stool, fondling his mother's alarm clock, and melded all the conversations between lovers into one great, deep conversation with a lover he didn't have. He was the one meeting a woman at the farthest corner of Woodview Park after work. He was the one jumping the fence and slinking into the slightly open kitchen door of a house in Unit Two. He was the one buying the taxi ticket to Verulam to meet and eat fried bhajias behind the tailor's shop before kissing with oily breath.

But all Anthony was was a keeper of time and of a bottomless pit of stories that he would never tell. And all Anthony got for policing the big black thing connected to the peeling wall was a cuff on his ear and a whack on the back of his head from his father when he handed the tin Pall Mall cigarette box filled with coins to him every night at nine.

'Finish your Matric, you useless bastard,' Dhanraj would say through drunken fumes. And Anthony wondered when, in all his conversation-collecting days, he would have the moments to finish that Matric. Never, Anthony, never. He would one day, in his twenties, end up getting a job as a waiter at one of the top-end 'White People' hotels on the beachfront. He would one day marry the girl from a few doors down the street and he would give her a beautiful son. But he would never one day finish his Matric. And by those days cellular phones would have arrived. On the day Anthony earned his first real working-man's wages – money he hid from his mother's waiting hands, lying to her about being mugged in Broad Street at the taxi rank – he used those waiter wages to buy a cellphone. His very own phone. Not a frog. But a prince now.

Gottlieb arrives at the tuck-shop table. He leans lazily on the table. He never speaks much to Thandi. He indicates with his clear brown eyes the items he wants. The items Thandi must scrawl into Anthony's breast-sex-emblazoned black book. The items Gottlieb will never ever pay for. Yet the list lengthens. What he owes to the drunk old Dhanraj grows into pages and pages.

Dhanraj lurks like a curmudgeon, shuffling towelling slippers into long grass to go and poke Gottlieb in the ribs with a long syringa-berry stick, stripped of leaves, stinking as only syringa berry can stink.

Time to go Blackie. He chases Gottlieb away. But Gottlieb keeps coming back. For his Fanta Grape, for his stolen 'inchie' – a piece of cigarette that Dhanraj has not completely smoked, and has thrown onto the overgrown lawn. Gottlieb knows the spot. Under the azalea bush that never flowers. He swishes his black fingers through hundreds of cigarette stubs, searching for the one Dhanraj has not finished. Maybe he can pull at least one drag from that filth.

He swigs on his loaned Fanta Grape and saunters away towards the building site where his beloved is a wheelbarrow. He is a carrier of broken bricks. He is a sorter of broken bricks. It is back-breaking work. He knows somewhere inside his head there is a child in Thandi.

He tells this secret to Vuyo, his partner in broken bricks. Vuyo tells him his son will be a born-free.

'What is this born-free, born-free you talk and talk about?' Gottlieb grunts impatiently in between brick sorting.

Vuyo, fifty and looking sixty, sorts bricks into completely broken, partly broken, and potentially breakable. He looks deep into the bush of the metropolis they are building. Homes for the Indian people. Phoenix.

He tells Gottlieb many things as rough black hands look for bricks that can never break. The world has gone mad, Vuyo tells him. Two years ago, the country and the world bayed for prison gates to open. Big, important pop stars sang songs about it. They released Mandela. They set him free. And now, says Vuyo, it is Freedom. One Man. One Vote.

But the people are still angry. They cry on the streets for what is rightfully theirs, what was stolen from them decades ago. Unrest between parties spreads into the townships. Vuyo tells Gottlieb not to worry, the Old Man will see everything right. In time.

Gottlieb thinks nothing of this news. He has never joined the marches or the stonings or the fists pumping green-gold-black air. He believes an old man is old. He must sit in peace. Anyway, he has sat in prison too long to know the real state of the angry country.

While the Grandfather Mandela had spent his days pruning trees and eating stale bread, a woman, his wife, had been stirring the pot.

And now, even though he is a free man, and everyone in the land is free, the world has indeed gone mad.

A woman who was once as beautiful as the moon now bears drawn, angry eyes and a black-green-gold headscarf. She whinnies to the people who gather in droves around her. She tells them to fight. To burn. To break. And to kill. An old man who had spent years reading books in a prison library cannot know of the young man's pain. Of the hatred between Zulus and Xhosas, of the bloodshed as they fight each other. The White Man is gone. But power is still contested with blood and pain.

Gottlieb knows. He knows of pain. And starvation. He listens to the woman in the headscarf. But no woman, no matter how beautiful, no matter how tortured, can tell a man how to run his country. Gottlieb believes another man will bring his unborn child its freedom. The man whose flag bears a sickle.

Non-violence does not appeal to Gottlieb. He knows the power of sweat mingled with blood. He used to be a miner.

He used to hawk and spit black tar out of his lungs when he emerged from pits digging and singing for platinum. He used to wrap his hands with old stolen T-shirts because they were too raw to do another day's digging. But he dug. And he dug. And he never knew what he was digging for. And he never knew its worth to the big White Man in the Glass Sky. A White Man who has been ousted from power but who still holds the purse strings.

And now he sorts bricks. And now he swears at the Indian man, not the White Man. The Indian man took his land. The Indian man gets food, clothes, car, job, school, cinema, road, music, trees, job job job. Job with pen. Job with book. Job with shirt collar. Job with no raw bleeding hands.

'Wait and see, change is here!' Vuyo tells him. 'Be patient, young boy. All of us will soon be One. We will stop our fighting and live like a family, a brotherhood. Calm your quivering liver. Change is coming to South Africa.'

Gottlieb rubs Zam-Buk lip balm on his torn knuckles and sorts bricks. He laughs at Vuyo. One day, he tells himself, those bricks will become weapons. And the Indian man will pay. Go back to India! Leave our land alone. Build your own homes for your old pensioners. Build your own brothels. Don't make us mix your cement. Don't make us build you bathrooms and toilets that actually flush. Build your own.

You Indians.

Gottlieb cannot see the white man with the book and pen, the one prodding the Indian man in his bony curry-back with mahogany canes procured from England during the last shipment of brown sauce, fish paste and lavender soap.

Gottlieb bows his head to the white man. He thanks him for allowing him to sort bricks. A strange situation. A love affair with a flag bearing a sickle and a marriage to a man with white skin. Gottlieb is confused. He seethes at the Dhanrajs of the world with their unplastered houses and well-paying jobs. Their street-sweeper jobs, their runner-clerk jobs, their drunk-postman jobs. Any job that doesn't mean breaking your back.

Gottlieb would have killed a man to carry Dhanraj's letter bag. Gottlieb would have killed a man to be bitten by a large mongrel as he deposited a letter from a debt collector into a rusty postbox. He hates the white white shirts, the shorts fashioned in khaki to cover bony Indian knees. Gottlieb would have killed the boys, the Indian boys, when they walked to school laughing and eating peanuts from packets bought at Dhanraj's tuck shop. Thandi has counted. Fifty-five peanuts only in one plastic packet. Only. Dhanraj's instructions.

Gottlieb hates the Indian boys who touch Thandi's hands as she hands over packets of peanuts and loose cigarettes that will be smoked inside schoolboys' toilets during lunch break. He hates Anthony.

He feels that one day he will kill Dhanraj. He will slit Anthony's throat. And he will rape the plaited sisters. One day he will.

Today, he finds whole bricks among broken ones. He stacks whole bricks in piles and wonders what it would feel like to enter the body of an Indian girl. He knows he won't like it, so he stacks more bricks.

Somebody, somewhere, told him Indian girls feel too soft inside. They cannot grip a man like a black woman can. He won't enjoy it.

But he will enjoy it.

Dhanraj has been volatile, wild in his rage when the bottles rattle with empty sounds. Basanti has ordered the plaited sisters to pour the alcohol down the outside drain. Where the smell of the cheapness of the liquor won't linger in her nostrils as she cooks a hot spicy curry of tinned sardines and dhal full of stones.

Dhanraj loses his mind when he finds out what the women have done. He grabs Basanti by her double-chinned throat and rips her only housecoat, the thin, worn-out pink one. The one she brought to his mother's house in her trousseau that many years ago. With a few silk saris and a flannel nightgown. And five bottles of Pond's Cold Cream. Back when she was a sixteen-year-old bride from a farm in Umzinto. Back when Dhanraj had sat next to her in a jerky ambassador car as they brought the bride home.

When home was Inanda. Before the White Man decided which group of which colour to place in which wasted township. Group Areas Act. Before the acting began.

Dhanraj remembers as he slaps Basanti's old face how young and soft her skin used to be. He remembers when he sucker-punches her eye how she had held her mother and cried at their wedding, and how her mother had wiped her tears with the corner of a brand-new orange Benares sari and whispered to Basanti to be good to her husband.

He remembers how drunk he was when the priest asked him to line her middle-pathed head with red sindoor vermilion. A ritual of marriage that made Basanti his property.

A wavy, snaky line that missed the path completely. Then he felt his sister-in-law Shanti's hands steady his and make him draw the line properly in the young Basanti's path.

But he still punches the old Basanti in the face, the breast, the rolls and rolls of stomach. He enjoys it. Maybe he should force himself on her. Maybe he should pull up the twenty-five-year-old housecoat to find her old hanging bits of flesh and penetrate the nothingness that is left.

He cannot. He is too drunk. Always, he could never become fully erect with Basanti. It still enthrals and surprises him how four fat babies grew large and swelled up her womb. Babies who came jumping with glee out of the swollen womb with barely a labour to speak of. All except Anthony, whom the midwife, having dug her hands in to the elbows, had pulled out by the head. Dhanraj is surprised daily when he looks at his big-eyed daughters and frail little son.

Where did these children come from? He had never penetrated Basanti deep enough to plant them there. But they had arrived from his oily sperm. They had arrived from his alcoholic breath on the young bride's neck. And here they were. Basanti had pulled it off.

She had extracted some essence from his unwilling penis and brought these useless girls and cowering boy into his life. He knew he loathed Basanti. He knew she loathed him.

Now, she stares at him straight in his face and wipes the blood away with a dishcloth that she will later use to wipe vegetables. Dhanraj chases the plaited sisters into all corners of the unplastered house, threatening to cut their throats for pouring his liquor down the drain.

Basanti tries to lock them into their room. Dhanraj yanks her thinning grey plait and the keys go flying across a dusty screed floor.

The girls run out of the door. They go to stand along the streets where he cannot get to them. They flirt with the bus conductors as they drive by. And they forget Dhanraj and how they will hide under blankets when they finally must go home. They hope against all hope that he has stolen the rent money that they collect from the two nurses who share the other unplastered room in the house and bought himself a bottle of cane spirit rum from Aunty Maymoona's shebeen before they cluster together to go home. After dusk.

They draw straws. Who will pick Basanti off the floor today? Who will wipe her cuts with Dettol and a dishcloth? Who will wrap bandages made of torn-up saris around her limbs today? Nobody wants to be the one.

Anthony. He must do it. Anthony. He must walk the streets of Unit Five looking for his drunk postman father and drag his slack, stinking body home amid jeers and laughter.

Anthony.

Meera arrives at this dirty, filthy house on the day Dhanraj's rage is bubbling like poison in a cauldron. He is angry. Like he has been angry for years.

The farm his grandfather had bought, the ten acres his indentured-labourer grandfather had used guineas wrapped in snotty handkerchiefs to buy, the farm in Inanda, is gone. Taken away in the mid-eighties by the orange-blue-white. And given over to become a black shantytown called Bambayi.

And Dhanraj has never forgotten. He uses this loss as a crutch, his reason for drinking, for hitting, for hating.

'What you want, girl?' He glares through a dangling cigarette. Meera clutches her bags like lifelines. Dhanraj doesn't stand up from the rickety garden chair. But even sitting down, he looks menacing.

Meera almost runs away. The place looks like a hellhole. And it is. She swears she sees a rat run across a patchy piece of weedy lawn. She eyes the bush near the rusty metal beach chair where the old man stations himself for hours. She knows what marijuana leaves look like.

A nasty, patchy dog walks lopingly towards the old man and places a yellow head full of mange in the corduroy lap.

'You fuck off, Bruno. You just fuck off!'

The old man pushes the dog's head away. The dog doesn't seem to mind at all. He'd much rather sit at the towelling-clad feet and lick his open wounds. Tasting blood.

'I said,' Dhanraj repeats to the frozen girl standing before him dressed in tight bootleg jeans and a Superman T-shirt, 'what the fuck you want here, girl?'

'Room,' is all Meera can mutter, shocking herself that she is even considering sleeping at this place.

Dhanraj indicates the open front door. Meera enters gingerly and is assaulted first by the chaos, and then, mostly, by Basanti's purple, bloated face. Basanti shows her the room she must share with the nurses. Basanti tells her through swollen, burst lips to find her own sponge mattress, her own blanket. Dhanraj sells them, she tells Meera, for thrice the price you could get them anywhere else. Meera is too tired, too wide-eyed in shock, to go elsewhere. She mumbles to Basanti to get Dhanraj to sell her a yellow sponge mattress and one thin grey blanket.

She hates that her life has come down to this. But strangely, she loves the destruction of it all. The dregs. They course like drugs in her veins. Now, she can self-destruct completely. Honestly.

This chattel is cheap and it is on the bus route to the hospital. The new shiny one they have recently built. Fat men have cut ribbons and shown photographers airy new rooms with green tubing hanging from ceilings, and cotton-wool balls packed neatly into rows in metal containers. Kidney dishes and sparkling new bedpans. Freshly painted metal beds with neat nursey box-turned corners of white starched sheets. Who knew?

Then, when the red shiny corridors smelt of lavender polish, who knew? That this homage to the Mahatma would turn so sour and ugly in such a short time. Who knew it would all just turn to shit? So fast. So many old Basantis dying in the passageways with no one to care.

Meera's cousin Shalini had fetched her from the airport, asking no questions, not really caring why the strange divorced girl had returned from some Island nobody had heard of. For two weeks Meera had slept like a big, round duvet-covered bump on Shalini's lounge floor. And nobody really asked any questions.

Meera called home twice. Once to tell her mother she had arrived. And once again to tell her parents she never wanted to see them again. She enjoyed the dreamlessness that came with Shalini's lounge floor. She never enjoyed forgetting her parents. But she proceeded to wipe the memories of them away.

She had no plans. She had no Plan B. She had a floor and a pillow and a duvet. And she gratefully ate what Shalini provided, happy in the silence of the hugging couple at the sink – Shalini and her soft, spectacled clerk of a husband, Santosh. Months could have passed happily. She had converted the few pounds she had brought back into rands and contributed a bag of rice to Shalini's grocery cupboard.

Until one morning Santosh, while looking for his clerky clunky shoe, the ones he shone with regularity and spit, tripped over the sleeping mound.

'Out!' he told Meera. 'You can't sleep on my floor forever. Decide what you want to do with your life. But get off my shoe. Get off my floor. Your mother says those … people will take you back. So, go back. You married that man so go back to his house. A woman has a place. And they have a place for you.'

Meera had slid Santosh's shoe out from under her buttock and knew then what had been troubling her the entire night. It was the inanimate deliverer of the kick.

The Boot.

Shalini heard from someone who knew another one who was friends with that one whose husband carpooled with a certain one – they were looking for people at the new hospital in Phoenix. Any people. Unqualified people would do just fine.

She helped Meera pack away her small suitcase. She gave her back her bag of rice. She drove her to the hospital gates. After dragging her suitcase bumpily along, after securing a job, Meera shyly asked strangers if they knew a place she could stay. A fat lady selling nectarines on a plastic plate pointed her in the direction of Dhanraj's digs.

She settled into Dhanraj's unplastered world so well, she felt she had been born there. She sat next to Anthony and never spoke. And work began.

28

The Indian Summer

THE DURBAN HEAT ASSAULTS YOU. TAKES YOU BY THE hand onto the dance floor. You're a reluctant debutante, tapping your foot to music that hasn't even started yet. Peeping from behind a thick humid fringe. You dance. But Durban people are always looking at each other across crowded dance floors, wanting to approach; they keep their distance, never really mixing and mingling, never becoming part of one.

The suburbs have strange names, the streets have changed names. The plush beachside enclaves of lavish sprawling houses sprout names that are so African: Umhlanga, Inchanga Umhlali. Ugly wasteland housing developments of poor semi-detached grey concrete claim names that are so English: Phoenix, Chatsworth, Mountbatten Drive. It's the schizophrenia of it all that can kill you, kick you in the guts.

Into the Durban heat, Meera had arrived back home, like an exile from ice-cold Dublin. Like an exile in Durban too. Back where she came from, back to hiding in corners.

She had to come back; there was nowhere else she could go. Dublin had chewed her up and spit her out. She realised too late that, in any town, it is so easy to lose who you are. And to lose your place in the world.

Work. She had found work. A golden word. A precious word. A pearl from her mouth.

Work. Money. Coins. Notes. A Pay Slip on the twenty-eighth of every month. Her heart swelled with joy. Never would she return, head bowed, to the family.

She enjoys her job at a wasted hospital, the one that

proudly bears the name of a Mahatma. Proud until the nameplate of brushed chrome falls off on one of its hinges and hangs like that for months, swinging the name of the Mahatma back and forth in the wind. The same Mahatma whose name is later given to a street in Durban City famed for its drug dens and brothels.

The hospital is her haven. She slowly begins to melt into its corridors, its dirty urine-smelling wards, its car parks filled with lavish machinery. Her work is easy. Simple labour. Assistant to the physiotherapists, help to transport patients whose legs are amputated, paraplegics, babies with tuberculosis. Help to move their limbs, follow instructions, don't sit in the doctors' lounge. Eat your lunch with the rest of the drones. She could easily have been a machine. An arms-and-legs mover, pusher of wheelchairs, the instructions punched into her keyboard, no questions asked.

She rarely talks to anybody. It really can't be said why or when she settled into silence. Silence and smoking. Nobody even sees her. Nobody really bothers in this hospital. They are too busy surviving. The trenches. Those wards.

She buys fresh fragrant peaches from the round black woman whose stall of plastic plates piled high with teetering freshness is at the entrance to the hospital. Fair, fast trade – the woman doles out blue plastic packets of vegetables and fruit she has procured at early-morning markets out on the farms. The doctors never buy from her. They prefer to drive twenty minutes away into the plushness of a shopping mall where shrink-wrapped organic avocados await their guacamole. Meera opts for deep-fried snacks from roadside vendors. She gains weight, begins spreading.

The poor people have set up their own shopping mall in a rainbow-coloured marquee across the manic street from the hospital. Anything can be bought here. Shampoo, toilet paper, oily samosas filled with dubious minced meat, herbs, potatoes still dredged in earth, bootlegged bottles of Old Brown Sherry.

Old drunk-man Dhanraj's house becomes her haven too. In Unit Five, Phoenix, Meera sleeps on a dusty sponge mattress, sharing the ugly room with a nurse named Savvy and a nurse assistant named Rochelle. Rochelle, who is also Mageshnie, but much prefers Rochelle. Just as Problem Mkhize Road in plush Morningside much prefers Cowey.

Savvy smokes. Rochelle chews betel nuts that stain her mouth red. They have lovers. Doctors. Middle-of-the-night doctors who are supposed to be on call.

They call on cellphones, and their gold-toothed smiles make a girl named Savvy not so street-smart. Promising herself he will leave his society wife one day, for her mismatched cheap Chinese-store Polo shirts, or her itchy scratchy red and black lace lingerie that never stays on too long.

Meera listens late into the screed brown walls – the conversations of deep-in-love Savvy and deep-in-lust Rochelle. Doctor-nurse love-lust. Typical. Apparently, they say, the surgeons are the worst lovers, the physicians are the stingiest, and the professors want the most depraved things of them all. Meera would never know otherwise.

But she knows exactly how, in a nearby Umhlanga hotel room, the good doctor will shower, washing Savvy's or Rochelle's cheap perfume off his skin, going freshly ground back to the wife in Umhlanga, the one who hosts coffee mornings in aid of Cancer Relief and is a fashionable patron of the Bone Marrow Registry.

Savvy will never realise it, but Doctor-Fast-Shower loves his life. He loves his wife, her fat rolls, her spreading body. He loves that she had been chosen for him by well-meaning relatives, and that she has plied him with three perfect children, two boys and a girl who attend the best private school.

Savvy dreams. Rochelle dreams. Mills & Boons dreams. One day I will sit in the front seat of his Mercedes-Benz. At least they have their dreams. One day … the front seat.

Meera's dreams take her to rosters where a man in a uniform is reading out names to a crowded hall. And she waits and she waits, but her name never comes up. And in her dreams, she hears clicking of fingers and beeping of trucks backing up. She sees a pixel hedgehog, and a dot on a screen. Both deleted. But never deleted. From her experience. We are a product. We become the things we cut out with scissors and paste with glue onto the canvases of what we think are our lives.

She lingers for hours in the intensive care unit. She often thinks of the funeral. The click-click funeral. Why had she gone to it? Dressed like a vagrant in old cheap jeans and an unfashionable black shirt, she had insulted his funeral. She had gone because she had wanted to torture herself even more. To see Ian's face contorted in grief.

One last time. Before leaving Dublin with the same incense-smelling suitcase, not so incense-smelling any longer. They had chased her away from the chapel. Anger and rage had flooded precious Ian's handsome face. She didn't need to be told twice. She stood at the chapel door amid shocked whispers, and then as Ian raced down the aisle followed by Teresa in a designer little black dress, Meera had run like the wind. Across the graveyards, the cobblestones, the highways and the lanes. Thinking somewhere that they were still chasing her. And, for days after leaving Dublin, still feeling that they were chasing her away.

She forgot Ian's face. She forgot Ian's body. All in one quick turn, she forgot Dublin had ever existed. But there were too many things in Meera's heaving brain to forget. And those things came to her in dreams.

The dreams of the funeral never left her. Dreams of sugar cane rolling in the wind, of black smoke that stained prayer-room walls, dreams of old men seated in the lotus position reaching clawed hands towards her, dreams of slithering over golden arms, of being kissed and fondled, of howls of masturbation and beeping hedgehogs.

Too many.

Back in Durban, she avoided sleep. She lingered for hours at the hospital, long after everyone had gone home.

She spent hours with Susan. They spoke about the dreams, dissecting them like cadavers of people whose bodies had never been claimed. Susan held her head every night, on the pancake-thin sponge mattress. It was Susan who told Meera, 'I will never go away from you. I will never abandon you.'

She tried not to finish a day's work in the working day. She tried to miss the last bus back to Dhanraj's den in Unit Five. She once fell asleep in the Casualty Department on an old plastic chair, and no one bothered to wake her till the morning cleaners shoved her body with their mops.

Go home, people wanted to tell her. But she persisted, wanting to touch the rough government-issued sheets of dying humanity, smell the odours that come from a body that is rapidly breathing the death rattle.

One morning in the Neurology ward, there was a teen-age boy, a thin boy lying supine on his cot. Her instructions had been to move his arms and legs in five times ten passive motions, much like a human robot. Just move him around. He was practically brain-dead anyway.

Just preventing pressure sores. She lowered the metal bars on his bed wondering why they would put metal bars on a bed filled with a boy who could barely flutter his eyelids. She placed her hands on his ankle, wanting to move the stiffness away. But she suddenly felt the need to place her hands on his rapid chest. And her gloved hands on his chest, the latex reality of disease, sat comfortably between the ribs, the lack of flesh, the taut skin.

In the instant she laid her hands on the rapid chest, a heave and a rattle, and he was dead. The chest rose to the ceiling and then fell, and, with wide open eyes, he simply died. She felt he had seen her. And she had given him permission to leave the world. Her hands had opened the gate. But she pulled up the metal bars and snapped off her gloves.

Why put up metal bars on a bed filled with a dead boy? Because that's just all we know here.

Epilogue

Branches of Acacia Trees

THERE ARE DEAD BRANCHES OF ACACIA TREES LITTERED all over this place. This hospital. In concrete courtyards and parking lots, finding their place among lustrous machinery, expensive cars of red and silver, and open garbage bags lavishly spilling their contents, there are dead branches of acacia trees all over this place. This hospital.

Tumbleweeds, they become, rolling their thorny shapes in the rare breeze of a boiling African summer. Plastic shopping packets, the colours of which have long ago faded, fly up, then down, and finally they settle, joining the rotting fruit peels, torn nappies, syringes. This hospital.

'What's with the branches?' Meera casually asks a busy nurse. For a moment, the nurse stops her hands that bear needles and vials. She widens her eyes and looks directly into space; the sharp black cornrows on her head glisten with sweat. The air conditioning doesn't work here. It never did.

'The branches,' Meera persists. 'What's with all those dead tree branches everywhere I look?'

'Sisi,' she huffs, and shakes her head, 'there are some things you people would never understand.'

Meera is affronted. Not because she refers to her as 'you people'. She is affronted because the nurse hasn't stopped her work to answer her question.

But here, in this hospital, nobody has the time. Scuttling through corridors that have been polished an earthy red, important diligent professionals go about their days. A herd of young doctors swarm anxiously around, pronouncing in whispered tones sizeable words in Latin, the language of love poetry, and the language of disease.

They are waiting for the alpha male, the uber-intelligent professor, to come charging through the doors, firing questions at them about Case no. 1 and Case no. 2. Often, while Meera performs the mundane tasks of moving almost-dead limbs, or of carrying gym mats from ward to ward, she nurtures the idea of stopping the professor's booming voice and asking him in a language we all understand if he knows the names of the people who are Case no. 1 and Case no. 2. But she joins the herd, possibly the weakest in it for wanting to ask these questions. The very bottom of the food chain. Invisible to those with an education.

She is learning fast these days: here, as in the rest of life, there is always hierarchy. Which must be respected. And there are divides. Which must be fostered. We all know our place. Quietly, she weaves around important people. People who never see her. Confident, happy professionals who always move in packs, always throw around comparisons between what they see with their own eyes and what they were taught in Course 364 and Course 365.

This filthy hospital is world renowned. Known for the most virulent of viruses. Passing through its wide-open doors, nobody here gets out alive. The science of disease in its relentless wards attracts academics the world over. They come from Michigan, New York, Maastricht, Newcastle upon Tyne. American and European researchers and egalitarian experts, all claiming publishing rights over their opinions of how to solve Africa's 'health issues'.

But a simpleton whose daily bread it is to perform the dirty mundane dance in a ward that is crowded to bursting with the sick and the dying asks, 'What the hell do they know about Africa's health issues anyway?'

The ward is dirty. They all are. Not just dirty in a ramshackle kind of way, the kind that comes with occasionally not doing the dusting. Dirty in the way that you tiptoe around blood-soaked sheets and piles of used bedpans. Nothing glossy and of great magnitude like Course 364.

It has been almost fifteen years now that she has been gainfully employed here at the Mahatma Gandhi Memorial Hospital. Her shocked eyes, glazed over from being booted out of a Dublin funeral, became horrified eyes and now, slowly, like everyone else's eyes she passes in the Passively Resistant corridors.

She has taken to becoming a watcher. A stalker. A peeping Tom. The shiny, happy doctors, the silly giggling physiotherapists, they know – actually they say often – that they are here to do time in the trenches and then to exit this world rapidly.

There's Kenneth, blond beautiful Kenneth, brought up in the luxury of a gated, manicured life in Durban's answer to the Cotswolds – Kloof. He raced through his years at university with the rambunctious vigour of a rugby lock. Maybe because Kenneth nurses constant dreams of becoming the team physio for the Sharks rugby team. And he's well on his way. His father has already sorted out his 'community service' in the Shark Tank, weekends of volunteering at Kings Park Stadium.

Marlini – a Bollywood princess. Meera often watches her navigate her designer-shod feet through piles of bedpans and broken x-ray machines and wonders how she ever found herself in this profession. A long-nailed, painted-on doctor, with a penchant for Polo shirts and Louis Vuitton.

She complains the loudest. About the stench, the belligerent nurses, the wet mattresses, the whiff of what's cooking in the patients' canteen … everything. She never complains about her fellow doctors. Her coiffed hair flicks in the direction of suitable husbands. That she will marry a bespectacled, skinny doctor with a mansion in Umhlanga, Meera has no doubt. This filthy hospital is her hunting ground.

That leaves Nokulunga, a hope, possibly, for devoting her life to service. But again, perhaps, Meera is playing to stereotypes. Brought up in Umlazi, a township girl to the core. Bantering with nurses in Zulu, uninterested in glamour, mildly shocked by the odorous diseased, lying in caged cots and on ward floors. A distant ugly voice inside Meera whispers 'Her people, after all ...'

Meera silences that voice with a reprimand from a rainbow nation. But Nokulunga disappoints, perhaps even more than Kenneth and Marlini. A brand-new private practice awaits her in all its polished glory. In Umlazi, it appears, there are not many GPs, and the people will be queuing outside her door. Her father has even started work on the interiors. He has even contacted all the medical aids.

Meera wishes this world were easier for her. Easy enough not to be touched in some way by the stench of the dying. It is a stench that she has come to love. Who will walk away from this war cool, calm, collected?

None of us.

She trudges daily from ward to ward. She watches dying babies who have as much chance of survival as mynah birds that have been driven over by taxis. Most of them are AIDS orphans, HIV positive themselves.

Almost everyone has TB, the newly discovered extra-strength variety. She moves the limbs of thieves who were shot in the buttocks when fleeing from police. She massages, with thick dark-brown antiseptic cream, the whip-ripped backs of men who raped babies. She makes boys who hijacked move their toes, after their spines have been sliced in two by bullets. Their ankles are shackled to the bed cages, making exercise and movement very near impossible. Paralysed eighty-year-old women with glassy eyes who refuse to remove their doeks during exercises, young fresh girls with amputated legs who sit in the long grass outside the ward, grooming each other's hair like a troop of vervet monkeys.

The taxis arrive often, like drone bees to the hive, in hooting crescendos. Diseased humanity spills out of their bowels onto the pavement outside the hospital's gates. Nobody even gets out to accompany the patients to the Casualty Department, artfully positioned as far away from the gates as the mortuary. Not even the security guard, who sucks at his teeth and continues reading the *Isolezwe* newspaper.

Ambulances never arrive. There are none. Or, at least, there are many, but very few actually run, and the ones that do have probably gone running errands to the Hungry Lion chicken outlet.

In the tea lounge, a nurse flops exhaustedly onto a fraying chair. Her shaking head and constant tut-tuts make Meera look in her direction. It is the same nurse she once asked about the dead tree branches?

'Eish, Sisi,' she says disconsolately, 'the fridges are full! There is no more place in the mortuary. Now they must lie on the streets, then someone upstairs will smell what KwaZulu-Natal smells like.'

Meera regards her intently. She sips tea from a chipped cup with faded blue words emblazoned on the side: 'Humane Healing for All. Conference 1998.'

'The tree branches …' she says distantly, and Meera knows she remembers her for her long-ago question:

What's with all these tree branches? Lying everywhere.

'Our people, they bring the branch of a tree to the place where a loved one has died. The spirit of the dead enters the branch, and the branch is taken back home to their village to find peace.'

Speechless, and stupid, Meera sits. No words come to her mouth. Everything would sound like banality. In silence she sips.

She knows that very few of these tree branches find their way back home. She knows because their gnarled corpses lie in courtyards and dusty parking lots in this hospital – forgotten, stepped on and driven over. She knows that there are many ghosts that haunt this place. Secretive ones that branch out towards the haves and the have-nots.

She does not know much about KwaZulu-Natal. She has lived here her entire life. She was born on a sugar-cane plantation in the deepest and most beautiful part of this place. Her childhood playground has been the grass, the sky, the streams and the trees.

But she does not know anything at all. Ask her about the beauty of the Drakensberg, the wild verdure of rural Zululand, the setting sun and the thunderous rivers. She will tell you nothing.

What she will tell you is that there are hundreds of villages dotted around this waste world. Places like Magudu, Kwambonambi, Babanango and Msinga. In these places there are many acacia trees, whose branches reach up to the beautiful heavens.

Their branches wait.

On the length of a red, snaky corridor, the squeak of a battered wheelchair breaks the silence of a lazy Friday afternoon. Meera is pushing an old man, onwards and forwards. She looks ahead, breathing in the smells of the familiar hospital.

The old man, paralysed from the waist down, hums a tune out loud. Meera recognises it. It is an old Mohamed Rafi song from a Hindi film she had often watched as a child. It is a song her father had sung to her. She recalls the words, their meanings not lost on her now. The song is of a traveller who comes, and goes. She joins the old man's song. Together they sing as she takes him back to his bed. Getting the words of the song wrong, Meera and the old man burst into laughter.

'Never mind, daughter,' the old man says. 'It's okay we get the words wrong. It's all okay.'

•